UNFORGETTABLE
JACKSON P. BURLEY HIGH SCHOOL
1951 – 1967

Lucille Smith

2022

Unforgettable Jackson P. Burley High School

Printed by Worth Higgins and Associates, Inc. Richmond, VA
Printed in the United States of America

Library of Congress Cataloging-in-Publication Data
ISBN (print) 978-0-578-95292-5

Cover Design by Anne Chesnut
Cover Photo of Jackson P. Burley High School, Anne Chesnut

Author Photo by Brandon R. Smith

Edited by Charlotte Matthews

UNFORGETTABLE
JACKSON P. BURLEY HIGH SCHOOL
1951 – 1967

Three area Negro High Schools in the City of Charlottesville and
Albemarle County united in 1951 to become
Jackson P. Burley High School

Lucille S. Smith

PREFACE

Black History Matters. We must continue to document and promote cultural awareness and historical preservation. This is essential to preserve the rich and brave story of African American students in the City of Charlottesville and Albemarle County.

Some of the photographs appearing in this book are more than 60 years old and were selected from yearbooks, newspaper articles, personal files and other sources. Even though some have begun to fade, they still illustrate the way things were during the era of Jackson P. Burley High School. In this way they provide a pictorial overview of the school.

Step back in time, and re-live this historical journey. This book is a compilation of astonishing, sometimes challenging, but proud, unforgettable memories of days gone by.

The interviews from students, faculty and administrators are their reflections and remembrance. They are raw, candid, and from the heart.

Never forget, as students, you persevered, because you were supported, nurtured, taught and inspired by your parents, members of the community and the staff and administrators at Albemarle Training School, Esmont High School, Jefferson High School and Jackson P. Burley High School. You were raised to be honorable, respectful, and responsible young adults. You became committed, hardworking students, who strived to receive an education with dreams of a better life.

Students of segregation were challenged and transformed from eager and dedicated teenagers to successful, productive adults. Those were the days, life was oh so simple, the days were brighter, smiles wider, hearts a little happier, and problems were smaller. Dreams of an equal education were beginning to come true.

Looking back, lasting friendships were made, you kept in touch, and over the years many of you have become better acquainted. Continue to take advantage of any opportunity to share and support the many events and special occasions sponsored by classmates and your school family.

The author of this book is not a former Jackson P. Burley High School student, but a student of the Pulaski County School District in the City of North Little Rock, Arkansas.

Lucille S. Smith, 2021

ACKNOWLEDGEMENTS

The completion of, "Unforgettable Jackson P. Burley High School," brings closure to a long time vision. Without the collaborative effort and assistance from many, the book would not have been possible. I am indebted to many people and offer a special thanks to everyone who provided support, feedback, artifacts, photographs, and yearbooks to complete a vibrant history of Jackson P. Burley High School. Writing this book has taken me on an extraordinary journey, as I met truly heartwarming people who assisted and encouraged me along the way.

To the many students, faculty, and staff who allowed me to interview them or those who provided reflections, your memories are priceless. I sincerely appreciate your kindness and selflessness in sharing your recollections of a time gone by. The memories linger and are highlighted in the pages from students of each graduating class. Many of the pictures in the book were taken from yearbooks of the 1952 – 1967 classes.

James "Jimmy" Hollins, class of 1965; thank you for your tireless support. The completion of this book would have been almost impossible without your encouragement, and assistance. You identified people to interview or contact for additional information, as well as providing telephone numbers and addresses. You were always just a telephone call away, and had the ability to open doors to people and priceless information.

Donald A. Byers, class of 1959; thank you for being a great "detective" in locating people and providing telephone numbers, addresses and names for pictures. You never failed to let me know if information was available, it could be found. You opened the door to a wealth of information, which allowed me to walk in and retrieve what was needed.

Rauzelle J. Smith, class of 1966; most of all, I am so grateful to you, my husband, for your critical editing, and the confidence you had in me as I worked diligently to complete this book. The appreciation you extended to me for documenting the history of your school will always be the motivation I needed to keep moving forward. Thank you for filling in the gaps, letting me interview and quiz you on people, places and things from more than 60 years ago.

My children, Crystal and Brandon Smith, provided support and understanding throughout this effort, which took longer than expected, because of the COVID-19 Pandemic shutdown. I appreciate your sincere understanding and patience, as I was not always readily available when needed.

I offer a special thank you to George Lindsay Jr., class of 1966 for his assistance in finding missing pieces needed to fill in gaps for the bus drivers, as well as other documentation. Mary Nicholas Nightengale, class of 1960; thank you for assisting Donald, and providing names for many of the pictures shown. A special thank you to Katherine Banks, class of 1957, Beatrice Washington Clark, class of 1956, Marcha Payne Howard, class of 1964, Patricia Bowler Edwards, class of 1966 and Maxine Holland, class of 1967. They were always readily available, and offered support from making telephone calls, to providing contact information, documentation or answering questions.

Dede Smith and Kay Slaughter; I treasure your friendship and support. You were eager to provide a warm dose of both, along with documentation, people to contact and much encouragement. Margaret T. Peters provided editing of the architectural and physical description of the school. She was also the inspiration I needed to keep moving forward. Peggy Denby, 'Friends of Esmont' provided information and contacts for Esmont High School, whereas much of the information will be used in a book to be published at a later date on the local Segregated High Schools.

The Four Seasons at Charlottesville Writer's Group provided much encouragement and interest throughout this endeavor. Thank you to special friends and neighbors, Hazel Sykes who wrote the perfect poem, 'Back in the Day' previewed in Chapter 1, and Diane Horvath who provided countless books to review on Virginia history.

Early in my research, I met Jeffrey B. Werner, AICP, Historic Preservation and Design Planner, City of Charlottesville. Jeffrey is a mover and shaker, who pointed me in the right direction to gain access to documents to continue research when I hit a snag. Thank you Kyna Thomas, City of Charlottesville Chief of Staff/Clerk of Council, for providing access to Council meeting minutes from 1946 – 1952.

Burley Middle School Staff, former principal James Asher and current principal, Kasaundra Blount and staff were generous with their time and with answers for many questions. Their enthusiasm was infectious and much needed.

Dr. Helen Dunn, Legislative and Public Affairs Officer for Albemarle County Public Schools periodically reached out to offer support and assistance with much enthusiasm. Dr. Bernard Hairston, Assistant Superintendent for School Community Empowerment, answered many questions and was always just a telephone call away. Leslie Thacker, Executive Assistant to the Superintendent and Deputy Clerk to the School Board for Charlottesville City Schools provided much needed personal assistance and support.

Dr. Andrea Douglas, Executive Director, Jefferson School African American Heritage Center, invited me in to view much needed documents for Jefferson and Burley High School. Regina Rush and George Riser, Special Collections Reference Coordinators at the University of Virginia's Albert and Shirley Small Special Collections Library provided access to pivotal material.

Many thanks to Miranda Burnett, Historical Collections Librarian, Albemarle Charlottesville Historical Society and Addison R. Patrick, Curatorial Specialist, Arthur J. Morris Law Library, University of Virginia for much assistance in my many visits to locate requested materials.

I am especially thankful to Prof. Ben Allen, Executive Director of the Equity Center at the University of Virginia for assistance in obtaining book Editor Prof. Charlotte Matthews.

This publication is made possible through the generous support of Preservation Piedmont and the Charlottesville Area Community Foundation (CACF).

INTRODUCTION

A Note about Diction:

In this history of Unforgettable Jackson P. Burley High School, I strive to be as accurate as possible. For that reason, I employ words that in 2021 are profanities; they are misguided, reprehensible words. However -- Colored and Negro -- were the terminology of the day. While I do not endorse usage of them, if I were to omit Colored and Negro from this history, I would be falsifying the nomenclatures. So, please read these words in a historical context. The use of Colored, Negro, Black and African American are used within their spoken times.

Jackson P. Burley High School is located at 901 Rose Hill Drive in Charlottesville, Virginia. With the forward thinking of the combined School Boards of the City of Charlottesville and Albemarle County, the school was built to unite the three area black high schools. The school was jointly operated by the City of Charlottesville and Albemarle County. For years the parents of black students had fought hard and prayed their children would receive a better education to prepare them for a brighter future. As black schools in the City of Charlottesville and Albemarle County were, separate and unequal, Jackson P. Burley High School strove to meet the educational needs of the students, offering cultural, athletic and educational opportunities.

This book contains a history of Jackson P. Burley High School from its opening in the fall of 1951 to the closing of the school during "desegregation" in the spring of 1967. It also contains a pictorial overview of the school from opening to closure.

This book allows the Burley Varsity Club to continue one of its goals, which is, "Dedicated to Preserving the Educational Legacy" of Jackson P. Burley High School. Seventy years later, documenting the history of one of the most memorable times for the students and their ancestors will make for a lasting legacy. It is of utmost importance to preserve history for the students who attended the school, as well as all faculty, administrators and others, who contributed to the success of the students.

A brief history of Albemarle Training School, Esmont High School and Jefferson High School is included in this book. A separate book will be published later to highlight the three area Negro high schools.

Currently there is sparse documentation on file for Jackson P. Burley High School, with the exception of a few articles on the internet, old newspaper articles, and council minutes from the City of Charlottesville and the Albemarle County Board of Supervisors. There are some school board meeting minutes from Charlottesville and Albemarle County available, but they only revealed a miniscule part of the history. The first class to graduate from Jackson P. Burley High School was in the spring of 1952. While many of the students and staff are no longer with us, the memories still linger. It is of utmost importance to preserve as much information as possible, and this book begins to accomplish that goal.

CONTENTS

Treasure the unforgettable memories you made as students,

and forever honor those who fought to make it possible.

CHAPTER 1

SEGREGATED HIGH SCHOOLS OF ALBEMARLE COUNTY AND THE CITY OF CHARLOTTESVILLE

Logo of Albemarle County Public Schools, *Courtesy of Dr. Matthew S. Haas, Superintendent*
Logo of Charlottesville City Schools, *Courtesy of James M. Henderson, Acting Superintendent*

BACK IN THE DAY

All aboard the big yellow bus
Passing by schools not meant for us.
Our fate in the hands of a young classmate
Speeding around curves, so we won't be late.

Picking up black youngsters from all around---
Keswick, Crozet, North Garden and Newtown.
Racing over roads packed with ice and snow,
Not enough time left to really go slow.

Children huddle in bunches three to a seat
With frostbitten fingers and frozen feet.
Headed for a school twenty some miles away---
A separate but equal one, so white folks say.

Singing, reading, or just conversing with a friend
Sharing wild tales from beginning to end.
Finally reaching our destination
Piling out quickly without hesitation.

For we know, waiting for us inside,
Are knowledgeable teachers with strong black pride.
Dedicated teachers, full of zest and zeal,
Who understand our plight and the way we feel.

Greeting us with kindness and warm tender smiles---
Sympathetic we had come those twenty some miles.
Instructing classes filled with gifted to LD,
Preparing all too someday get a high school degree.

Laying a good foundation to help build dreams,
Improving behaviors and self-esteem.
Teaching about never before seen places,
Reading from books without any black faces.

Using old equipment a far cry from new,
Waiting for supplies that are long overdue.
Still keeping morale and expectations high,
Letting us know we can succeed if we try.

But, of course, with racially biased tests
Most of the scores are mediocre at best.
For tests aren't designed for a minority
Who has to make survival its priority?

Then comes the "Great Black Hope" called integration
That at first only masks discrimination.
But finally, our struggle for civil rights
Gives us a choice to go to school with whites.

Should we go or should we stay?
That is the big question of the day.
So, we search the depths of our heart, mind, and soul,
For there's no one right answer if the truth be told.

Hazel Sykes
Ruckersville, VA

Segregation in Albemarle County and Charlottesville

The end of the Civil War ushered in a new era for the education of Black children all over the South. The racially segregated society that developed in Virginia after Reconstruction denied political, economic, educational, and social equality to Black citizens. So called Jim Crow laws mandated the segregation of public schools, and public places such as restaurants, theaters, libraries, parks, public transportation, and neighborhoods.[1]

Though full high school instruction was not available, beginning in the 1890s, Black students from Albemarle and surrounding counties could continue their education beyond grade school at the Albemarle Training School. Primary grades through high school classes were taught in the same school with as many as three or four grades in the same classroom. During segregation, Albemarle Training School was the first black school in the area to offer a vocational curriculum.

A formal education for Black children was the result of aggressive determination and tireless persistence by parents and local Black leaders. The parents were dedicated and worked diligently to improve schools for their children. They used the assistance of community leaders, church clergy, Parent Teacher Association (PTA), the NAACP, as well as engaging the local white power structure to support their cause. Throughout countless cities and counties in the South, many small one and two room schools were built in the Black communities, which allowed the children to walk to school.

For years, Black children attended separate and unequal schools, where improvements in facilities, teaching resources and course offerings lagged behind those funded for white students. As a result, many black schools relied on the Freedmen's Bureau, Rosenwald Fund, and community and philanthropic support. These programs subsidized the insufficient aid provided by the cities and counties. The students were provided worn, second-hand books and the schools had no heat, poor ventilation, little natural light, no indoor facilities or running water. The facilities were heated by coal or wood on potbelly stoves. The parents and students performed all the maintenance for the school. Although early black schools shared the same problems as some of their white counterparts, there were greater challenges to face: inadequate facilities, few teachers, and fewer resources. Over the years, the first schools for Black children, particularly in Albemarle County, lagged far behind schools for white students. Black schools were sometimes mere makeshift one or two room buildings or cabins in desperate need of repair.

In the fall of 1951, students from Albemarle Training School, Esmont High School, and Jefferson High School, united and became Jackson P. Burley High School. The school was located in the City of Charlottesville. There were also some students in attendance from the counties of Greene and Nelson. For the first time, a school curriculum was added to educate Black students through twelfth grade.

---

[1] Michael R. Gardner. *Harry Truman and Civil rights.* SIU Press, Page 108.

Segregated High Schools in
The City of Charlottesville and Albemarle County

From 1926 to 1951, there were three high schools for Black students, located in the City of Charlottesville and Albemarle County. In 1947, formal discussions began between the two school systems to unite the three area high schools.

In September 1951, Jackson P. Burley High School became the high school for all Black students in the City of Charlottesville, Albemarle County and some students in Greene and Nelson Counties.

Albemarle Training School
(1926 – 1951)

Esmont Colored School / Esmont High School
1930's – 1951

Jefferson School / Jefferson High School
1926 – 1951

Albemarle Training School

In 1886, fifteen years after free public education became law in Virginia, Albemarle County purchased land for the Union Ridge School for Colored children. In 1912, a new seven room school was built to replace the old Albemarle Training School. It included a primary structure for classrooms, a small library, as well as a separate Industrial Education building. The school followed an educational program advocated by Booker T. Washington. It offered a basic elementary education, followed by two years of training in vocational agriculture, domestic science, or industrial education. The school combined vocational education, such as home economics, agriculture, and shop, with various academic courses, including English, math, chemistry, biology, history, French, and Latin.[1] In 1915 the school was expanded into a teacher training school with a high school curriculum, as well as instructions in carpentry, cookery, farming and other trades. For years it was the only school in a five-county area to offer African American children an education beyond seventh grade.[2]

In 1926, Albemarle Training School became the county's first four year high school for African American students with John G. Shelton serving as the first high school principal. It served grades seventh through tenth, with as many as 244 students in attendance. It was the only school in a five-county area to offer African American children an education beyond grade seven.[3]

A foreign language, physical education and domestic science, were soon introduced into the curriculum. Domestic science was directed by rural supervisor, Maggie P. Burley, wife of educator Jackson P. Burley. Shortly thereafter, music and drama were added to the curriculum. But, due to a lack of space, drama, chorus and operettas were presented in the sanctuary of the all-black, Union Ridge Baptist Church. The church was located on Hydraulic Road, a short distance from the school. While Mr. Shelton taught industrial education and shop, he also directed "Annual Operettas" that required months of practice. The students looked forward to the event each year with eager anticipation. Graduations at the Training School were also held at Union Ridge Baptist Church.

In 1930, after teaching Domestic Science at Albemarle Training School for 15 years, Mary Carr Greer became the second principal of the high school, serving from 1930 – 1950. The high school was located a short distance from her home at River View Farm in Charlottesville. Mary continued to attend summer school at Hampton Institute and Fisk and Cornell Universities, qualifying herself to teach English, History, and Government. During the 1940s the school included a home room for each of the five grades (seven through eleven), as well as a library and a detached industrial education building.

---

[1] A.L. Bennett, *"Schools: An Economic and Social Survey of Albemarle County,"* University of Virginia Record, Extension Series 7 (Oct, 1922)
[2] *Education for Colored children within five counties. The Daily Progress*, August 4, 1915, page 6
[3] *Albemarle Training School (ATS), first high School for Black students. The Daily Progress*, August 4, 1915, page 6.

During the tenure of Mrs. Greer, a period of both physical and academic expansion and growth occurred. She encouraged extracurricular activities, which included: Lyric Club, 4-H Club, and annual events such as the Father and Son Banquet, Field Day, and May Day. The annual Field Day was held at Washington Park where African American schools from all over the region met for a picnic, games and wonderful camaraderie. Over the years, the school's band and choral group won several state competitions. The band members trained after hours at the old Jefferson High School in the City of Charlottesville.

After fifteen years of teaching, Mrs. Greer worked to develop an accredited four year curriculum similar to that in white high schools. She pushed for the merging of the Training School with the Charlottesville and Albemarle Public School Systems to include students from Jefferson High School and Esmont High School.

Ethel Payne Nicholas became the third and last high school principal, as it students united with Esmont High and Jefferson High School to attend Jackson P. Burley High School in 1951.

Esmont High School

Between 1906 and 1907, a School League of men and women in Esmont was organized, and led by Mr. Benjamin F. Yancey. The league purchased three acres of land in 1913. The County of Albemarle built a six-room school in 1916 on the land, and the school was known as the Esmont Colored School. The school was built at a cost of $4,000. In the early 1930s, the Esmont Colored School served Black students from all the Esmont communities. The school soon became overcrowded, and a two-room house nearby on Porters Road was converted into more classroom space. The converted house was known as "The Little School" and served grades first through fourth. The Esmont Colored School was later renamed "Esmont High School" and educated students in fifth through eleventh grade.[4] At any given time, as many as 182 students were in attendance. The high school graduation ceremonies for the school alternated between the New Hope Baptist Church and the New Green Mountain Baptist Church, located in Esmont, Virginia.

Rev. Warner J. Jones was the first principal of Esmont High School in the early 1930s, serving until 1937. In the fall of 1937, five educators were on staff at the high school and Henry L. Summerall became the second principal. Mr. Isaac D. Faulkner became the third principal in 1943, serving through the opening of Jackson P. Burley High School in 1951.

Parents of Esmont High School students continued to provide financial support for education, forming the Parent-Teacher League in 1937, which combined the previously separate men's and women's leagues. There were very few clubs and activities for the students. They participated in Student Patrol (organized in 1938). The Student Council was formed in 1944. The students participated in the Girls' Glee Club, Boys' and Girls' singing Quartets, Oratory, A Capella Choir, Choral Club, Editorial Staff for the student newspaper, and the "Esmont High School Journal." There was a Girls' and Boys' Basketball Team, and a Girls' and Boys' Softball Team. The teams would participate in competitions annually with Albemarle Training School at Washington Park. Other competitions included Pole, Block and Hoop Relays.

During the mid-1940s, the six-room Esmont High School was overcrowded and in poor physical condition. The Esmont Black community formed a Parent Teacher Association (PTA) and purchased four additional acres of land next to the current school building to permit future expansion, which would better accommodate the growing student population. The PTA had hopes that Albemarle County would replace their old high school building with a "fine brick structure." Over the years, teachers at Esmont High School came from many different communities in Albemarle and surrounding counties, as well as the City of Charlottesville.

By 1947, plans were in the works with the Charlottesville School Board and the Albemarle County School Board to unite the three area black high schools. Many of the Esmont teachers would eventually become teachers at the newly opened Jackson P. Burley High School in Charlottesville.

---

[4] *Esmont Colored School renamed Esmont High School*, ca. 1930s. Esmont High School Reunion Booklet, Sep 27–29, 1991.

Jefferson High School

In September 1922, School Superintendent, James G. Johnson reported there were more than 694 students attending the Jefferson School. Only the children in grades six, seven and eight were able to attend school full-day, the balance attended half-days. Around 1924, eighty-six parents and interested individuals submitted a petition to the Superintendent and members of the City School Board for the building of a Negro high school in Charlottesville. Because no high school classes were offered to Negro students at that time, their families were forced to send them away to schools outside of Charlottesville or the state; where they could obtain high school-level training. Among the petitioners were the leadership of most of the Negro churches, fraternal organizations, store keepers, as well as individual parents. The petition stated: [5]

Petition to the Charlottesville School Board requesting the establishment of a "High School for colored Youth," c. 1921. *Courtesy of the Albert and Shirley Small Special Collections Library, University of Virginia*

The city decided in 1924 to honor the request for a "Negro" high school that would house three high school grades. Meeting minutes for the Charlottesville School Board in November of 1924 revealed that the board was anxious to get the plans for the new colored school from the State education department architect, Mr. Raymond B. Long. By December of 1924, the Board had received the plans.[6] The architectural firm of Calrow, Browne, and Fitz-Gibbons Architects of Norfolk, Virginia were selected to oversee the construction of the new building, with Charles Calrow serving as the architect. In March of 1925, Motley Construction Company was awarded the building contract for a cost of $47,777.86. The school included an office, library, seven

---

[5] *Petition to the Charlottesville School Board to establish High School for Colored youth*. Records of Charlottesville City School Board, c. 1921.

[6] Request honored to build school. Meeting minutes of the Charlottesville School Board, November 1924.

classrooms, an auditorium, home economics room, and cafeteria. The original structure is brick, with distinctive detailing in the Classical Revivalist style and was completed in 1926. When construction began, the Jefferson School bordered the Charlottesville's Vinegar Hill neighborhood, an African American residential and commercial area, which was demolished during the period of urban renewal in the mid-1960s.

In 1926, three additional grades, nine through eleven, were added to further the education of Black students, and the school became Jefferson High School. Four subjects were offered in each grade, eight through eleven. Only sixteen units were available and sixteen were required for graduation. At the time, Jefferson was one of only 10 accredited black high schools in Virginia. In the fall of 1927 the existing building had eight classrooms built around the auditorium with a seating capacity of 200. The course subjects offered in grades eight through eleven were: English I, II, III and IV, general mathematics, (algebra and geometry), general (environmental) science, biology and chemistry, French I and II and U.S. and World History.[7]

The principals of Jefferson High School were: Maude M. Gamble, Cora B. Duke and Owen J. Duncan, Jr. Jefferson High School was awarded accreditation as a high school by the State Department of Education in 1929. The school celebrated its first graduating class in 1930 and marked the first time a group of African American pupils had ever graduated from an accredited high school in the history of the City of Charlottesville.

The large two-story brick building, was built in four sections; 1926, 1938–39, 1958 and 1959. The Jefferson Graded School and Jefferson High School was located in the Starr Hill neighborhood on the western edge of Vinegar Hill, a predominantly African American neighborhood, with residential, commercial and civic buildings. This was Charlottesville's economic and social core for African Americans during the first half of the 20th century. Between 1938 and 1939, as the demand and student population grew, as well as the African American community's desire for access to public library services, the high school underwent its first expansion. The 1938 addition closely matched the original structure. The expansion included an enclosed open air courtyard at the rear of the original building. Additional classroom space, library and industrial arts shop; all built through the use of Federal Public Works funds. The later additions of 1958–1959 complemented the original structure and reflected a more modern style and materials.[8]

By the end of the 1940s, the African American student population had outgrown its school and in 1946 the school boards from the City of Charlottesville and Albemarle County began formal discussions to build a new high school to serve Black students from both the city and the county. The new Jackson P. Burley High School opened in the fall of 1951, serving grades eight through eleven and Jefferson High School ceased to function as a secondary school. It became known as Jefferson Elementary School, housing African American students in grades first through seventh.

---

[7] *Courses offered at Jefferson High School.* Jefferson Handbook, 24-26. Albemarle Charlottesville Historical Society.
[8] *Additions to Jefferson High School.* Summary Description, Section 7, page 2, VDHR #104-5087

CHAPTER 2

ABOUT JACKSON P. BURLEY
HIGH SCHOOL

Charlottesville and Albemarle County
School Superintendents

In 1946, early planning began between the City of Charlottesville and Albemarle County to unite the three area Negro high schools (Albemarle Training School, Esmont High School and Jefferson High School). In January 1947, the City of Charlottesville and Albemarle County moved forward to acquire land on Rose Hill Drive in the City of Charlottesville for their joint venture. The school superintendents were: Rufus Claude Graham, Albemarle County Public Schools and Robert C. Jennings, City of Charlottesville Public Schools. On January 18, 1947 and January 30, 1947 the City of Charlottesville and County of Albemarle appropriated funds to pay $10,000 each for land, defined in resolutions for the proposed high school for Negro pupils. The resolution established the school would be operated jointly by the City and County.

Through completion of the building and full school desegregation in 1967, Albemarle County and the City of Charlottesville, had several changes in their Superintendents.

Rufus Claude Graham
Albemarle County Public Schools
Superintendent, 1937 – 1947

Paul H. Cale
Albemarle County Public Schools
Superintendent, 1947 – 1969

Robert C. Jennings
Charlottesville Public Schools
Superintendent, 1946 – 1949

Hugh L. Sulfridge
Charlottesville Public Schools
Superintendent, 1949 – 1953

Fendall R. Ellis
Charlottesville Public Schools
Superintendent, 1953 – 1963

George C. Tramontin
Charlottesville Public Schools
Superintendent, 1963 – 1966

Inspection Report for the Proposed Location of the Regional Negro High School

Dated, December 11, 1946

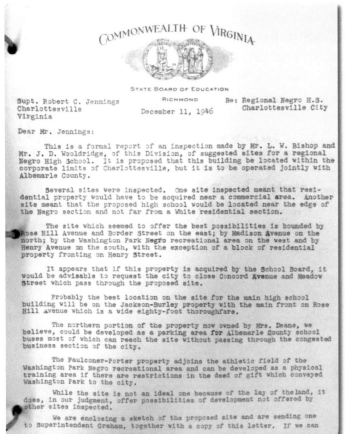

COMMONWEALTH OF VIRGINIA

STATE BOARD OF EDUCATION

RICHMOND

Supt. Robert C. Jennings
Charlottesville
Virginia

December 11, 1946

Re: Regional Negro H.S.
Charlottesville City

Dear Mr. Jennings:

This is a formal report of an inspection made by Mr. L. W. Bishop and Mr. J. D. Wooldridge, of this Division, of suggested sites for a regional Negro High School. It is proposed that this building be located within the corporate limits of Charlottesville, but it is to be operated jointly with Albemarle County.

Several sites were inspected. One site inspected meant that residential property would have to be acquired near a commercial area. Another site meant that the proposed high school would be located near the edge of the Negro section and not far from a White residential section.

The site which seemed to offer the best possibilities is bounded by Rose Hill Avenue and Border Street on the east; by Madison Avenue on the north; by the Washington Park Negro recreational area on the west and by Henry Avenue on the south, with the exception of a block of residential property fronting on Henry Street.

It appears that if this property is acquired by the School Board, it would be advisable to request the city to close Concord Avenue and Meadow Street which pass through the proposed site.

Probably the best location on the site for the main high school building will be on the Jackson-Burley property with the main front on Rose Hill Avenue which is a wide eighty-foot thoroughfare.

The northern portion of the property now owned by Mrs. Deane, we believe, could be developed as a parking area for Albemarle County school buses most of which can reach the site without passing through the congested business section of the city.

The Faulconer-Porter property adjoins the athletic field of the Washington Park Negro recreational area and can be developed as a physical training area if there are restrictions in the deed of gift which conveyed Washington Park to the city.

While the site is not an ideal one because of the lay of the land, it does, in our judgment, offer possibilities of development not offered by other sites inspected.

We are enclosing a sketch of the proposed site and are sending one to Superintendent Graham, together with a copy of this letter. If we can

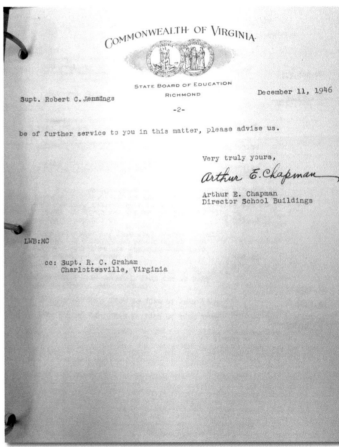

COMMONWEALTH OF VIRGINIA

STATE BOARD OF EDUCATION

RICHMOND

Supt. Robert C. Jennings

December 11, 1946

-2-

be of further service to you in this matter, please advise us.

Very truly yours,

Arthur E. Chapman

Arthur E. Chapman
Director School Buildings

LWB:MC

cc: Supt. R. C. Graham
Charlottesville, Virginia

Charlottesville City School Board
Meeting Minutes - December 1946

City of Charlottesville Council Meeting Minutes
Timeline of Uniting the Three Area Negro High Schools

As early as 1944, a discussion was recorded in the Charlottesville City Planning Commission meeting minutes concerning consideration of "the site of a Colored High School and playground," but no action was taken.

In January of 1947, discussions between the County of Albemarle and the City of Charlottesville on uniting the three area Negro High Schools moved forward. The move would provide better facilities and more varied programs and instructions, for Negro students in the area.

The Charlottesville President/Mayor of the Council was, Roscoe S. Adams. Robert C. Jennings was the Superintendent of the Charlottesville Public Schools.

Charlottesville City Council Members, 1946 – 47	Charlottesville School Board Members – 1947
Roscoe S. Adams, Mayor/President of the Council	Robert C. Jennings, Superintendent
J. Emmett Gleason	First Ward – Mrs. Mason Byrd
Charles P. Nash	Second Ward – W. T. Dettor
Gus K. Tebell	Third Ward – J. Fred Harlan
Fred L. Watson	Fourth Ward Dr. A. G. A. Balz
James E. Bowen, Jr., Clerk of the Council	

January 18, 1947 – Council meeting for the City of Charlottesville, $10,000 was appropriated for payment by the School Board of the City of Charlottesville. It would pay one–half of the cost of acquisition of a site of approximately twelve (12) acres as defined in the resolution of the School Board for a proposed high school for Negro pupils to be established and operated jointly with the County of Albemarle.

February 3, 1947 – Charlottesville Council meeting, the resolution appropriating the $10,000 for one-half of the cost of the site for the joint colored high school was unanimously adopted by recorded vote of the council: Mr. Roscoe S. Adams, Mr. J. Emmett Gleason, Mr. Charles P. Nash, Mr. Gus K. Tebell and Mr. Fred L. Watson. Mr. James E. Bowen, Jr. was the Clerk of the Council.

March 6, 1947 – Charlottesville Council meeting, Mayor Adams advised he had appointed a committee to study a joint school system in accordance with communication from Mr. E. O. McCue, Jr. The committee was comprised of Dr. William R. Smithey, Dr. Loren A. Thompson, and Mr. William, S. Hildreth.

A document related to the Burley property and its ultimate transfer to the City is a typed letter from Maggie P. Burley to Seth Burnley, City Manager, and members of the City and County school boards, dated March 17, 1947. In the letter, Maggie P. Burley states unequivocally that her property in Block 32 is not for sale. She would, however, be willing to sell other parcels to the City. She did not want to sell her home because it would be a "great sacrifice." Before moving to the Rose Hill neighborhood, the Burleys had lived on Free Bridge Road in Albemarle County and the adjacent golf club had bought it. She states they were "younger" then but that now it would be a great hardship for her to give up her residence. The March 1947 letter goes on to state that she and her husband had opened their property and offered "demonstrations for the benefit of school children and adults," suggesting that her reluctance to sell her house was not for lack of caring about children and their education. She closed her letter by declaring, "We, as well as some of our close neighbors, are in the midst of spending and planning in order to improve our homes, for more healthful living, and I am sure you would not think of moving these homes when there are so many slum areas."

The Burleys also owned lots 33 and 34 in Block 34 and lots 1 through 6 in Block 35. Maggie was willing to sell other parcels of her land to the City.

April 7, 1947 – Charlottesville Council meeting, the following Resolution was unanimously adopted:
BE IT RESOLVED, by the Council of the City of Charlottesville that the plan for the joint ownership and operation of a high school for Negro pupils proposed by the School Board of the City of Charlottesville and the County of Albemarle be and the same is hereby approved, and it is recommended that the said Board proceed to acquire a suitable site for the establishment of such joint high school.

May 19, 1947 – Charlottesville Council meeting, Mr. Robert C. Jennings, Superintendent of Charlottesville Schools addressed the Council and presented a resolution from the Charlottesville School Board requesting the City authorized the School Board to enter into a joint contract with the Albemarle County School Board to employ an architect to prepare plans for the new joint colored high school.

June 16, 1947 – Charlottesville Council meeting, Mayor Adams advised he had appointed Mr. Fred Watson, Mr. J. Emmett Gleason, Mr. Charles P. Nash and Mr. James E. Bowen, Jr., as a committee to work with a committee from the Board of Supervisors of Albemarle County in the matter of employing an architect for the proposed joint city-county colored high school.

August 4, 1947 – Charlottesville Council meeting, the Council appropriated $500 for legal cost in connection with acquiring property for the new joint colored high school.

September 12, 1947 – Charlottesville Council meeting, the Council appropriated $200 for a survey at the proposed Joint County-City colored high school site.

The land needed for the new high school site was owned by distinguished citizen, Jackson P. Burley. Jackson was a teacher and devoted church worker in Charlottesville and Albemarle County. The desired Burley land was eventually secured by the City of Charlottesville using the Right of Eminent Domain on September 25, 1948.

It appeared that additional property other than the Burley dwelling site was conveyed to the City of Charlottesville in the summer of 1948. There was a reference in the Planning Commission Meeting Minutes of August 18, 1948, stating, "Particular investigation was made of the area on Rose Hill

Street adjacent to the newly acquired school site, and of the areas to the north and south of Route 250, and west of Route 29." [1]

Additional property acquired was owned by:[2]

- Lucy C. Deane, 6.33 acres more or less, all of Block 33 and 34 excepts lots 12, 13 and 14 and lots 1 to 13 inclusive, Block 42, and all right, title and interest in Cynthianna Avenue west of Rose Hill Street

- Sally Fry Wood sold .84 acres, more or less, Lot 19, Block 35, and all right, title and interest in all adjoining or abutting streets and alleys.

- Sallie H. Smith and Nettis S. Burgess sold .21 acres more or less, Lots 12 and 13, Block 34, and all right, title and interest in all adjoining or abutting streets and alleys.

- William A. McClung and Rosser J. Eastman, 1.48 and more particularly described as Lots 13 to 19 inclusive and Lots 26 and 27 on a plat of Beachtree Subdivision.

A final decree was issued on October 15, 1948, in the matter of the City of Charlottesville and the County School Board of Albemarle County (for school purposes) versus Maggie Payne Burley et als, ". . . that the aforesaid condemnors on September 25, 1948 paid to the Clerk of this Court the sum of $14,000.00 as ascertained and awarded by said Commissioners in said report. . . confirms unto the School Board of the City of Charlottesville and the County School Board of Albemarle County as provided by Statute the fee simple title to all of the following property . . . all that certain tract of land in the City of Charlottesville, Virginia, containing 2.16 acres more or less and particularly described as all of Block 32. . ." Thus it appears that Maggie P. Burley, who had contested the sale of her home for the purposes of completing the parcel for the new high school, had to accept condemnation of her property and payment for it. Such transactions are suggestive of the unequal relationship between African American landowners and local governments during the Jim Crow era. [3]

At a meeting of the Council on September 19, 1949, Mr. Randolph H. Perry, and other members of the City School Board appeared before the Council and presented a Resolution, which had been adopted by the body at said meeting. The resolution passed by judgement of the Board the **construction and school's equipment** for the City's half of the Joint Negro High School would be $600,000.

---

[1] Minute Book H, Charlottesville City Council, Sep 1, 1938 – Apr 1, 1947 and Minute Book I, Charlottesville City Council, Apr 1, 1947 – Aug 31, 1953. *Timeline of uniting the three area Negro High Schools.* Meeting Minutes of Planning Commission, City of Charlottesville, Dec 15, 1944

[2] Charlottesville Deeds, DB: 39–476–478, Plat of a sub-division of Rose Hill known as Lincoln Heights. DB 140, page 488, Deed Book B 52, page 262, Deed Book 97, pages 348-49, Deed Book 126, pages 231-232. *Additional property purchased for Jackson P. Burley School site.*

[3] Charlottesville Circuit Court Real Property Data, Final Decree recorded in Deed Book, 141:33 (1948).

The vision was realized and Jackson P. Burley High School would become a reality. The school was built in 1950 by J.W. Daniels Construction Company at a cost of $748,066.47.

In 1951, the newly constructed Jackson P. Burley High School would end the operation of Albemarle Training School, Esmont High School and Jefferson High School. Students from the City of Charlottesville, Albemarle County and some students from Greene and Nelson counties would be in attendance.

In 1951, Mr. Leander Shaw became the first Principal of Jackson P. Burley High School. In 1952, Mr. Eugene Mobley became the Principal and Mr. Edwin A. Simmons became the Assistant Principal. Mr. Alexander Scott served as Principal from 1960 until 1967.

Jackson P. Burley High School proved to be the last substantial project prior to the 1954 Supreme Court's *Brown v. Board of Education* decision that outlawed school segregation. In 1958 the NAACP filed a lawsuit on behalf of Burley students who sought the opportunity to transfer to all white Lane High School. This resulted in the City joining the massive resistance strategy that prevailed throughout the commonwealth. Despite students being offered admission to attend Lane High School as early as 1962, some students chose to attend Burley instead. [4]

On September 4, 1958, the Charlottesville School Board met to consider applications for the transfer of thirty-three Black pupils who were residents of Charlottesville. The Board resolved unanimously that each applicant be refused permission to transfer, offering as reasons that twenty-four lived in the Jefferson Elementary School District, sixteen were not academically qualified, and three were likely to have social adjustment problems. [5]

For sixteen years (1951 – 1967), Jackson P. Burley was the only high school in the immediate Charlottesville/Albemarle area serving Black students. Desegregation closed the school in 1967 and the school became the Jack Jouett Junior Annex before going back to its original name of Jackson P. Burley in 1973.

---

[4] Virginia Foundation for the Humanities. *In 1958 the NAACP filed a lawsuit on behalf of Burley students who sought the opportunity to transfer to the all –white Lane High School.*

[5] School Board Meeting minutes, September 4, 1958. *Charlottesville School Board met to consider applications for the transfer of thirty-three Black pupils who were residents of Charlottesville.*

Albemarle County Board of Supervisors Meeting Minutes Timeline of Uniting the Three Area Negro High Schools

In April 1946, a resolution was adopted by the School Board of Albemarle County, Virginia that determined it was necessary to construct, furnish and equip a Negro high school building.

In January of 1947, discussions between the County of Albemarle and the City of Charlottesville had become serious in moving forward on uniting the three area Negro High Schools.

The Chairman of the Albemarle County Board of Supervisors was, P. H. Gentry. Rufus Claude Graham was the Superintendent of the Albemarle County Public Schools.

Albemarle County Board of Supervisors	Albemarle County School Board Members
P. H. Gentry, **Chairman of the Board**	Rufus Claude Graham, **Superintendent**
W. Warren Wood, Rivanna District	Joseph T. Henley, **Chairman**
E. J. Ballard, Ivy District	W. A. Dawson, Jr.
C. Purcell McCue – Samuel Miller District	Earnest J. Oglesby
T. E. Bruce, Scottsville District	Karl R. Wallace
Henry Chiles, White Hall District	Robert E. Turner
June T. Via, Clerk of the Board	Paul H. Cale, Clerk
D. A. Robinson, Director of Finance	

April 17, 1946 – Meeting of the Albemarle County Board of Supervisors, the following Resolution was approved:

> **"BE IT RESOLVED**, *by the County Board of Albemarle County, Virginia as follows: It is hereby determined that it is necessary to purchase sites and to construct and to furnish and equip one White high school building and one Negro high school building;*

January 15, 1947 – Meeting of the Albemarle County Board of Supervisors of Albemarle County, Virginia, a notice of a special meeting to be held at 7:00 o'clock P.M., on the 30th day of January, at the Board Room in the County Office Building, on Court Square, in the City of Charlottesville, Virginia, for the purpose of considering and acting upon a plan for the joint ownership and operation of a high school for Negro pupils proposed by the School Boards of the City of Charlottesville and the County of Albemarle; considering and making an appropriation toward cost of acquiring a site for such proposed high school.

January 30, 1947 – Meeting of the Albemarle County Board of Supervisors the following Resolution was unanimously adopted:

> BE IT RESOLVED, *by the Board of County Supervisors of Albemarle County that the plan for the joint ownership and operation of a high school for Negro pupils proposed by the School Boards of the City of Charlottesville and the County of Albemarle be and the same is hereby approved, and it is recommended that the said Boards proceed to acquire a suitable site for the establishment of such joint high school.*

BE IT RESOLVED, *by the Board of County Supervisors of Albemarle County that $10,000.00, or so much as may be necessary, be and the same is hereby appropriated for the payment by the County School Board of Albemarle County of one-half of the cost of acquiring a site for a proposed high school for Negro pupils to be established and operated jointly with the city of Charlottesville.*

February 26, 1947 – Meeting of the Albemarle County Board of Supervisors, Mr. E. O. McCue presented a request to appoint a committee to study the school systems of the County of Albemarle and the City of Charlottesville. Mr. Gentry appointed, Gen. P. B. Peyton, Mr. E.H. Bain, and Mr. F. E. Paulett to serve on the committee.

August 20, 1947 – Meeting of the Albemarle County Board of Supervisors, $250 was appropriated out of the Unappropriated Reserve to be used for a contour map for the Joint Negro High School.

April 21, 1948 – Meeting of the Albemarle County Board of Supervisors, Mr. Paul H. Cale, Superintendent of County Schools, appeared concerning the condemnations proceedings in connection with the purchase of a site for the proposed Joint Negro High School. Upon motion, made by Mrs. W.W. Wood and seconded by Mr. Henry Chiles, the following resolution was unanimously adopted:

> **BE IT RESOLVED**, *by the Board of County Supervisors of Albemarle County, Virginia, that the Albemarle County School Board be and it is hereby authorized to proceed with the purchase of a site for the proposed Joint Negro High School, and*
>
> **BE IT FURTHER RESOLVED** *that $16,377.50 be appropriated from the Unappropriated Reserve of the General Fund to be used by the School Board in purchasing a site for the aforesaid school.*

September 15, 1948 – Meeting of the Albemarle County Board of Supervisors, and Mr. D. A. Robinson, Director of Finance presented a statement of the cost of land for the Joint Colored High School showing $38,260.25 as the total cost of the land, not including the architect fees previously paid, nor court costs, recording fees, and attorney fees still to be paid. Upon action, made by Mr. Chiles and seconded by Mr. Ballard, the following resolution was unanimously adopted:

> **BE IT RESOLVED**, *by the Board of County Supervisors of Albemarle County, Virginia, that $1,770.20 or as much thereof as may be necessary be and is hereby appropriated from the Unappropriated Reserve of the General Fund to be used in payment of the County's share of court cost, recording fees and attorney fees in connection with the purchase of land for the Joint Colored High School.*

November 17, 1948 – Meeting of the Albemarle County Board of Supervisors, Mr. Paul H. Cale, Superintendent of Schools, and Mr. J.T. Henley, Chairman of the School Board appeared before the Board and requested that funds be made available to pay for the County's share of architectural fees for the Joint Negro High School. Mr. D. A. Robinson, Director of Finance suggested that as a means these funds the Board might consider making available to the School Fund the amount of their current levy as shown by the original current assessment books of his office.

January 19, 1949 – Meeting of the Albemarle County Board of Supervisors, Chairman, Mr. P.H. Gentry and Mr. C. Purcell McCue, appointed a committee to work with the committee from the City of Charlottesville in making a survey of the costs of the Joint Negro High School Project. Committee members were: Mr. C. R. Dorrier, Mr. W. W. Wood, Gen. P. B. Peyton, and Mr. W. O. Fife.

Upon a motion made by Mr. Wood and seconded by Mr. Ballard, a resolution was unanimously adopted for the County to appropriate $180.00 from the Unappropriated Reserve of the General Fund to cover the County's share of the premium on an additional $25,000.00 bond approved by the Director of Finance at a meeting held on December 15, 1948. The motion was made by Mr. Chiles and seconded by Mr. Dorrier.

July 20, 1949 – Meeting of the Albemarle County Board of Supervisors, a letter from B. C. Baker addressed to Superintendent Paul H. Cale was presented advising that August 15, 1949 had been set aside as the completion date for the working drawings and specifications of the Joint Negro High School. In connection with this matter, the following resolution was received from the City Council:

> **"BE IT RESOLVED** *by the Council of the City of Charlottesville that the City Attorney be and he is hereby authorized to prepare an ordinance authorizing the issuance of bonds for the purpose of improvement to the Public School System of Charlottesville, and,*
>
> **BE IT FURTHER RESOLVED** *that the Mayor and the City Manager be and are hereby required to confer with proper Albemarle County officials relative to the date of the bond issue election pertaining to the New Joint Colored High School."*

Upon motion made by Mr. Dorrier and seconded by Mr. Ballard, the action of the School Board taken at its last regular meeting was approved.

August 17, 1949 – Meeting of the Albemarle County Board of Supervisors, Mr. Paul H. Cale, Superintendent of Schools, appeared regarding the proposed bond issue for the Joint Negro High School. After a discussion of the matter, the following resolution was introduced by Mr. J. W. Williams and seconded by Mr. C. R. Dorrier, it was unanimously adopted.

> **"BE IT RESOLVED** *by the County School Board of Albemarle County, Virginia, as follows:*
>
> **(1)** *It is hereby determined that is necessary to construct jointly with the City of Charlottesville, Virginia, a Negro high school building and jointly furnish and equip the same for the joint use of the County of Albemarle and the City of Charlottesville; and hereby determined that one-half of the costs of construction and one-half costs of the furnishing and equipping said building be at the expense of said County.*
>
> **(2)** *It is hereby determined that it is necessary and expedient to contract a loan on the credit of the County of Albemarle in an amount not to exceed $600,000.00 in order to carry out the purposes referred to in the foregoing, and to issue School Bonds of Albemarle County*

to evidence said loan in the amount not to exceed $600,000.00, pursuant to Section 673, 2738, 2739, 2740, 2741 and 2741b, of the Code of Virginia, which said bonds shall bear interest at a rate not exceeding five per centum per annum, and shall mature in such annual, or semi-annual installments, as may hereafter be determined by resolution of this Board, the last installment of which shall be payable not more than thirty years from the date of such bonds, provided, however, that at least four per centum of the principal amount of said bonds shall, beginning not later than five years after date of issue, be payable annually, together with all due interest. A tax sufficient to pay the principal and interest of said bonds as the same nature shall be levied upon all of the property subject to taxation by said County.

January 18, 1950 – Meeting of the Albemarle County Board of Supervisors, a request was received to establish a School Construction Bond Fund for the Joint Negro High School. Upon motion by Mr. Chiles and seconded by Mr. Williams, a School Construction Bond Fund was established.

July 19, 1950 – Meeting of the Albemarle County Board of Supervisors, a request was received from the Albemarle County School Board to make a written offer of $1,500 for four lots extending 160 feet, facing Henry Avenue, owned by William Johnson, in order that the land might be added to the Joint Negro High School site. The Charlottesville City School Board and the Albemarle County School Board would each pay one–half the cost of the land. The resolution was offered by Mr. Williams and seconded by Mr. Wood was unanimously adopted.

July 19, 1950 – Meeting of the Albemarle County Board of Supervisors, a request was received from the Albemarle County School Board to make a written offer of $1,500 for four lots extending 160 feet, facing Henry Avenue, owned by William Johnson, in order that the land might be added to the Joint Negro High School site. The Charlottesville City School Board and the Albemarle County School Board would each pay one–half the cost of the land. The resolution was offered by Mr. Williams and seconded by Mr. Wood was unanimously adopted. [6]

---

[6] Albemarle County Board of Supervisors Meeting Minutes, January 1946 – December 1949 and Albemarle County School Board Minutes, January 1946 – July 1951. *Timeline of uniting the three area Negro High Schools.*

1947 Joint School Board Representatives from Albemarle County and the City of Charlottesville

Albemarle County School Board Members
Joseph T. Henley, **Chairman**
Earnest J. Oglesby
Leslie H. Walton

City of Charlottesville School Board Members
Randolph Perry, **Chairman**
H. W. Walsh
Harry A. Wright

Drawing of Jackson P. Burley High School
Charlottesville Daily Progress
October 14, 1950

Architects: Pendleton S. Clark of Lynchburg, VA and Associated Architects, Baker, Heyward and Llorens of Charlottesville, VA

Completed Jackson P. Burley High School 1951

Naming of Jackson P. Burley High School

Appropriate Names For Two Virginia Schools

THE school boards of two widely separated Virginia communities have acted wisely in their choice of persons they will honor in naming two schools for colored pupils. In both instances there can hardly be any doubt that the honorees symbolize quite admirably a high calibre of citizenship and devotion to the cause of public education.

In Richmond, the City School Board has announced that the GEORGE THORPE School on the city's North Side which is being made available to colored pupils, will be renamed in honor of the late ALBERT V. NORRELL, pioneer Richmond educator and outstanding citizen.

In Charlottesville, the new colored high school being built jointly by Albemarle County and the City of Charlottesville at a cost of $1,200,-000, will be named in memory of the late JACKSON PRICE BURLEY, educator, of Albemarle County. The name, which was recommended by a special committee appointed for the purpose, has been unanimously approved by the two school boards.

Mr. NORRELL's long and constructive career was linked closely with the progress of public education for his race in Richmond and throughout Virginia for more than a half century. It was said of him that as both teacher and principal in Richmond's public schools, he had the rare capacity of inspiring his pupils simply by the wholesome influence of his personality, and his career as an educator is probably without parallel in the State's capital city.

Mr. NORRELL was associated with the city's public schools in one capacity or another for 65 years, until his retirement in 1939 at the age of 82, just two years before his death. He also served as president, secretary and treasurer of the Richmond Teachers Association.

Mr. BURLEY, a native of Albemarle County, graduated from Hampton Institute in 1889. For the following twelve years he taught at Stony Point in Albermarle County, and at Eastham in 1917-18. When he retired in 1937, he had been teaching agriculture at the Albemarle Training School for 19 years. He died on July 2, 1945 at his home which is part of the present site of the new high school.

The naming of these two schools will undoubtedly serve to remind the citizens of Richmond and Charlottesville and Albermarle County specifically, as well as Virginians generally, of two notable figures whose devotion to the cause of public education paid large dividends for future generations.

New Journal and Guide, June 17, 1950
ProQuest Historical Newspapers:
Newspaper Collection pg. 12A
*Courtesy of Albemarle Charlottesville
Historical Society*

New Joint School Will Honor Name Of Jackson Burley

The joint Negro High School being built by the County of Albemarle and the City of Charlottesville will be known as the Jackson P. Burley High School. This name, recommended by a committee appointed to select a name, has been approved by the two school boards.

Jackson Price Burley, native of Albemarle County, was born February 12, 1863. He attended Hampton Institute and was graduated in 1889. For the next 12 years he taught at Stony Point and for the following 17 years operated a store at the intersection of Free Bridge Road and Meade Avenue. He taught at Eastham in 1917-18, and in 1918 moved to the Albemarle Training School, where he taught agriculture for 19 years until his retirement in 1937.

He spent his years of retirement before his death on July 2, 1945, at his home, which is part of the present site of the Joint Negro High School. He was highly respected as a teacher and as a citizen by a large number of people with whom he had dealings.

Daily Progress - June 2, 1950
*Courtesy of Albemarle
Charlottesville Historical Society*

Charlottesville Dedicates New $1,400,000 Hi School

By T. J. SELLERS

CHARLOTTESVILLE, Va.—The governor of Virginia came back to his home town Friday night of last week as guest of honor at the dedication ceremonies of the new $1,400,000 Jackson P. Burley High School.

Governor Battle praised the Albemarle and Charlottesville school boards for this new venture in city-county cooperation and pointed out that this was the first educational plant in Virginia to be jointly sponsored by a city and a county.

He also reminded the mixed audience of an observation that he had made in his message to the General Assembly earlier this year.

"In that message I said that we must have just as good schools for our Negro citizens as we have for our white citizens, and I said that must be done not because of any impelling force from the federal courts but because of its right."

THIS ASSERTION brought scattered applause from both the white and Negro sections of the spacious auditorium.

Earlier during the program Homan W. Walsh, new chairman of the city school board, had described the Negro school as one of the finest of its kind in the state or nation in accepting it from Contractor John W. Daniel.

Mr. Walsh also gave his views on the fundamentals of democracy. "Here is evidenced the functioning of a fundamental tenet of our concept of democracy, of American democracy. In dedicating this property to the education of Negroes, so that they may enjoy these fundamental rights of man, the obligation inherent in the rights of the majority is thus recognized and fulfilled."

There are 26 class rooms, which include science laboratories, band, choral, art, homemaking, commerce, and nursing rooms, as well as standard class rooms. The library is located on the first floor just opposite the central school entrance.

THE AUDITORIUM in which the dedicatory program was held, is situated at the end of the building near the corner of Henry street and Rose Hill drive and seats 900. It has a modern stage and light facilities for drama presentations and can be cut off from the class room area. There is also a separate lobby which makes the auditorium useful for other groups engaged in community activities.

The gymnasium, at the opposite end of the building from the auditorium, is located adjacent to the playing areas. It has folding bleachers which seat 720 and is equipped with a motorized partition which divides the standard playing court into two areas for use by boys and girls at the same time.

The cafeteria is located below the gymnasium and has a modern kitchen with a walk-in ice box and refrigerated garbage room.

The shops are housed in a separate building across the parking lot from the rear of the main building.

THE STRUCTURE was designed by the architectural firms of Baker, Heyward, and Lorens, of Charlottesville and Pendleton S. Clarke, of Lynchburg.

A highlight of the dedication program was the presence of Mrs. Jackson P. Burley, widow of the man for whom the school was named. Jackson P. Burley taught in the Albemarle county schools until his retirement in 1935, and Mrs. Burley once served as supervisor in the same system. Mr. Burley died here in 1945, and Mrs. Burley now makes her home in Atlanta, Ga., with her daughter. The new school is located on the former home site of the Burley family.

The joint high school opened last fall, and has an enrollment of 543 pupils and a faculty of 26. Leander J. Shaw is principal.

EDUCATOR and school officials seated on the platform included: Colgate W. Darden, Jr., president of the University of Virginia; Dowell J. Howard, state superintendent of public instruction, and Dr. J. Rupert Picott, executive secretary, Virginia Teachers Association.

Joseph T. Henly, chairman, school board of the county of Albemarle, presided, and special music was furnished by the Jackson P. Burley Band and Chorus. Dr. E. D. McCreary gave the invocation, and the Rev. Waddell Ward pronounced the benediction.

New Journal and Guide (1916-2003); Mar 29, 1952; *ProQuest Historical Newspapers: Black Newspaper Collection* pg. 26
By T. J. Sellers

Application for Building Permit – 1950

City of Charlottesville – Application for Building Permit, "Joint Negro School, Charlottesville and Albemarle County"

Diagram of Burley High School – 1950

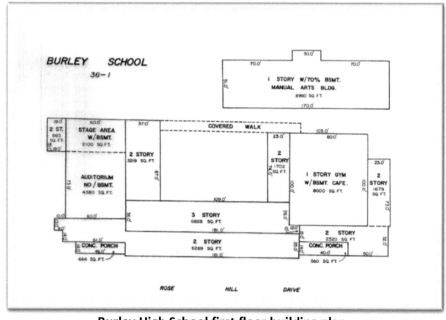

Burley High School first floor building plan
Courtesy of City of Charlottesville

About Jackson P. Burley High School

Jackson P. Burley High School is located at 901 Rose Hill Drive in Charlottesville, VA on a 17.6 acre site. Burley is one of three operating Virginia schools that had once been all-black. The school was built in an urban setting in the Rose Hill Drive neighborhood, historically known as Rose Hill. A portion of Rose Hill was sold to the Charlottesville Industrial and Land Improvement Company in the late 19th century. Rose Hill was a late 18th century Albemarle County plantation, built by William and Mildred Gilmer Wirt.

For many years the parents of Black students attending overcrowded, inadequate, and poorly funded high schools in the City of Charlottesville and Albemarle County had assembled in their small schools, homes, and churches for answers. They discussed what could be done to assist them in helping their children to receive a better education, which would prepare them for a future other than domestic work. Black parents continued to provide out of pocket financial support to subsidize the education of their children. As early as 1937, they began to form Parent-Teacher Leagues, Men and Women Leagues, as well as, sought support from the NAACP. Very little of their tax dollars helped in the educating of their children and providing adequate facilities.

Educational opportunities for Black children in Albemarle County was severely limited prior to desegregation. Well into the first half of the 20th century, it remained common for students to stop their education after primary school. In addition, due to segregationist policies, black public high schools tended to promote vocational education, which allowed for very limited economic power. Community involvement played a significant role in creating and supporting the early education of Black students. Outside philanthropic entities, like the Jeanes Fund, which provided teachers in rural black schools financial support. The Jeanes Foundation, also known as the Negro Rural School Fund or Jeanes Fund, helped support education and vocational programs for African American in rural communities from 1908 to the 1960s. The fund was founded in 1907 by Anna T. Jeanes, a white Quaker who endowed the fund with $1,000,000. Booker T. Washington helped to create a Board of Trustees to manage the fund. The Jeanes teachers were mostly women.

Two localities, the City of Charlottesville and the County of Albemarle sought to achieve equal educational facilities during the era of segregation. Absent any pending legal challenges that were common throughout the Commonwealth during the 1940s, an agreement between the City of Charlottesville and neighboring Albemarle County was reached for the two political jurisdictions to work together. The building of a school to be owned and operated jointly by the City and the County was constructed to serve African American high school students from both jurisdictions. [7]

In Virginia, unlike in other states, counties and cities are completely separate jurisdictions, a condition that dates to colonial times when the basic government unit was the county. Cities only exist when a charter was granted by the Virginia General Assembly, and as a rule spanning the years

---

[7] Albemarle Charlottesville Historical Society, Jackson P. Burley collections folder. *Two localities, City of Charlottesville and County of Albemarle builds school.*

since the colonial period, cities and counties have maintained separate government facilities, including schools.

Jackson P. Burley High School is significant, as a symbol with a unique history. It serves as an emblem, of herculean efforts in Virginia (prior to the historic Brown v. Board of Education Supreme Court decision) to address the lack of equal facilities for high-school aged African American youths. The agreement to construct a new high school to provide nominally equal, but segregated, educational facilities for African American youth, resulted from the overcrowded and seriously insufficient facilities for African American students in both jurisdictions, notably Esmont High School, Albemarle County Training School, and Jefferson High School in the City.[8]

The new Lane High School opened in 1940. It was a large modern building constructed to serve white students in Charlottesville. The school was built on Preston Avenue and McIntire Road when the student population outgrew the Midway School. The building of Lane High School, likely stimulated broad support in the African American community for an adequate high school for its youth. In an environment around the Commonwealth where challenges due to the lack of equal facilities for African American students and serious overcrowding were being successfully litigated, the construction of a new and well-equipped high school building for African American students was viewed as mandatory. It is also likely that financial demands on a small city and a county to build separate high school buildings for each jurisdiction would have been prohibitive. The building and opening of Jackson P. Burley High School proved to be the last substantial effort in Virginia prior to the 1954 Supreme Court's ruling in the Plessy v. Ferguson that overturned "separate but equal" in both public accommodations and in schools. [9]

It was at this time that the City of Charlottesville and Albemarle County began to look at land off Rose Hill Drive to build a school. The area west of Rose Hill Drive was one of several neighborhoods in the City that was marketed to African Americans. These included the historic Charlottesville neighborhoods, known as 'Lincoln Heights' and 'Preston Park.' The land on which the school sits was part of the neighborhood known as Lincoln Heights. Preston Park was a subdivision developed in 1913. The area included present-day Booker Street, part of the south side of Charlton Avenue (then known as Carlton Avenue), and part of the west side of Rose Hill Drive (then known as Rose Hill Street/Avenue). In the minutes of a meeting of the Planning Commission of the City of Charlottesville, held on March 8, 1949 a communication addressed to the City Council from Radio Station WCHV, dated February 24, 1949, with reference to the requested re-naming of Rose Hill Avenue was considered, and after full discussion the Commission agreed to recommend to the City Council that the thoroughfare extending northward from Preston Avenue to the city limits, including that portion now known as Gentry Road, be hereafter designated as Rose Hill Drive. [10]

---

[8] Maral S. Kalbian, LLC and Margaret T. Peters. Nomination for National Register of Historic Places, 2020. Charlottesville, DHR No. 104-5276-0064, *Construct new high school*. Section 8, page 13.

[9] Statement of Significance, Sec 8, para 13, National Park Service/National Register of Historic Places *(OMB No. 1024-0018.)* Nov 2020. *Challenges to Albemarle County to build a second high school*.

[10] *Plans to build Jackson P. Burley High School*. Meeting minutes of the Planning Commission of Charlottesville, Mar 8, 1949.

By pooling resources of both Charlottesville and Albemarle County, it became possible to construct a school building that in many ways, sought to equal the all-white Lane High School built in 1940. Lane High School, now used as the Albemarle County Office Building, epitomized the monumental public school, so common in the second quarter of the 20th century. It was a three–part symmetrical brick block with side wings, it is of the Classical Revival Style and is an imposing presence. Schools, such as Lane high School were meant to illustrate a community's commitment to public education and to be local landmarks.

Clark S. Pendleton of Lynchburg designed Lane High School and is also listed as an Associate Architect for Jackson P. Burley High School, although the extent of his contribution is not certain. Both schools are brick, but Burley is not symmetrical and features large expanses of ribbon windows and a flat roof. The minimalist aesthetic of the Stripped Classical Modernism Style is expressed in Burley in its flat-roofed, rectangular forms, with limited exterior decoration that alludes to classical motifs. However, Burley was not of the traditional Colonial Revival Style, but rather a more subdued institutional design, based on classical forms with limited decorations. Modern fireproof materials were used, that may have not been available at the time Lane High School was constructed, a decade earlier. One can speculate that the environment in a community, which was home to a major university would have been more conducive to pursuing this challenge. Large cities like Richmond, Norfolk, and Roanoke already had substantial high school buildings for African American students, but small communities and rural counties with fewer revenue sources would have been far more hard-pressed to erect such buildings. Moreover, the constituency calling for such improvements would have been considerably smaller and less vocal and influential.

The most interesting document related to the Burley property and its ultimate transfer to the City is a typed letter from Maggie P. Burley to Seth Burnley, Charlottesville City Manager, and members of the City and County School Boards, dated March 17, 1947. In the letter, Maggie P. Burley states unequivocally, that her property in Block 32 is not for sale. She did not want to sell her home, because it would be a "great sacrifice." The Burleys home was built on Block 32.

Additional property, other than the Burley dwelling, was conveyed to the City of Charlottesville in the summer of 1948. There was a reference in the Planning Commissiion Meeting Minutes of August 18, 1948, stating, "Particular investigation was made of the area on Rose Hill Street adjacent to the newly acquired school site." A final decree was issued on October 15, 1948, in the matter of the City of Charlottesville and the County School Board of Albemarle County (for school purposes) versus Maggie Payne Burley et als, "that the aforesaid condemnors on September 25, 1948 paid to the Clerk of this Court the sum of $14,000.00 as ascertained and awarded by said Commissioners in said report. confirms unto the School Board of the City of Charlottesville and the County School Board of Albemarle County as provided by Statue the fee simple title to all the following property ... all that certain tract of land in the City of Charlottesville, Virginia, containing 2.16 acres more or less and particularly described as all of Block 32 ..."[11] Thus it appears that Maggie P. Burley, who had

---

[11] *Final Decree for Land.* Recorded in Charlottesville Deed book 141:33 (1948)

contested the sale of her home for the purposes of completing the parcel for the new high school, had to accept condemnation of her property and payment for it. [12]

By August of the following year, 1949 plans for the "Joint Negro High School" for the City of Charlottesville and for the County of Albemarle were in place.

The new school was named for Maggie P. Burley's late husband, Jackson P. Burley by a special committee appointed and approved by the school boards of both jurisdictions. According to the *Daily Progress* article, dated June 2, 1950, Burley was a native of Albemarle County born in 1863. He studied at Hampton Institute and following his graduation began his long career as a teacher. He later moved back to Albemarle County, and taught Agriculture at the Albemarle Training School for nineteen years before retiring in 1937. As a life-long educator and community leader, the committee agreed, it was most fitting to name the new high school for him. It was also appropriate as most of the land where Burley stands had belonged to Jackson P. Burley and his family.[13]

Segregation continued in Charlottesville and Albemarle County following the 1954 *Brown v. Board of Education of Topeka* decision (by the U. S. Supreme Court), and Black residents who requested transfers to white schools in 1955 were denied. . . . A Black student who wished to transfer from Burley High School to Lane High School had to submit a written application and meet certain residential and academic qualifications, and other criteria that did not apply to white students. In July of 1958, the city School Board "adopted a resolution establishing a pupil assignment plan." It called for attendance zones with the boundaries drawn in such a way that the majority of the Negro students living in the Jefferson School zone. The plan also included the administration of an achievement test for any Negro student wishing to attend a school outside his or her residential zone. It was believed that such tests would eliminate many Negro pupils wishing to transfer to previously all-white schools. An interview with the student and his or her parent was also required, with students denied transfer who appeared to have "hostile attitudes or indifference." During the summer and early fall of 1958, the Charlottesville City School Board examined the applications of 22 Black students, 10 at Burley and 12 at Jefferson for admission to Lane High School, and Venable Elementary School, and in two cases, McGuffey School. The School Board denied all of the applications based on geographical location (the student lived closer to the school in which they were already enrolled), test results which the Board believed showed that the students were not qualified to keep up with the work, and a personal interview with both the students and their parents. In all cases, the evaluation closed with the statement, "for the foregoing reasons, this application is denied." [14]

---

[12] Charlottesville Deeds, DB: 39–476–478, Plat of a sub-division of Rose Hill known as Lincoln Heights. Deed Book 140, page 488, Deed Book 52, page 262, Deed Book 97, pages 348-49, Deed Book 126, pages 231-232. *Additional property needed to purchase the site for Jackson P. Burley School.*

[13] The Daily Progress, June 2, 1950. *Naming of Burley High school.*

[14] Virginia Foundation for the Humanities. *Segregation continues in Charlottesville and Albemarle County.*

Architectural Description of
Jackson P. Burley High School

The architectural plans for the building of the "Joint Negro School," were approved by the Joint Board of Control from the City of Charlottesville and Albemarle County in 1949. The plans were signed by members of the Joint Board for Control; Hugh L. Sulfridge, Division Superintendent for the City of Charlottesville Schools and Paul H. Cale, Division Superintendent for the County of Albemarle Schools; J.T. Henley, Chairman of the Albemarle County School Board and Randolph Perry, Chairman of the Charlottesville School Board also signed off on the plans.

Topographic Map: Completed by, A. R. Sweet and Associates, Engineers-Surveyors in Charlottesville, Virginia. Completed on October 9, 1947. The South/East Section was revised on July 13, 1949.

Architects: The architects for the design of the "Joint Negro School" were: Pendleton S. Clark of Lynchburg, Virginia and Associated Architects, Baker, Heyward and Llorens of Charlottesville, VA. The architectural design was completed on August 25, 1949, with revisions in December 1949.

Consulting Engineers: Engineers, Watson and Hart completed Structural and Electrical work and Wiley and Wilson completed the Heating and Ventilation work.

Construction Company and Builder: The building of the school began in 1950, by John W. Daniels Construction Company of Danville, VA.

Cost to build: Structure – ($622,733.57), plumbing and heating – ($83,332.90) and electrical work – ($42,000). The total cost to build was: $748,066.47. The total cost was $15,000 more than originally estimated.

Architectural Classification: Modern Movement: **Other:** Stripped Classical Modernism Style

Materials: Brick, concrete, steel, metal, aluminum, and other

General Characteristics: The school was built in a residential neighborhood in northwest Charlottesville. The front of the school faces east toward Rose Hill Drive. The large U-shaped school is minimally set back from the concrete sidewalk, which runs along the Rose Hill Drive front and Henry Avenue sides, which is north of its junction. The small front lawn allows for a few ornamental trees, a grassy area, and planting beds. Poured concrete walkways lead from the sidewalk to the central main entrance and to the auditorium and gymnasium entrances. Three steps lead up to the main entrance doors.

The vernacular International–style architecture for the school takes the form of a rectangle with a central block marked by a two-story, three bay, projecting cast stone entry with recessed modern aluminum doors and windows. On either side are matching brick wings with secondary entries marked by one-story multi-bay porticos. The wing to the north is the gymnasium, and the one to the south houses the auditorium. The side and rear walls of this sprawling building are all brick, and the flat roofs are at multiple levels due to the downward–sloping site toward the rear of the building.

The primary entrance along Rose Hill Drive is through a monumental, two-story, projecting entrance of cast stone. In deep contrast to the red brick walls, it features a prominent inscription of "Jackson P. Burley High School" at the top of the lintel. This tripartite main entrance displays an abstracted interpretation of classical elements. Divided into three bays by plain full–height pilasters and surrounded by a concave architrave, the double-leaf front doors are flanked by windows on the first floor. Each window feature a stepped cast stone architrave with raised panels beneath them. Three wide reeded bands of green stone (perhaps cast stone with green aggregate) separate the first and second floors. All the original wooden doors and steel windows were replaced with aluminum during a 1987 remodeling, although in most cases, the original openings were retained with their cast stone surrounds. The flat roofs are covered in a built up material, have cast stone coping, and contain interior gutter systems with exterior downspouts. [15]

The long, two-story, brick-veneered building has a multi bay central block flanked by recessed two-story wings that house a gymnasium and auditorium. The building's tripartite massing references classical forms, while its use of traditional classical decoration is restrained. The U–shaped school footprint follows the contours of a sloping site, resulting in the rear of the building being three stories in height with two-story classrooms opening out into an open air courtyard. The original open-air, grassy courtyard remains intact. It is now enclosed on four sides, whereas originally the west side was open. Multiple additions connect an original, two-story, free–standing, brick "manual arts" building to the rear of the school. A covered walkway originally ran along the west side of the open courtyard. It was removed when additions were made to the rear of the building in 2001, which connected the main part of the school to the detached, former manual arts building. The original grass courtyard, now enclosed on all sides, remains.[16]

The school is constructed of cinder block with a brick veneer. The horizontal massing of the building, with bays of windows and a flat roof, is broken up by the cast stone detailing between the window bays on the primary and secondary entrances, creating an impressive and elegant building. The property overall has a very good integrity of location, setting, design, workmanship, materials, feeling, and association.

The site slopes dramatically down to the west, allowing for multi-level additions in the rear. It then flattens out to a large expanse of open land containing a baseball diamond, which was once part of a football field, and a running track, surrounded by a chain link fence. Three sets of concrete steps lead up from the flat area to the back of the school building. The area north of the school is sloping and has been terraced. It now contains a track and basketball court surrounded by a chain link fence.

---

[15] Maral S. Kalbian, LLC and Margaret T. Peters. Nomination for National Register of Historic Places, 2020. Charlottesville, DHR No. 104-5276-0064, *Primary entrance*. Section 7, page 6.

[16] Ibid. *Description of two-story brick veneer building*. Section 7, page 4.

There are 120 paved parking spaces in the rear of the school off the Henry Avenue entrance and off the north, Rose Hill Drive entrance. Madison Avenue runs along the northern boundary of the school parcel. The 12 acre, City owned, Booker T. Washington Park adjoins the school property to the west. It was established in 1926 on land that was part of the original 400–acre Rose Hill tract. It is located directly west of the Preston Park and Lincoln Heights subdivisions. Paul Goodloe McIntire, donated it as a "public park and playground for the colored people of the City of Charlottesville." It is still an active community resource, the park contains a large public swimming pool and bathhouse (1968), a recreation building, and multiple playing fields that were easily accessible for the students of Burley High School.

The original stairwells of the school have tile wainscot, a metal balustrade with rectangular balusters, a metal handrail, and lower wooden handrails. Some areas still maintain the original mastic black tile flooring. All the floors, with the exception of the gymnasium, are covered in vinyl composition tiles. The plastered ceilings have surfaced-mounted lights. Many stairwells feature windows allowing for natural light.

The walls of Burley High School are constructed of concrete and steel with a brick veneer, laid in a six-course stretcher bond, with a Flemish–bond variant. The concrete foundation is also brick veneered. The 1950 building permit application describes the materials of the school, as "fire-proof" and the flat roof as "built up." The architectural plans are housed in the Albemarle County School Board offices. The imposing, two-story, flat-roofed, Stripped Classical Modernism–Style institutional building was completed in time to open for the 1951 school year.[17]

Constructed at the same time as the main school building, the one–story, western-most part of the school was originally a free-standing building housing the "manual arts" classrooms. In 2001, additions were made to the rear of the original school that filled in the space between it and the detached building. A one-story brick hyphen provides access from the rear of the school to this building, which now houses some sixth and seventh grade classrooms. Built into a banked site, and measuring 170 feet long by 51 feet wide, it stands a full two storeys on the west side and features the same brick work and detailing as found in the main part of the school. One of its most prominent features is the tall, free-standing brick chimney along its west side. The walk-out basement along the west side leads to the parking area at the rear of the school. Three sets of concrete steps with metal hand railings lead up from this parking area to the current bus–loading area along the north side of the school.

The original building was designed and constructed in three levels and three distinct entry sections: (1) Auditorium (2) Administrative and Academic and (3) Gymnasium. The two story front faced Rose Hill Drive. The back of the school was accessible from Henry Avenue, where the full three story structure was visible. Burley High School can be described as an institutional brick-veneered building with classical references in its massing and stripped-down ornamentation. Its footprint is U-shaped,

---

[17] Maral S. Kalbian, LLC and Margaret T. Peters. Nomination for National Register of Historic Places, 2020. DHR No. 104-5276-0064, *Walls of Burley High School*, section 7, page 5.

but the façade presents as a fairly continuous rectangle with a prominent, central, symmetrical entrance bay. Most of the decorative elements are confined to the façade and have been simplified to a degree where they merely allude to classical motifs.

The original footprint of this sprawling building has three main components: the long two and three-story main block which measures 181 feet in length; the two-story south auditorium wing, which measures 60 feet wide by 73 feet deep and includes a stage area with a basement and a balcony on the second floor and is fronted by a 46 feet wide by 14 feet deep porch; and the north gymnasium wing, which measures 80 feet wide by 100 feet deep with the cafeteria in the basement, that is fronted by a 40 feet wide by 14 feet deep porch. The south end of the façade terminates in a recessed brick wing that houses the auditorium. It is fronted by a three-bay portico with rectangular cast stone posts and a flat roof. The front of the two central posts are fluted, adding visual interest to the otherwise simple portico. Three bays of doors open to the lobby of the auditorium. [18]

Overall, Burley High School retains a high degree of architectural integrity. As one of the earliest examples in the region of the application of the Modern Movement to an educational building, Burley is also one of the first schools in the region to embrace Stripped Classical Modernism in its execution. Burley High School was one of the first instances in the region where elements of an architectural style of the Modern Movement were used for a high school. Most local public schools before World War II were designed using an architectural vocabulary based on traditional popular revival styles of the late 19th and early 20th centuries. The Stripped Classicism mode straddled the architectural vocabulary of Classicism and Modernism and had been a popular style for institutional and government buildings since the 1930s. Although, some changes have been made, the horizontal emphasis, flat roof, ribbon windows framed by cast stone, and limited architectural ornamentation are still part of the school's visual character.[19]

On September 4, 1951, Jackson P. Burley High School opened with some areas still under construction. It was built for a capacity of 600 students, serving grades eight through twelve. The school opened with 542 students from the City of Charlottesville, County of Albemarle and some students from Greene and Nelson counties. Twenty–six teachers, a principal, assistant principal, secretary, two cafeteria workers and six bus drivers comprised the staff.

When the school opened it consisted of an auditorium, administrative and guidance offices, academic classrooms, library, audio visual room, infirmary, band room, art room, home economic suite, practical nursing room, gymnasium, locker rooms, equipment storage, gymnasium, shower

---

[18] Maral S. Kalbian, LLC and Margaret T. Peters, Nomination for National Register of Historic Places, 2020. DHR No. 104-5276-0064. *Original footprint of building*. Section 7, page 6. Albemarle County Public Schools Building Services. *1949 Building and Site Plans for the Joint Negro High School, blueprints*, dated August 1949, revisions, December 1949.

[19] Ibid. *Architectural description of Jackson P. Burley High School*. Section 7, page 9.

rooms, restrooms, agriculture and Industrial shop, choral room, journalism room, cafeteria and custodial storage.

Main Level:

- The main level of the school housed the academic section, which contained classrooms for English, social sciences, mathematics, foreign language, fine arts, speech and drama, and a Journalism Room for school publications.

- The Administrative and Guidance offices were accessible from the main entrance of the school.

- The Library was located across from the Administrative Office and had a seating capacity for 90 students.

- A small faculty alcove was located on the main hallway.

- The Auditorium had a separate entrance. There are 2 ticket booths, located outside the lounge area with a check room. The two–aisle auditorium has a raised wooden stage, framed by a segmental arch with a stepped cornice. The auditorium has a seating capacity for 720 in the main area and 180 in the balcony. There is a lighting sound booth and a 30 X 61 foot stage with scene dock, lounge, and restrooms.

- The full-size gymnasium is located on the north wing of the school. It had a high-gloss hardwood floor with markings for a basketball court, retractable backboards and hoops, retractable bleachers along both the north and south walls, large windows on the west end, and an exposed bar joist ceiling. The lobby of the gym has two double-leaf doors leading out to the front portico. There are both locker rooms and equipment storage rooms and showers. A folded partition divided the floor space into separate units for boys' and girls' physical education classes.

Third Level:

- The English and natural science departments, an audiovisual room, 8th and 9th grade mathematics, 9th grade Science, 10th and 11th grade English, Latin, algebra, geometry, trigonometry, chemistry and physics were located on the third level, along with the infirmary.

Lower Level:

- The home economics department, business classes and typing room were located beneath the academic section of the building.

- The Practical Nurses' Room was located on the lower level.

- The band room, dressing and practice areas, with storage space for instruments and uniforms were located on the lower level and were also accessible from the breezeway.

- The choral room was located on this level.

- Rooms for equipment and storage, dressing rooms and showers for athletes were located on this level.

- The kitchen facilities and rooms for storage were located towards the rear of the building.

- The cafeteria is in its original location. It is located below the gymnasium capable of seating 230 students per lunch period. There were two lunch periods each day. It featured a large room with multiple rectangular pillars set on tall plinths covered in the same yellow wainscot tile that lines the walls. A curved, wooden stage is located in the southeast corner of the room, which can be set-up as a small auditorium. The walls are painted above the wainscot, the floors are modern VCT tile, and the ceilings are dropped acoustical tile with modern lights.
- The faculty alcove located on the lower level had a seating capacity of 20.

- The custodian's shop with storage was located on the lower level.

Detached Outside Entry: (Trade and Industrial Building)
- The large Agriculture and Industrial Shops were located at the rear of the building, which included a classroom, tool and storage room and an office.

- Rooms for Auto mechanics, carpentry and brick masonry, Drafting, and Farming were accessible from the back outside of the school.

- The Shop was a detached building located in the back of the school across the parking lot.

- The Athletic Field for football, baseball, as well as track and field were located at the back of the school. Washington Park was accessible from the rear of the athletic field.

- The school had a duel heating plant.

Secondary Resources:[20]
Baseball Diamond: The ca. 1951 diamond–shaped softball field is located down the hill (west) from the school building and is enclosed with a chain link fence. The 1949 site plan shows its location as part of the football field and a running track that are no longer there (Contributing Site).

Restroom: The one-story, shed roofed brick restroom building appears to have been remodeled in the 1970s and has a shed roof with metal coping, overhanging eaves, paired windows with cast stone surround, and side integral porches with brick supports. It stands at the southern edge of the property behind one of the dugouts (Non-contributing building).

Secondary Dwelling: The one-story, T-shaped, cross-gable-roofed, frame building is a modular building and was built by students at the Charlottesville Albemarle Technical Education Center. It was used as offices and later as the Post High School for those who qualify for special education

---

[20] Maral S. Kalbian, LLC. *Secondary Resources*. Nomination for Department of Historic Resources (DHR No. 104-5276-0064), 2020. Albemarle County Public Schools Building Services.

purposes. Constructed ca. 2000, the building is covered in vinyl siding, and has asphalt shingle roofing, vinyl one-over-one-sash windows, and a five-bay front porch with wooden posts and balusters. The building rests on a raised formed concrete foundation (Non-contributing building).

Dugouts: The two, concrete block, shed-roofed dugouts are identical. One is located east of the baseball diamond, and the other to the south. They appear to date to the 1970s (2 noncontributing structures).

Basketball Court: Constructed ca. 2000, this paved basketball court is located north of the school and is surrounded by a chain link fence. It contains multiple backboards and hoops and painted markings (Non-contributing structure).

Running Track: This five-lane oval running track is located north of the school and appears to have been constructed ca. 2010 (Non–contributing structure).

Memorial Wall: Installed in 2018, this memorial features a concrete pad with a three stone memorial plaques and 2 benches (Non-contributing structure). The left sectionof the wall contains the names of all administrators, faculty, staff, custodians, and cafeteria workers. The middle section of the wall honors Mr. Jackson P. Burley. The right section of the wall contains the names of all alumni and special participants.

Alumni of Jackson P. Burley High School have been very active in keeping the history of their beloved school alive. The Burley Varsity Club, a non-profit organization, has been instrumental in providing recognition of the school's accomplishments, including the recently installed monument wall in the front lawn that features the names of many former students, faculty, and staff.

Jackson P. Burley High School operated as an important educational resource for the African American community of both Charlottesville and Albemarle County during the tumultuous years of integration mandated by the Supreme Court in 1954 and Virginia's Massive Resistance, launched to avoid any racial integration in public schools in the years following *Brown vs Board of Education*. When Virginia's Governor, J. Lindsay Almond chose to close Charlottesville's public schools in 1958 rather than integrate the all-white Lane High School and Venable Elementary School, Burley's students who had integrated the schools were left with no schooling at all for a year from September 1958 to September 1959. African-American families were forced, along with White families, to scramble to provide some education for their students.[21]

When desegregation finally occurred in Charlottesville, the all-black Jackson P. Burley High School was closed and repurposed. The Charlottesville School Board divested itself of any relationship to the school, renting its portion of the jointly–owned building to Albemarle County for $10,000. On April 18, 1968, Albemarle County purchased the City's portion of the school for $700,000.

---

[21] Encyclopedia Virginia, Virginia Humanities, *Closure of Charlottesville Public Schools in 1958*.

Jackson P. Burley High School
1952 Dedication Ceremony

The dedication ceremony for Jackson P. Burley High School was held on March 21, 1952, in the newly opened school auditorium. The Burley Band and Chorus provided the music for the program. Mr. Joseph T. Henley, Chairman of the Albemarle County School Board, presided over the service. Division Superintendent, Hugh L. Sulfridge of the Charlottesville City Schools and Division Superintendent, Paul H. Cale of the Albemarle County Schools were in attendance.

Maggie P. Burley, widow of Mr. Jackson P. Burley, traveled from Atlanta, Georgia to attend the dedicatory ceremony. The 720 seats on the main floor of the auditorium were filled by students, parents, guests and faculty. The 180 seats in the balcony were half filled.

Virginia Governor, Honorable John Stewart Battle, gave the dedication address. Governor Battle had served in both the Virginia House of Delegates, (1929–1934) and the State Senate, (1934–1949) before being elected Governor. In a news article entitled, "Battle Terms School Realization of a Dream in that the City and County have united." According to the article, the construction of Burley High School, was "the first school" in the Commonwealth built under an amendment to a law introduced by Governor Battle when he was in the Senate. It allowed for a city and its neighboring county to jointly build and operate a school.

In his speech, which was quoted extensively in the Charlottesville *Daily Progress*, Governor Battle said: "In thus dedicating this property to the education of Negroes . . . so that they may enjoy these fundamental rights of man, the obligation inherent in the rights of the majority is recognized and fulfilled... Segregation is a social arrangement for the betterment of relations between the different races living under a democracy as we conceive it." It should be added that after leaving the governor's office, John Battle returned to Charlottesville and his law practice where he represented Albemarle County Public Schools, as they confronted desegregation lawsuits filed by the NAACP. An editorial in the same March 22, 1952 edition of *The Daily Progress* printed: [22]

> *Assuming as we do, that the City (Charlottesville) and County (Albemarle) administrations will discharge their duty to see that it is properly staffed, it (the opening of Burley) goes far toward discharging the obligation of Charlottesville and Albemarle to provide full equality in educational opportunity for their Negro citizens. So far as Charlottesville is concerned, that equality was achieved with the opening of this school, which in some respects has facilities superior to those provided for White children at Lane High School."*

Following the ceremony attendees toured the school building.

---

[22] Governor John Battle's remarks at the Jackson P. Burley's 1952 Dedication Ceremony. *Daily Progress*, Mar 22, 1952 edition.

1952 Dedication Program for Jackson P. Burley High School

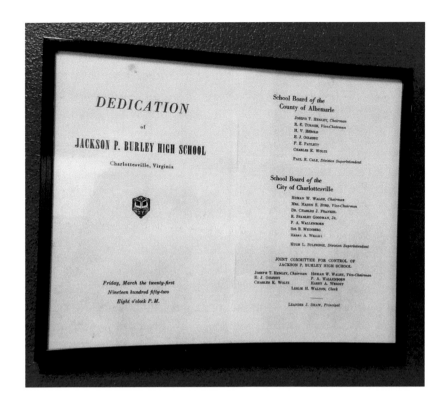

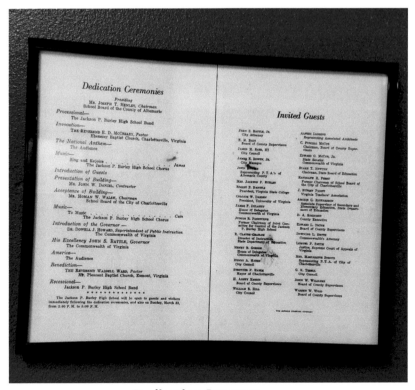

Dedication Program
Courtesy of Burley Varsity Club

1952 Replica of Dedication Program for Jackson P. Burley High School

DEDICATION

Of

JACKSON P. BURLEY HIGH SCHOOL

Charlottesville, Virginia

Friday, March the twenty-first

Nineteen hundred fifty-two

Eight o'clock P.M.

School Board of the
County of Albemarle

JOSEPH T. HENLEY, *Chairman*
R.E. TURNER, *Vice-Chairman*
H.V. HEROLD
E.J. OGLESBY
F.E. PAULETT
CHARLES K. WOLTZ

PAUL H. CALE, *Division Superintendent*

School Board of the
City of Charlottesville

HOMAN W. WALSH, *Chairman*
MRS. MASON S. BYRD, *Vice-Chairman*
DR. CHARLES J. FRANKEL
R. STANLEY GOODMAN, JR.
P.A. WALLENBORN
SOL B. WEINBERG
HARRY A. WRIGHT

HUGH L. SULFRIDGE, *Division Superintendent*

JOINT COMMITTEE FOR CONTROL OF
JACKSON P. BURLEY HIGH SCHOOL

JOSEPH T. HENLEY, *Chairman*   HOMAN W. WALSH, Vice-Chairman
E.J. OGLESBY   P.A. WALLENBORN
CHARLES K. WOLTZ   HARRY A. WRIGHT
              LESLIE H. WALTON, *Clerk*

LEANDER J. SHAW, *Principal*

Dedication Ceremonies

Presiding
MR. JOSEPH T. HENLEY, *Chairman*
School Board of the County of Albemarle

Processional—
The Jackson P. Burley High School Band
Invocation—
THE REVEREND E.D. MCCREARY, *Pastor*
Ebenezer Baptist Church, Charlottesville, Virginia
The National Anthem—
The Audience
Music—
Sing and Rejoice . . . . *James*
The Jackson P. Burley High School Chorus
Introduction of Guests
Presentation of Building—
MR. JOHN W. DANIEL, *Contractor*
Acceptance of Building—
MR. HOMAN W. WALSH, *Chairman*
School Board of the City of Charlottesville
Music—
To Music . . . . *Cain*
The Jackson P. Burley High School Chorus
Introduction of the Governor—
DR. DOWELL J. HOWARD, *Superintendent of Public Instruction*
The Commonwealth of Virginia
His Excellency JOHN S. BATTLE, *Governor*
The Commonwealth of Virginia
America—
The Audience
Benediction—
THE REVEREND WADDELL WARD, Pastor
Mt. Pleasant Baptist Church, Esmont, Virginia
Recessional—
Jackson P. Burley High School Band
* * * * * * * * * *

The Jackson P. Burley High School will be open to guests and visitors
immediately following the dedication ceremonies, and also on Sunday, March 23,
from 2:00 P.M. to 5:00 P.M.

Invited Guests

JOHN S. BATTLE, JR.
City Attorney

E. H. BAIN
Board of County Supervisors

JAMES M. BARR, III
City Council

JAMES E. BOWEN, JR.
City Manager

JOHN BOWLES
Representing P.T.A.'S of
Albemarle County

MRS. JACKSON P. BURLEY

ROBERT P. DANIELS
President, Virginia State College

COLGATE W. DARDEN
President, University of Virginia

JAMES F. DULANEY
House of Delegates
Commonwealth of Virginia

JUNIUS R. FISHBURNE
Former Chairman of Joint Com-
mittee for Control of the Jackson
P. Burley High School

R. CLAUDE GRAHAM
Director of Instruction
State Department of Education

HENRY B. GORDON
House of Delegates
Commonwealth of Virginia

HENRY A. HADEN
City Council

STROTHER F. HAMN
Mayor of Charlottesville

H. ASHBY HARRIS
Board of County Supervisors

WILLIAM R. HILL
City Council

ALFRED LLORENS
Representing Associated Architects

C. PURCELL MCCUE
Chairman, County Board of Supervisors

EDWARD O. MCCUE, JR.
State Senator
Commonwealth of Virginia

BLAKE T. NEWTON
Chairman, State Board of Education

RANDOLPH H. PERRY
Former Chairman of School Board of
the City of Charlottesville

J. RUPERT PICOTT
Virginia Teachers' Association

ARCHIE G. RICHARDSON
Associate Supervisor of Secondary and
Elementary Education, State Depart-
ment of Education

D. A. ROBINSON
County Executive

EDWARD L. SMITH
Board of County Supervisors

DOWNING L. SMITH
Commonwealth's Attorney

LEMUEL F. SMITH
Justice, Supreme Court of Appeals of
Virginia

MRS. MARGARETTE STROUD
Representing P.T.A. of City of
Charlottesville

G. K. TERELL
City Council

JOHN W. WILLIAMS
Board of County Supervisors

WARREN W. WOOD
Board of County Supervisors

THE JARMAN PRINTING COMPANY

Replica Dedication Program
Created by Lucille S. Smith, 2020

Jackson P. Burley High School - 1951

Jackson P. Burley High School - 1952

Jackson P. Burley High School - 1963

Entrance to Auditorium – Senior Class of 1953

Entrance to Auditorium Advanced Band - 1961

Bus pick-up in back of school - 1955 **Walkway view back of School - 1956**

Interior courtyard walkway view - 1951

Interior courtyard without walkway – 2017

The primary monumental, two story, projecting entrance to the school is of cast stone. The school inscription is visible from Rose Hill Drive.

Plaque at Entrance of School

Plaque donated by City of Charlottesville - 2010

Campus Views

Front Entrance - 2011

Front Entrance - 2020

View of Entrance to Gym - 2019
Photo by Maral Kalbian

Rose Hill Drive Northern View – 2021
Photo by Anne Chesnut

Entrance View of School - 2012

Aerial view of school – 2018 *by Skyclad Aerial*

View of school with Monument Wall - 2019

Front Entrance of School - 2021

Photo by Anne Chesnut

View of Monument Wall – 2021
Photo by Anne Chesnut

Dr. Bernard Hairston
Jackson P. Burley Middle School, Principal

In 2001 and 2002, Dr. Bernard Hairston successfully advocated keeping Jackson P. Burley Middle School on Rose Hill Drive to continue the legacy of Burley High School. Subsequently, a $7 million building renovation and remodeling included major upgrades to the auditorium, connecting the annex to the main building, adding the seventh-grade wing, a new media center, technology lab, broadcast studio, and modernizing the flooring and ceilings to preserve the integrity of Burley.

Dr. Bernard Hairston joined Albemarle County Public Schools in 1992 as an associate principal at Western Albemarle High School. He became the Principal of Burley Middle School in 1997 where he developed and led the division's first formal anti-bullying program. During his tenure, there were significant academic gains by Burley students. He holds the longest tenure of any principal who walked the halls of Burley High or Middle school.

Dr. Hairston became the school's division Executive Director of Community Engagement in 2006 and Chief of Community Engagement in 2017. From 1997–2006, Dr. Hairston served as the first African American Principal of Jackson P. Burley Middle School. Thirty years after Mr. Alexander Scott closed Burley High School as the principal. He was appointed Assistant Superintendent for School Community Empowerment in 2018. The second African American to serve in the role of Assistant Superintendent. Once again, following the footsteps of Mr. Alexander Scott. He is responsible for expanding the participation and input of students, teachers, administrators, staff, and community partners in developing school division policies, programs, and budget initiatives to meet School Board priorities.

"Dr. Hairston has been a highly influential advocate for equity and diversity in educational opportunities in our school division and in our region for many years," said County School Superintendent, Dr. Matthew Haas. "More than that, he has developed programs that have brought more equity into our classrooms and, with that, higher academic achievement by students. His contributions will be very influential to the success of all of our schools, but most immediately, in the collaborative work we have ahead of us with the Charlottesville City Schools. His leadership led to Albemarle County as the first school division nationally to approve an anti-racism policy and a culturally responsive teaching evidence based model designed to close achievement gaps."

Several of the school division's most accomplished programs originated with Dr. Hairston. As the founding president of the African American Teaching Fellows, he helped to develop a partnership that has increased the number of teachers of color in county and city schools. Other programs initiated by Dr. Hairston include the national award-winning M-Cubed (Math, Men, Mission) Program, which has significantly increased the number of African American middle school males who enroll and succeed in advanced math classes. Prior to the program's debut, only one African

American middle school male student was enrolled in an advanced math class, which often is an indicator of academic success in high school. In addition to providing leadership to the High School Scholars program that significantly increased grade point averages of African American males and their participation in upper level classes and leadership positions. He is the founding President of the 100 Black Men of Central Virginia and a member of the Omega Psi Phi Fraternity.

Dr. Hairston received his undergraduate degree in Industrial Arts Education from Norfolk State University and his Masters in Industrial Education from Virginia State University. He also holds a Doctor of Education degree from Virginia Tech.

Jackson P. Burley Middle School

In 1967, Jackson P. Burley High School became known as the Jack Jouett Junior Annex, housing an overflow of seventh grade students from Jack Jouett Middle School in Albemarle County. Albemarle County purchased Charlottesville's part of the Burley School property in 1968 and in the fall of 1973, the school re-opened as Jackson P. Burley Middle School, housing 841 students in grades six through eight. The school continued to include all three grades except for the 1976 – 1977 school year, when it operated as a middle school with only seventh and eighth graders. In the fall of 1977, Burley became a middle school again serving grades six through eight.

During the summer of 1987, a $2.8 million building renovation project was launched. Air conditioning and new energy efficient aluminum windows were installed. The project continued during the summer of 1988 with the installation of an elevator and a complete remodeling of the administrative, guidance, and annex areas. Smithey & Boynton from Roanoke were the architects.

In the summer of 1991, the building renovations continued with the gym and auditorium to include heating, air conditioning, and new lighting.

Additional refurbishments were completed during the summer of 1995, to include a new cafeteria floor and furniture, carpeting in the auditorium and main office, new bathroom stalls in the main building, new risers in the band room, and a partial roof replacement.

The auditorium underwent a major renovation in the summer of 2001. The acoustics were greatly improved, new seats were installed, and the entire area was painted.

Over $7 million in building renovations and new additions were initiated in the summer of 2002. BCWH Architects (now Quinn Evans) of Richmond completed the designs. The annex was renovated, a two story addition was built connecting the annex to the main building. The second floor of the new addition became the seventh grade wing. The new addition also included a media center with a broadcasting studio, a technology room, a new functional skills classroom and a courtyard located between the new addition and the main building. Floors and ceiling in the existing building were refurbished and air conditioning was installed in the gym. The renovation provided each grade level with a science room and lab.

Jackson P. Burley Middle School was assessed at $16,779,300 in 2020.

Timeline of Principals for Jackson P. Burley High School, Jack Jouett Junior Annex and Burley Middle School
1951 – Present

Leander Shaw
1951 – 1952

Eugene Mobley
1952 – 1959

Alexander L. Scott
1959 – 1967

Robert H. Thraves
1967 – 1971

Joseph Trice
1971 – 1982

Ronald Broadbent
1982 – 1987

Thomas Zimorski
1987 – 1994

Sherrard Howen
1994 – 1997

Dr. Bernard Hairston
1997 – 2006

Marcha P. Howard
2006 – 2009

Sharon Amato-Wilcox
2009 – 2012

James Asher
2012 – 2020

Kasaundra E. Blount
2020 – Present

CHAPTER 3

THE BURLEY FAMILY

Jackson Price Burley

Maggie Lena Payne Burley

Frederick Price Burley
(Son)

Grace Lena Ann Burley
(Daughter)

Frederick Price Burley, Jr.
(Grandson)

Dr. Olivia M. Boggs
(Granddaughter)

Jackson Price Burley

Jackson Price was born on February 22, 1863[1] in Stony Point, Virginia to George Price of Culpeper, Virginia and Lucy Woodson of Stony Point, Virginia. He was raised by his stepfather and mother, Hardin and Lucy Burley, taking the Burley name and becoming Jackson Price Burley.

Jackson graduated from Hampton Institute in 1889 as the class valedictorian. As a young man, he travelled to Cuba, where he became fluent in Spanish. He taught for 12 years at Stony Point School and for two years at Eastham School. He began teaching Agriculture at Albemarle Training School in 1918 remaining for 19 years, until retirement in 1937. He served as a farm agent for Albemarle County.

Jackson married Willie Goodloe on November 24, 1897. They had one daughter, Harriet Beecher Burley, born June 30, 1899. Harriet died at the young age of two and one-half years on January 7, 1902. At the death of wife Willie in 1913, Jackson married Maggie Lena Payne on April 29, 1914. Jackson and Maggie had two children: Frederick Price Burley and Grace Lena Ann Burley.

The Burley family owned and operated a store/market for 17 years at the intersection of Free Bridge Road and Meade Avenue. At the age of 19, Jackson bought land on Rose Hill Drive. The land became the site of Jackson P. Burley High School, which is now an "Unforgettable" History.

Mr. Burley was a member, faithful worker, Sunday school teacher, and Deacon at First Baptist Church on West Main Street. He was a member of the "Four Hundred Club", which was comprised of prominent African American businessmen.[2]

Mr. Burley died on July 1, 1945 at the age of 80, and is buried in the Oakwood Cemetery in Charlottesville, Virginia.

In 1950, a special committee recommended naming the new colored school, Jackson P. Burley High School in honor of distinguished educator, church worker, community leader and businessman. The school name was unanimously approved by the Joint Board for Control from the City of Charlottesville and Albemarle County. [3]

The original portrait of Mr. Burley was painted in 1953 by Fine Arts teacher, Waldo Johnson. Over the years the portrait began to fade. In 1997, Burley Middle School Principal, Dr. Bernard Hairston commissioned artist, Frank Walker to repaint the portrait. As a teenager, on many evenings Frank would come to the school to meet his mother, Business teacher, Mrs. Teresa Walker Price. During those visits, Frank was inspired by Mr. Waldo Johnson to become an artist. The portrait of Mr. Burley hangs proudly in the lobby of the auditorium, high above the trophy cases, where he looks proudly out at all visitors.

---

[1] DOB (2/22/1863 & DOD 7/1/1945) for Mr. Burley from the Burley Family Bible. Courtesy of Olivia Boggs.
[2] The Four Hundred Club. *The Reflector*, February 17, 1934
[3] New Joint School will Honor Name of Jackson Burley. *Daily Progress*, June 2, 1950

Jackson Price Burley
February 22, 1863 – July 1, 1945

Portrait re–painted by Frank Walker
Original art by Waldo Johnson

Home of Jackson Price Burley

In 1949, the Burley home was moved from its original location to 810 Concord Avenue at the corner of Rose Hill Drive, where it still stands.

Original home of Jackson P. Burley - front view
Concord Avenue

Original home of Jackson P. Burley - side view
Rose Hill Drive

Remodeled home front view – 2020
Concord Avenue

Remodeled home side view – 2020
Rose Hill Drive

Honorary Jackson P. Burley Drive

On October 7, 2011, under the leadership of Mayor Dave Norris a Proclamation was passed for Rose Hill Drive to receive the honorary name of Jackson P. Burley Drive.

Buried at Oakwood Cemetery
1st Street South • Charlottesville, VA 22902

HOUSE RESOLUTION NO. 528
Offered April 11, 2018
Prefiled April 10, 2018

Celebrating the life of Jackson P. Burley.

Patron-- Toscano

WHEREAS, Jackson P. Burley, a dedicated educator in Albemarle County, died on July 1, 1945; and

WHEREAS, a native of Stony Point, where he was born in 1863, Jackson Burley attended Hampton Institute and graduated as valedictorian in 1889; and

WHEREAS, fluent in Spanish, Jackson Burley taught at the Stony Point School for 12 years and the Eastham School for two years; he later taught agriculture at Albemarle Training School for 19 years, until his retirement in 1937; and

WHEREAS, Jackson Burley enjoyed fellowship and worship with the community as a member of First Baptist Church, where he served as a deacon; and

WHEREAS, in 1950, a new high school for African American students in Charlottesville, and the Counties of Albemarle, Greene, and Nelson, was built on the former site of the Burley home and named Jackson P. Burley High School; the school is now known as Burley Middle School; and

WHEREAS, Jackson P. Burley is fondly remembered by numerous family members and the students of the school that bears his name; now, therefore, be it

RESOLVED, That the House of Delegates hereby note with great sadness the loss of Jackson P. Burley; and, be it

RESOLVED FURTHER, That the Clerk of the House of Delegates prepare a copy of this resolution for presentation to the family of Jackson P. Burley as an expression of the House of Delegates' respect for his memory.

Maggie Lena Payne Burley

  **Maggie Lena Payne** was born on September 14, 1875 in Scottsville, Virginia. Maggie was the youngest of the 10 children of Ann Johnson and Nathan Payne.[4]

In 1910, following graduation from Hampton Institute in Hampton, Virginia, Maggie Payne was employed by the Albemarle County Public Schools to serve as a Jeanes Supervisor.

Maggie Lena Payne married Jackson Price Burley on April 29, 1914. She and Mr. Burley worked for many years, side by side at Albemarle Training School.

Mrs. Burley taught sewing, basket-making, weaving, cooking, canning and domestic art. She spent time teaching Domestic Science at many of the Negro schools in Albemarle County. She also taught the students to make shuck mats for chairs and white oak baskets, as well as upholstery and furniture making. The money needed for the material was raised by the families through community fund raising. The older students assisted with teaching different trades to the younger students. Several stores in Charlottesville were supplied with the shuck mats for their chairs.

A Jeanes Supervisor was a group of African American teachers who worked in southern rural schools and communities throughout the United States between 1908 and 1968. They also assisted the ladies in the community to improve the quality of their homes. The teachers were funded by the Jeanes Foundation, also known as the Negro Rural School Fund or Jeanes Fund. It was founded in 1907 by Anna T. Jeanes with help from Booker T. Washington.[5] Anna T. Jeanes was an American philanthropist and Quaker who wanted to establish a fund to improve the educational opportunities of rural African Americans.[6]

In 1949, Mrs. Burley moved from Virginia to Georgia to live with daughter, Grace Boggs.

Maggie Lena Payne Burley died in Atlanta, Georgia on May 13, 1959 at the age of 83.

---

[4] The Burley-Boggs-Woodson-Payne Family, Genealogy.com
[5] Jeanes Foundation and Jeanes Supervisors. Linda B. Pincham. Journal of Negro Education (2005) page 112-113
[6] Anna T. Jeanes. Lance G. E. Jones, (1937). The Jeanes Teachers in the United States 1908 – 1933.

Frederick Price Burley

Frederick Price Burley, son of Jackson Price Burley and Maggie Lena Payne Burley, was born on February 13, 1915 in Charlottesville, Virginia.

As a youth, Frederick was a student cadet at Rock Castle (a boarding military academy in Virginia). The academy was renamed, St. Emma Military Academy, also called "Belmead." St. Emma's was an Industrial and Agricultural Institute and first opened in 1895, admitting only African-American boys from the South.

Frederick became a gifted tailor who lived in Virginia and briefly in Atlanta, Georgia.

Frederick married Rebecca Pride Bowling of Hampton, Virginia. They had one son, Frederick P. Burley Jr., who was born in Norfolk, Virginia in 1941.

Frederick Sr., died at the age of 50 on December 12, 1965 at his residence of 303 5th Street S.E., Charlottesville, Virginia. Frederick is buried next to his father, Jackson at Oakwood Cemetery in Charlottesville, Virginia.

Belmead is the main house that remains on the former St. Emma's Military Academy property in Powhatan County. In 2011, it was listed on the National trust for Historic Preservation's 11 Most Endangered Places. The property is comprised of 2,265 acres. St. Emma's was a Catholic Boarding School for African Americans. It closed in 1972.

Aerial View of St. Emma Academy
Photos by Preservation Nation

Grace Burley Boggs Smith

Grace Lena Burley was born in Charlottesville, Virginia on December 26, 1917. She was the youngest child of Jackson Price and Maggie Payne Burley. Grace demonstrated at an early age a love for music and a thirst for education. Her desires were encouraged by her parents who were both educators.

Grace graduated from Jefferson High School in the City of Charlottesville. In 1938 Grace graduated with highest honors from

Hampton Institute, now Hampton University, earning a B.S. Degree in Music Education. She earned a Master's Degree in Music in 1940 from Columbia University in New York.

Grace moved to Atlanta, Georgia in 1944 and obtained a teaching position in the Music Department at Morris Brown College. In 1945, she married Professor Herbert Boggs of Selma, Alabama. They had one daughter, Olivia Boggs. Professor Herbert Boggs died in 1949.

In 1955, a Rockefeller Foundation Fellowship allowed Grace to complete a Doctorate in Music Education from Columbia University in New York. Dr. Boggs returned to Atlanta to teach at Spelman College. In 1962, she married Dr. Barnett Smith, Sr., a colleague and fellow professor.

Dr. Boggs received the first teacher of the year award at Spelman during the 1967 – 68 school year and became the Head of the Spelman College Music Department. In both college classes and church choirs, Dr. Smith was known for her powerful arrangements of spirituals, known as, "The Grace Smith Sound." Her arrangements were full and rich. She did a great deal with shading, emphasis and enunciation. She said, "We're talking about songs that came out of the slave experience". Dr. Boggs retired in 1983.[7]

Dr. Grace Burley Boggs Smith died in Atlanta, Georgia on March 26, 1999 at the age of 81. She was survived by daughter, Dr. Olivia Boggs, stepson, Barnett F. Smith Jr., and two step-grandchildren.

---

[7] Digital Library of Georgia. *Celebration of Life for Grace Burley Boggs Smith*, March 1999

Frederick Price Burley, Jr., is the elder of Jackson Burley's two grandchildren. He was born on June 9, 1941 in Norfolk, Virginia to Frederick Price Burley, Sr., a tailor, and Rebecca Pride Bowling, a public school teacher. His maternal grandparents were Reverend and Mrs. Richard Hausber Bowling (Rebecca L. Pride) and his paternal grandparents were Mr. and Mrs. Jackson Price Burley (Maggie L. Payne).

Frederick Jr., attended Oglethorpe Elementary School in Atlanta, Booker T. Washington High School in Norfolk, and Norfolk State College (now University).

He spent his career in the Washington, DC hospitality industry, working for the Hilton Hotels Corporation and later, for the Hyatt Hotels Corporation. Frederick was a champion swimmer and aficionado of jazz. He passed on January 29, 2012, following a brief illness, and was survived by his wife of 43 years, Thelma Halstead Burley and three first cousins, Charles Fox, Jr. of Norfolk, Olivia Boggs of Atlanta, and Annette Givens of Midway, Georgia.

Olivia Magdalyn Boggs was born on January 7, 1947 in Charlottesville, Virginia to Herbert C. Boggs and Grace Burley Boggs; both were professors at Morris Brown College in Atlanta., Georgia. From the age of 8-months, Olivia was raised in Atlanta. She has an undergraduate degree in mathematics from Hampton Institute (now University), a Master's degree in rehabilitation counseling from Boston University, and a Doctorate in administration and policy from Harvard University where she was elected to the Editorial Board of the Harvard Educational Review.

She is a tenured faculty member at Mercer University and a Registered Civil Mediator with the State Courts of Georgia. She is a former Ford Foundation Fellow, recipient of the Cathryn Futral Excellence in Teaching Award, and was a 2017 Governor's Teaching Fellow at the University of Georgia. Olivia is an active member of Atlanta's Friendship Baptist Church, several civic and service organizations, and a life member of the NAACP.

CHAPTER 4

ADMINISTRATORS, FACULTY AND STAFF 1951 – 1967

Pictures of the Administrators, Faculty and Staff are from the Jackson P. Burley High School Yearbooks, "Jay Pee Bee."

Principals

Leander Shaw, Principal
1951 – 1952

Eugene Mobley, Principal
1952 – 1959

Alexander L. Scott, Principal
1959 – 1967

Chelsie Clark
Veterans Education

 **Leander Jerry Shaw (1904 – 1978)**, born in DeKalb, Kershaw, County, South Carolina, was the son of Benjamin and Henrietta Lolley Shaw. Leander had six siblings, Eirea, Mary, Elma, Benjamin, Fred and Booker Shaw. He graduated from Lee County Training School, also known as the W. B. Wicker School. He graduated from college with a Master's Degree in Business Education. After graduation, Leander taught for a short time in Nashville, Tennessee before moving to Salem, Virginia and teaching in the Lexington School System.

Leander married, Margaret Wysong Shaw of Maysville, Buckingham, Virginia in 1928. Their two children, Leander J. Shaw Jr., and Jacqueline Shaw Willis, were born in Salem, Virginia.

Mr. Leander J. Shaw, was the first principal of Jackson P. Burley High School when it opened in the fall of 1951. He served in the position for one year, leaving in the spring of 1952. He was succeeded by Eugene Mobley.

Mr. Shaw and wife Margaret would later move to Tallahassee, Florida, where he became the Dean of the Florida Agricultural and Mechanical University (FAMU) Graduate School. Wife, Margaret Shaw, began her career as a high school teacher and retired from Lylburn Downing High School in Lexington, Virginia.

Mr. Shaw's son, Leander Shaw Jr. (1930 – 2015), began his education at West Virginia State College, where he earned a Bachelor of Arts Degree. Upon graduation, he enlisted in the United States Army, and served as an Artillery Officer during the Korean War. He was honorably discharged from the army. After the war, he attended Howard University in Washington, DC and received a Juris Doctorate Degree. Leander Jr., was employed by Florida A&M University School of Law as Assistant Professor of Law from 1957 – 1960. After leaving Florida A&M University School of Law, he established a private practice. He worked as Assistant Public Defender and Assistant State's Attorney in Jacksonville, Florida. On November 15, 1963, Leander Jr., was appointed the first African American Prosecuting District Attorney for non-capital cases. In January 1983, he made history when Governor Bob Graham appointed him to the Florida Supreme Court. Leander Shaw Jr. became the first Black Florida Supreme Court Chief Justice, serving from 1990 – 1992.

Leander Jerry Shaw, Sr. died on Jun 12, 1978 in Tallahassee, Florida. He is buried in the Memorial Gardens in Tallahassee, Florida.

Eugene Gary Mobley (1916 – 1988) was born in Chester County, South Carolina. He was the son of Tony Hudson Mobley and Maggie Curbeam Mobley. Eugene had two siblings, William and Jesse Mobley. Eugene graduated from the Pryor School and attended South Carolina State in Orangeburg, South Carolina, graduating with a Bachelor of Science Degree in Agricultural Education. After graduation he enlisted in the U.S. Army, during World War II. His first teaching job was in the segregated school system in the town of Fort Lawn in Chester County, South Carolina.

Eugene married, Honor C. Greene of Charlotte, North Carolina. They had one son, Michael Mobley.

Mr. Eugene G. Mobley was the second principal of Jackson P. Burley High School, serving in the position from 1952 – 1959. While serving as the principal, he also taught Vocational and Industrial Education. He was succeeded by Mr. Alexander Scott in the fall of 1959. He retired as an educator in the City of Lynchburg, Virginia.

Eugene Gary Mobley died on August 29, 1988 in Lynchburg, Virginia. He is buried in the Benson Cemetery in Chester County, South Carolina.

Alexander Livingston Scott (1904 – 1981) was born in the town of Murfreesboro, North Carolina. He was the son of John Scott, Sr., and Emma Branch Scott. Alexander had seven siblings, John Jr., George, Lloyd, Jesse, Teddy, Levister and Althea.

Alexander graduated with honors from the C.S. Brown School in Murfreesboro, North Carolina. He attended Hampton Institute in Hampton, Virginia. After graduation, he worked for the Spotsylvania County School Board in Spotsylvania, Virginia.

Alexander married Edith Pelham Scott and they had one son, John Scott.

Mr. Alexander L. Scott was the third and last principal of Jackson P. Burley High School. He served in the position from 1959 through desegregation and closing in 1967. While at Burley High School, many students said, "He was a stern disciplinarian. His goal was for Burley High School students and faculty to always display a positive image at home and away from school." After the closing of Burley High School, Mr. Scott remained in Charlottesville and worked for the City School System until retiring.

Alexander Livingston Scott, died on April 23, 1981 in Charlottesville, Virginia. He is buried in the Scott Family Cemetery in Hertford County, North Carolina.

Assistant Principals and Athletic Director

Samuel E. Smith
Assistant Principal
1951 – 1958

Edwin A. Simmons
Assistant Principal
1959 – 1960

Samuel F. Griffin
Assistant Principal
1960 – 1967

Robert "Bob" Smith
Athletic Director
1951 – 1960

Walter "Rock" Greene
Athletic Director
1960 – 1963

Clevester Logan
Athletic Director
1963 – 1967

Administrative Staff

Zelda H. Murray, Secretary
1951 – 1967

Pauline H. Garrett
Head Guidance Counselor

Alberta Faulkner, Librarian
1951 – 1967

William Johnson
Guidance Counselor

Patricia Crittenden
Guidance Counselor

Connie Rawlins
Guidance Counselor

Thelma McCreary
Guidance Counselor

Vanessa Venable
Guidance Counselor

Business Department

Lorraine Williams

Teresa Walker

Gloria Thaxton

Rosemary Byers

Alfreda Saunders

Roseanna Hillian

English Department

Inez Bowler

Thelma H. McCreary

Dorothy Alston

Vanessa Venable

Pauline Garrett

Geneva Wright

Gladys W. McCoy

Margaret Smith

Vernell Lipscomb

English Department

Ellen Bigger

Marjorie Whitcraft

Lois Porter

Steven D. Waters

Cynthia DeSue

Irvine Gordon

Gladys Jones

Yvonne Nichols

Lola Amis

Shirley Batts

English Department

Annie Henderson

Eugene Williams

Sarah Barnes

Shirley Pope

Louise Pankey

Patricia A. Crittenden

Thelma Smith

Anna Patterson

Florence Bryant

Dorothy Searles

Fine Arts

Virginia Word

Waldo E. Johnson

Alice Wesley Ivory

Henry Shegog

Mattie Logan

Donald Willard

Charles Rogers

Foreign Language Department

Gladys W. McCoy

Thelma Smith

Alfreda Saunders

Dorothy Alston

Susan B. McCaffery

Yvonne Nichols

Margaret Smith

Homemaking Department

Lyria B. Hailstork

Phyllis A. Dent

Henrietta Spotts

Elenora Hawkins

Dorothy Harraway

Margaret Taylor Jefferson

Mathematics Department

Commora Snowden

Lillie Mae Brown

Pauline Garrett

Samuel E. Smith

Samuel F. Griffin

Vanessa R. Venable

Phyllis Carter

Josephine Y. Willis

W. J. Graham

Mathematics Department

Felicia P Rowe

Marvin Carrington

Susan B. Piepho

Wanda Fleming

Mozelle Frazier

Parnell Avery

Barbara Williamson

Music Department

George Maxey

Virginia Word

Henry L. Shegog

Virginia Wilson

Willis E. Keeling

J.W. Joyner

Horace Cooke

Elmer Sampson

Cynthia M. DeSue

Physical Education Department

Alma Pleasants

Robert Smith

Albert Moore

Clarence Jones

Walter Greene

Saundra Norrell

Doris M. Clark

Emma Jackson

Bobbie P. Richardson

George Quarles

Virginia Hunter

Science Department

Commora Snowden

Lorenzo Collins

Harold Green

James Stanton

Melvyn Jackson

Parnell Avery

Science Department

Rosalind Wright

Clarence Watson

Henrietta Spotts

Janice Mason

C. L. Poindexter

Barbara Williamson

Social Studies Department

Thelma H. McCreary

Inez Bowler

Gladys W. McCoy

J.H. Hunt

Lois Porter

Alicia Bowler

Mattie Pleasants

Lorraine Williams

Sarah Barnes

Social Studies Department

Irvine Gordon

Connie Rawlins

Florence Bryant

James Clay

Clarence Watson

Alonzo Davis

Felicia P Rowe

Vocational – Industrial Arts

Eugene Mobley

Clevester Logan

Bishop Patterson

James McDaniel, Jr.

Willard Robinson

William Johnson

James S. Roye

A.R. Crittenden

Morris Taylor

Cafeteria Staff

Eliza Brooks   Lula Bowles   Izetta Williams Neal

David Burns   Josephine Fortune   Carolyn Taylor   George Tinsley

Continuing the Legacy
Patricia Bowler Edwards, Class of 1966

I had hopes of attending the newly integrated Lane High School; however, my parents would not allow it. I was devastated then, but since, have thanked God over and over for my experiences at Burley High. The thirteen-year-old me, adjusted quickly, as I was very familiar with the "Burley life" because my mother and several of her closest friends taught there, and my sister, Alicia had graduated as valedictorian in the class of 1959.

That being said, I entered those hallowed halls "running"... anticipating that I would be compared with my sister, Alicia. Instead, I found my teachers to be supportive and encouraging. Oh yes, there were many characters among them, like Mrs. Snowden, my "Aunt Mae" who was always Mrs. Brown in class, Elmer "Sonny" Sampson, Madame McCoy, and Mr. Alexander Scott, our stern principal and my Sunday School teacher. These individuals always expected the best effort from me, and readily communicated their confidence and belief in my abilities.

The atmosphere at Burley exuded pride in our accomplishments and our potential to be the best. I joined a number of extra-curricular organizations (something I would not have been allowed to do at Lane High School). My favorite was the band! When we marched in parades, people would follow along on the sidewalks with us. The Science and Math Clubs required us to study and prepare together after school hours, something we didn't mind doing. When English teacher, Mr. Stephen Waters organized the Quill and Scroll, it felt like we were already in college. These opportunities allowed us to be leaders and organizers preparing us for our rapidly evolving communities.

I continued the legacy of my mom, Mrs. Inez Bowler, sister Alicia Bowler Lugo and Aunt Lillie Mae Brown, and became a teacher.

I spent the last half of my own teaching career at Charlottesville High School, the successor to Lane and Burley. While many of my colleagues were dedicated and caring, I always felt there were two schools at CHS...unlike Burley, a large group of students were routinely tracked into classes which dimmed their expectations. It was not the same overall, and I ached for the warm nurturing cocoon for my students, which was our dear Burley High.

Pathway to Becoming a Teacher
M. Maxine Holland, Class of 1967

I grew up during a time in which children used their imagination and creativity. The forest was among the safe spaces for us to explore and create. There, we could build the ideal house, play school, or doctor. We gathered things from the neighborhood trash piles to be used on our playground. When we were not doing chores, or not in the forest, we engaged in other forms of play. Some of them were: jumping rope, marbles, playing Annie Over, hide-go-seek, hopscotch, jack rocks, foot racing, Little Sally Ann, climbing trees, catching fireflies, and softball. Rarely, were we without something to do. Of all the things we did, I enjoyed being "the teacher." I found myself imitating my second-grade teacher, Mrs. Robinette Poindexter. I watched Mrs. Poindexter as she stirred the soup, stoke the fire in the pot belly stove and teach. She made an arduous task appear to be easy. I credit her and many of my childhood experiences to instilling resilience and innovation in me, which has guided my teaching since the beginning.

I really thought my respect for nature and the animals that I shared the environment with would lead me to Veterinary Science. Beginning as early as the ninth grade at Burley High School, I was encouraged to join the Future Teachers of America Club. According to Mrs. Vanessa Venable, club sponsor, I had "potential." She along with most of my teachers motivated me and served as exemplary models. They gave me opportunities to develop my talents. Mrs. Inez Bowler was instrumental in helping me with public speaking. Mrs. Dorothy Harraway and Mrs. Lyria Hailstork tactfully handled personal appearance and dress code. Mrs. Lillie Mae Brown did not accept failure in her Math/Algebra class. Therefore, she was willing to go above and beyond to help students achieve success. Mrs. Gladys McCoy taught French, but made sure that we learned the history of Charlottesville. They all practiced teaching the whole child/learner.

Years after high school, I enrolled into Hampton Institute (now Hampton University) and pursued a teacher preparatory program. I successfully completed the requirements and earned a B.S. and a Master's degree. I was endorsed to teach kindergarten through high school and college. My teaching experiences include: Kentucky State University, Spelman College, Atlanta Public Schools, Yancey Elementary, Albemarle High School and Fluvanna County High School. At every level, I found myself incorporating some of the methods and strategies my teachers used, especially the classroom management techniques. Although public education tends to be limited to preparing students primarily for jobs and consumerism, teachers at Burley included an agenda for transformation, character development and self-sufficiency. As a result, many of us enjoy a quality life. I thank them and my parents for guiding me along the winding path that led me to teaching.

Burley Bus Drivers

The bus drivers for Jackson P. Burley High School spans 16 years. Students from the many communities throughout the County of Albemarle, as well as some students from Nelson and Greene Counties required bus or private transportation to school. Students from the City of Charlottesville walked to school, or used public or personal transportation.

The typical start time for a bus driver began as early as 7:20 A.M each school day. The drivers were seasonal drivers, substitute drivers and student drivers. Some student drivers said they began driving as early as 16 years of age. They received their license from the Department of Motor Vehicles with little or no training for operating a bus. The adult drivers, along with the student drivers, were dedicated employees and true disciplinarians. The drivers were compensated monthly. Vocational Instructor, Mr. James McDaniel, was the Supervisor for the bus drivers.

Mr. George Green, Mr. George Lindsay, Sr., and Mr. Norris Monroe, fueled the buses as needed at the shop, which was located at the back of the school. Maintenance for the buses was provided at the shop located behind McIntire School and later at the site off Hydraulic Road, adjacent to Albemarle High School.

1954 Fleet of buses

Burley Bus Drivers (1951 – 1967)

Routes	Drivers and Substitutes	Student Drivers
Advance Mills, Earlysville, Proffit Road and Rio Road	George Lindsay Sr., Luther Sims and George Blakey (Substitute)	George Lindsay Jr., and Franklin Jackson
Barboursville, Stony Point and Eastham	Rev. Joseph Walker, Randolph Walker, James Thomas and Abell Brock	Sterling Walker, and Sherman Walker
Browns Cove, Free Union, White Hall and Ivy	Harold Barbour, Rev. Albert Walker and Samuel Howard	None
Buck Island, Milton, Monticello Mountain and Wake Forest	Bernard Curry, Junius Jordan Sr. and Millard Payne Ivan Nightengale (Substitute)	Nelson Jones, Phillip Jones, and James Thompson
Cismont, Cobham, Keswick and Shadwell	Joe Curry, George Ragland, Rev. John Smith, Dudley Quarles, Leroy Quarles, Harold Jones	Archie Bowler, Johnny Carr, Walter Johnson and Frank Dickerson
Covesville and North Garden	Joe Martin, Curtis Dowell, William Early, Earl Smith, Harold Brackett	Clinton Byers
Crozet, Free Union and Barracks Road	Eddie Howard and Wilbert Howard	None
Buck Mountain, Earlysville, Free Union and White Hall	Leslie Cato and William Thomas	None
Esmont and Scottsville	Jake Brown, Leo Thomas and Ray Watkins	None
Esmont, North Garden, Old Lynchburg Road and South Garden	Daniel Cowan, Harrison Cowan, Gene Burton and Howard Carter	James Whindleton and Curtis Byers
Greene County	Harry Brock, Leroy Grayson and James Morton (substitute) and John Carpenter	None
Greenwood, Newtown, and Hillsboro	Richard Brown, George Green and Norris Monroe	Benjamin Washington
Howardsville, Esmont and Scottsville	John Anderson, McArthur Brown and Lawrence Russell	None

CHAPTER 5

REFLECTIONS FROM FACULTY AND STAFF

Theresa Walker Price

Clevester Logan

Lorraine P. Williams

Dr. Eugene Williams, Sr.

Lyria Hailstork

James McDaniel, Jr.

**Reflections
1951 – 1967**

Gloria Thaxton

Coach Walter Greene

Willis E. Keeling, Jr.

Charles L. Rogers, Sr.

Harold Green

Cynthia DeSue-Grady

George Tinsley

I am a Charlottesville native and a 1942 graduate of Jefferson High School. I attended Hampton Institute in Hampton Virginia, graduating with a Bachelor of Science Degree in Business Education.

Upon walking into Burley High School, one savors a well-kept building and "separate but equal" equipped classrooms. You sense a spirit of joy and calmness among the student body and a faculty ready to make pathways for students to move into early adulthood. The faculties of the segregated schools are heroes and have amazed me in their effort to provide experiences and care for their students; the demands of the contract were met; and, the extra motivation and nurturing were outstanding. These factors were obvious as I entered that world.

Also, standing out in my memory, was the support of parents (PTA), Band Boosters, Sports Boosters and the like.

Our Business Department successfully taught personal and marketable skills that enabled students to perform their own clerical tasks. We also developed our own job placement, routing students into main-stream careers (with benefits) right out of high school.

In 1966, I was hired to teach at Lane High School as one of the cadre of African American teachers assigned to formerly white schools. Later, I worked as a Librarian at Clark School, I eased the transition for many black elementary school aged children. Teresa still picks up her phone to round up volunteers for Clark School.

Working at Jackson P. Burley High School was a rewarding career for me. My friendships, adult and students, are held in highest esteem.

Teresa Walker Price, Business Department

I attended Virginia State College in Petersburg, Virginia. I graduated with a Bachelor of Science Degree in Agriculture Education.

I was the Athletic Director at Burley High School from opening in 1953 through the closing of the school in 1967.

I taught vocational education at Burley High School, which was very rewarding for me. The young men who were enrolled in my agricultural mechanics and farm mechanics classes thrived. They were eager to develop skills they could use in everyday life. The students were quick learners and had pride in their work. The Vocational Program prepared the students to go out into society and begin work immediately. I especially enjoyed teaching farm mechanics and managerial abilities for modern farming. I also taught agricultural mechanics for electrical projects. The young men were dedicated and wanted to use their skills to build. Many said their goal was to build homes.

I was sorry when the school closed in 1967. After the Burley closure, I became the Assistant Principal at Jack Jouett Junior High School in the County of Albemarle. Years later, I became the Assistant Principal at the Charlottesville-Albemarle Technical Education Center (CATEC). While at CATEC, I had the opportunity to teach vocational education and share the skills I loved.

Clevester Logan, Vocational Education and Athletic Director, 1953 – 1967

I grew up in Ivy, Virginia and attended the small segregated Terry School. When it was time to attend high school, I moved to Charlottesville to live with my aunt so I could attend Jefferson School.

After graduating from Jefferson School, I enrolled at Hampton Institute and received a B.S. Degree in Commercial Education.

I taught at Burley High School from its opening in 1951 until it closed during Desegregation in 1967. I taught social studies, typing and shorthand.

The students at Burley High School, were glad to be there and were focused and eager to learn. The business teachers worked very hard to prepare the students for life after high school, whether they sought to seek a higher education or to go into the workforce after high school graduation.

There was much concern when the school was scheduled to close. We loved being at Burley High and teaching students who came prepared and were willing to work hard.

During Desegregation, the teachers were re-assigned, where needed. I taught Business at Lane High School. I also taught at Walker Junior High School and later taught at Buford Junior High School in the City of Charlottesville. I taught social studies at both schools.

I married my high school sweetheart, Eugene Williams in 1949. Eugene is a social activist and community leader. While teaching at Jackson P. Burley High School, Eugene and I worked together to form a committee of parents to integrate the Charlottesville Public Schools. Our two daughters, Karol and Scheryl were apart of desegregation of Johnson Elementary in 1962. The City of Charlottesville held an Unveiling ceremony on October 23, 2019 to honor students, and parents who desegregated Johnson Elementary. A historical marker was placed in the front of the school recognizing the efforts.

We have two daughters, Karol Williams Biglow who resides in Washington, D.C. with her husband, they have three children. Daughter Scheryl Williams Glanton resides in Philadelphia with her husband, they have a daughter who lives in Philadelphia and a son who lives in Seattle Washington. I have two great-grandchildren.

Teaching was a rewarding career for me. My warmest memories from teaching takes me back to the lasting friendships I gained and the difference I made, working with the students at Jackson P. Burley High School.

Lorraine Payne Williams, Business Department

I grew up in a large family in Orange County, Virginia. I am a 1960 graduate of the George Washington Carver Regional High School in Rapidan, Virginia. During segregation, the school served the educational needs of Black students from the four-county region of Culpeper, Madison, Orange and Rappahannock.

In the fall of 1960, I was the first in my family to attend college. I enrolled at Saint Paul's College in Lawrenceville, Virginia. While there, I had every intention to study biology, but was persuaded by my English Professor to pursue English. I have never regretted the choice. I received a B.A. Degree in English in 1964.

Upon graduation, I declined a teaching position offered by my high school. I had high regards for Burley High School in the City of Charlottesville, therefore I accepted a position there for my first teaching position. My time there was short, teaching from the fall of 1964 through the spring of 1966. I always dreamed of being a teacher and was not disappointed by the experience.

Teaching at Burley High School was a very positive experience. I taught some of the very best students, who were prepared, ready, willing and able to learn. Although, there were challenges, the students were well mannered and disciplined. I believed all students could learn and I gave my best, because I had a love and appreciation for education. One of my fondest memories is a challenge by Principal, Alexander Scott to sponsor the Debate Team. I was very doubtful, but did not refuse the challenge. Two of the most outstanding students to make up the team were, Otis Lee and John Ragland. I took the team to Hampton Institute for a competition and with poise and preparation, they won the trophy.

My stay at Burley High School was short, as I enrolled at the University of Virginia in the fall of 1966. I received a Master's Degree in Administration and Supervision in 1968 and a Doctorate in Curriculum and Instruction from the University of Miami in 1972. After completion of my Doctorate Degree, I became the Coordinator of Secondary Education at Howard University from 1972 to 1978.

I worked hard and became a well-known public school and college teacher, author, researcher, and administrator. As the Director of Academic Enhancement in the Washington, D.C. Public Schools, I implemented a highly effective test improvement program, which has dramatically increased National Merit and Achievement finalists in the D.C. Schools. I am a writer and I have spoken at several national conventions. My work has been featured in Newsweek, the Washington Post, the Washington Times, and on CNN.

Several years ago, while sitting in my living room in Clinton, Maryland, I had an epiphany. I knew the National Anthem was performed at most NBA games. But, what about "Lift Every Voice and Sing"—the song often called the "Black National Anthem," which comes from a poem by civil rights activist, **James Weldon Johnson.** I launched a campaign to convince teams and schools across the country to play the Black Anthem. To date, I've had success with some NBA teams, the Washington Wizards, the Golden State Warriors and the Brooklyn Nets, as well as many colleges in the District of Columbia, Maryland and Virginia (DMV.) I think the song belongs everywhere—in classrooms and on the court. The anthem could serve as a way for players to express both pride and protest. This song liberates my thinking about being a Black person in America, and I think it can do the same for others. I laud this as one of my proudest achievements.

I am married to Dr. Mary H. Johnson, the first principal and co-founder of the Washington Math Science Technology Public Charter High School. She has been involved in education for over thirty years. The school is one of the few such charter schools in the United States, which opened in September 1998, the school is located in southwest Washington, D.C. and serves 200 students from throughout the city. Dr. Williams is sometimes referred to as the "Marva Collins" of Washington, D.C., because of her reputation for working hard and enhancing the quality of life for her students. Dr. Johnson, a professor of Mathematics and Education at the University of The District of Columbia, and retired from the D.C. Public School System after many years as a mathematics teacher and school administrator. Mary is one of my biggest supporters.

My son, **Eugene Williams, Jr.** is an educator, writer, motivational speaker, and entertainer. He is a former child actor who played the role of the purple grape in the very first "Fruit of the Loom" back to school ad campaign. At the age of 12, he served as the children's correspondent for PM Magazine on WUSA (Washington, DC/CBS). As a child, he was featured in Ebony Magazine, People Magazine, and Soap Opera Digest. He also appeared on stage and television with such celebrities as Ray Charles, Pearl Bailey, and Stephanie Mills. Eugene is the Principal at Cumberland High School, Cumberland, Virginia.

Dr. Eugene Williams Sr., English Department, 1964 – 1966

I grew up in Campbell County, located a few miles outside of the City of Lynchburg, Virginia. I graduated in 1949 from Virginia State University, in Petersburg, Virginia with a Bachelor of Science Degree in Industrial Arts. After graduation, I worked for 1 ½ years before being drafted into the U. S. Army, serving during the Korean War.

I began my first teaching job in 1953 at Jackson P. Burley High School in the City of Charlottesville. I remained at Burley High until the school closed in 1967. Burley High School was a great place to teach. I taught vocational education to students beginning in 8th grade through 12th grade. The students were eager to learn and excelled.

All my students loved working with wood and constructing different projects. I remember one of my top students in particular, Lloyd Feggans. Each year, I would take students to Virginia State University and Hampton University to compete in carpentry with students from other black high schools. One year, Lloyd won the top prize for his carpentry exhibit. He was really hands on and loved carpentry.

While at Burley, I also worked with the school bus drivers. It was my responsibility to keep records for the drivers. I made sure the buses were maintained and inspected. I tracked the routes the drivers were assigned, and how many students rode their bus. There were adult and student drivers. At the end of each month, I provided a detailed written report to the Assistant Superintendent of Schools on the bus schedules and the drivers for Burley High School.

Teaching at Burley High prepared me for what was to come after desegregation. In the fall of 1967, when Burley closed, I was assigned to teach at Buford Middle School. At Buford, I taught vocational arts to 7th and 8th graders. I was there from 1967 through 1973. From Buford I went to the Charlottesville-Albemarle Technical Education Center (CATEC) and continued teaching vocational arts. At CATEC, I was a teacher and coordinator. During my 15 year teaching career at CATEC, my class built 12 houses throughout the City of Charlottesville and County of Albemarle.

I married Marian L. Washington (deceased) in 1952. I have two children; daughters, Wilhelmina and Marilyn. Both are married, but chose to keep their maiden names. Marilyn and son, James Peters lives in Bowie, Maryland. James is an honor student at DeMatha Catholic High School.

Teaching left me with many fond memories. I still remember many of my students at Burley and occasionally speak with some of them.

I now reside at the Colonnades-Sunrise Senior Living. Charlottesville is home, and I am enjoying independent, retirement living.

James McDaniel, Jr., Vocational–Industrial Arts Department, 1953 – 1967

I am a Charlottesville native and graduated from the Jefferson School in 1946. I attended Virginia State College in Petersburg, Virginia, graduating in 1950 with a Bachelor of Science Degree in Vocational Home Economics.

My first teaching assignments were substitute positions at (Albemarle Training School and Esmont School.) In 1953, I began teaching at Esmont Elementary School in Albemarle County, teaching for 3 years. I taught vocational home economics for one year at S.C. Abrams School in Palmyra, Virginia. Superintendent Paul Cale of the Albemarle County Public School System, assisted me in getting transferred in 1956 from Abrams School to Jackson P. Burley, my tenure lasted for 11 years.

Beginning in July 1956, I taught vocational education in the summer program at Burley High. The classes trained young women, as well as men, how to preserve and can food products. My position also included home visits to provide assistance to families. The Home Economics Program had a suite of classrooms located in the basement of the school.

I enjoyed teaching, and the relationships I developed with the students. We worked closely together to make things work. I also worked with parents solving many problems. I had fond memories working at Esmont Elementary School, because I developed a bond with many of the students who would later attend Burley High School.

I was so proud of my brother, Roosevelt "Rosey" Brown Jr. who also attended the Jefferson School in the City of Charlottesville. Rosey, played college football for Morgan State University in Baltimore, Maryland. He was an American football player and was drafted as an offensive tackle in the National Football League for the New York Giants. He played from 1953 to 1965. Rosey was inducted into the Pro Football Hall of Fame in 1974. A Historical Marker in Rosey's honor was erected in 2009 at 10th & Page Street in Charlottesville, referred to as the intersection of Roosevelt Brown Boulevard and Main Street

I married Adolphus Hailstork in 1956 in Ithaca, New York. We returned to Charlottesville where our two children were born; Lyria Belle, now the Assistant Director of the Victim/Witness Program in Charlottesville. Lyria received her B.S. Degree from Roberts Wesleyan College in Rochester, New York, and received her Master's Degree from Longwood University in Farmville, Virginia. Son, Roger Cunningham attended Syracuse University in Syracuse, New York for undergraduate studies and received his graduate degree from Virginia State University in Petersburg. Roger is the Director of the Syracuse University Book Store.

I enjoyed working at Burley High School. Growing up in the City of Charlottesville, I thought Jackson P. Burley High was the 'Be all and end all' of schools. After desegregation closed Burley in 1967, I returned to Ithaca, New York and taught in the Ithaca City School District, Ithaca, New York and the Rush-Henrietta Central School District, Rush, New York. I enrolled in graduate school at Cornell University and received a graduate Degree. I am finally home again, in Charlottesville the city I love.

Lyria Hailstork, Vocational Home Economics, 1956 – 1967

Coach Walter 'Rock' Greene, was the Head Baseball and Basketball Coach and the Assistant Football Coach at Burley High School from 1957–1963. Coach Greene is still recognized with great respect by all that knew him. He is a very well-spoken, humble, and gracious gentleman. He speaks very candidly and was eager to share his experiences and memories while at the much loved Burley High School.

Coach Greene said he chose to come to the City of Charlottesville to teach physical education in 1957, it was his first teaching assignment. He wanted to visit the city he had heard so much about, and to see how others were living further south of him. He grew up in the Washington, D.C. area and graduated from Phelps Vocational School. He attended Delaware State College, graduating in 1957. He has been a lifetime member of the Kappa Alpha Psi Fraternity.

Coach Greene said, teaching and coaching at Burley High School, was one of the greatest experiences of his life. Working with the young students who were so well mannered and respectful, meant so much to him. He knew God had helped him by sending him to this wonderful school. To this day, many of his students still keep in touch with him.

While at Burley High School, he had the highest respect for student trainer and manager Thomas Carey, who assisted him with the Baseball Team. He still communicates with Thomas, who later became a trainer and manager while attending college at Delaware State. After graduation, Thomas became a teacher and later a principal in the New Jersey Public School System.

One of Coach Greene's biggest disappointments was leaving Burley High so abruptly and not telling anyone he was leaving. He said, "I just didn't have the heart to tell anyone." He left Burley after the 1963 school year and returned to his Alma Mater, Phelps Vocational High School. The Assistant Superintendent of Adult Vocational Education for the District of Columbia Public Schools, Mr. Lemuel A. Penn wanted him to return home to teach and coach, as he had earned so much success at Jackson P. Burley High School. Coach Greene returned and taught physical education and later became the Assistant Basketball Coach. He was the first student to return to the school as a teacher and Coach.

The saddest experience of Coach Greene's young life was losing his mentor, Mr. Lemuel A. Penn. During the summer of 1964, Lt. Col. Penn was at Fort Benning, Georgia, on Army reserve duty, along with two other reserve officers. After two weeks of reserve duty, they headed home to Washington, DC, with hopes of driving straight home, and plans to stop only for food and fuel. Col. Penn was murdered by a Ku Klux Klan sniper after changing drivers. The tragedy occurred nine days after the passage of the Civil Rights Act of 1964. The murder occurred in Madison County Georgia, near the city of Athens. A local jury failed to convict the Klansman, but the federal government successfully prosecuted the case and the Klansman served six months in federal prison. In 1973 the Lemuel A. Penn Career Development Center was named in honor of Coach Greene's mentor.

Coach Greene married Estelle Lockert in 1969. Estelle was a Librarian at Phelps Vocational High School and is now retired. Walter and Estelle have two children: Walter Greene Jr. a retired Air Force Chief Master Sergeant, with 30 years of service and resides in San Antonio, Texas. Daughter, Lisa Greene, graduated from the University of Maryland Eastern Shore, in Princess Anne, Maryland. Lisa is the Director of Early Childhood Development. Granddaughter, Jaylin is a student at Virginia Union University in Richmond, Virginia. Coach Greene has retired and resides in Hyattsville, Maryland.

Walter Greene, Physical Education, Head Baseball and Basketball Coach and Assistant Football Coach, 1957 – 1963

I taught at Burley High School from 1963 – 1967, and love being there. The students, were focused and dedicated. Although, some were just typical students trying to find their way. I taught in the Business Department, preparing the students for a successful life after graduation. Many of the students were prepared to go out into the workforce when they left Burley, but many others were prepared for a higher education.

There was much concern from the students and teachers when the school was scheduled to close in 1967. Some of the students wanted to know where they would go and how they would succeed. I could only calm them and say, we have prepared you to go to any school and succeed.

During desegregation, the teachers were re-assigned, where needed. I was assigned to J.T. Henley Middle School in Crozet, and later to Jack Jouett Middle School, where I taught Keyboarding and Introduction to Business.

Teaching was a rewarding career for me. My fondest memories from teaching takes me back to my friends and the students at Jackson P. Burley High School.

Gloria Thaxton, Business Department, 1963 – 1967

I grew up on Grove Street in Charlottesville, Virginia and graduated from the Jefferson School. I received my B.S. Degree in Music Education from Virginia State College in Petersburg, Virginia and a Master's in Music Education from the University of Michigan.

My first teaching job was at Jackson P. Burley High School as a Fine Arts teacher. I also held the position of Band Director during the 1954-1955 school year.

The students at Burley High School were well-mannered and responsible students. It was a wonderful school in which to work and I loved teaching there.

After leaving Burley High School, I was hired as the Head of the Music Department at Shaw University in Raleigh, North Carolina. While at Shaw University, I taught Music Education and was the Band Director.

I later moved to Wilmington, Delaware and worked at the Pierre S. DuPont High School in the Brandywine School District. While at DuPont, I taught Music Education and was the Band Director. I was later hired to be the Fine Arts Supervisor in the Brandywine School District, teaching at Hanby Middle School in Wilmington, Delaware. My position at Hanby Middle School was my last teaching job before retirement.

I am married to Janice Davis Rogers and we have one son, Charles Lawler Rogers, Jr.; two grandsons, Charles Lawler Rogers, III and DeCarlo Rogers, two granddaughters; Chloe Rogers and Alicia Wivecon.

Teaching music has left me with many fond memories. My music education training from the Jefferson School to Virginia State College to the University of Michigan, provided me the motivation that served me through my teaching career. I owe a very special thanks to all my music teachers.

Teaching at Jackson P. Burley High School was the start of the path that led me to a successful music career.

Charles Lawler Rogers, Sr., Fine Arts and Band Director

Jackson P. Burley High School was my first teaching job. I taught there from 1956 – 1960. Upon graduation from Virginia Union University, in Richmond, Virginia, I enlisted in the Army, serving during the Korean War. I returned to Richmond and worked at the Medical College of Virginia. One of my professors at Virginia Union assisted me in getting a teaching position at Jackson P. Burley High School in Charlottesville. I loved being at Burley High, as I was doing what I always wanted to do, teach science.

While at Burley High, I enjoyed working with the students on Science projects. They were so excited and eager to learn. I travelled all around the state with some of the students, where they competed with other schools on science projects. I still have memories of a very ambitious student, Alicia Bowler who always went above and beyond on her projects. Many of the students were very successful in their studies and received scholarships to attend college.

Teaching at Burley High was the best thing to ever happen to me. It prepared me for other teaching jobs to come. After four years, I left Burley for a teaching position at Maggie Walker High School and later at John Marshall High School, both in Richmond. I taught science at both schools.

Teaching Science led me to work in medical research, where I worked for the next 20 years at A.H. Robins Pharmaceuticals Company in Richmond. My son also worked in medical research and I assisted him as an X-Ray Technician.

I married Lucille Williams on June 13, 1952. We have three children; sons, Harold Jr. and Terone and daughter Denita. Teaching was a rewarding career for me with many fond memories.

Harold Green, Science Department, 1956 – 1960

I enrolled in Norfolk State College in 1959 and attended for two years. I attended Virginia State College in 1961 for one year. I returned to Norfolk State College, graduating in 1964, receiving a Bachelor of Music Degree in Vocal Music Education, with a minor in English.

In 1964, I met Mr. Alexander Scott, Principal of Jackson P. Burley High School at a professional meeting. Through discussions, he got to know me, and said Burley High School was seeking a Music teacher. He asked if I was interested. At the time, I had committed to my first teaching assignment at West Moreland Middle School in Danville, Virginia as a music teacher. I never forgot Mr. Scott, and a year later, in 1965, I was hired as the Choir Director at Jackson P. Burley High School. I later entered the Master's Program at the University of Virginia.

When I first moved to Charlottesville, I lived in the home of Mary Battle, on 5th Street N.W. across from Jefferson School. I had no car at the time and rode to Burley each morning with local resident and Burley High School teacher, Mrs. Teresa Walker. We have remained the best of friends and keep in touch to this day. My first apartment in Charlottesville was on Rose Hill Drive, walking distance from Burley High School.

The Burley music program had an outstanding reputation. There were always new goals from each Music Director and my first goal, was to continue with the outstanding program already established. I also had my ideas of what would make the program great, and had many opportunities to apply them. The choir continued to travel and remained successful, performing in local, district and state festivals. The students were proud of their achievements.

I was re-assigned to Albemarle High School in 1969, with no promises of being a music teacher. I made it very clear, I was interested in a job teaching music. I later became the Choir Director at Albemarle High School, and taught music for seven years. After leaving Albemarle High School, I married and moved to New York.

One of my fondest memories in Charlottesville is meeting Rev. James Hamilton of Mt. Zion Baptist Church. Rev. Hamilton told Mr. Scott he needed a Director of Music at the Church, as Mr. Scott had told Rev. Hamilton about me. Rev. Hamilton told me the church's Music Directors were always teachers from Burley High School. I accepted the job and later performed my first Cantata at Mt. Zion Baptist Church. The day of the performance was, "Standing Room Only." I had a good relationship with the people I met, and I was doing what I loved, musical performances.

I have one son, Onaje Grady and three grandsons; Onaje, Jaylen and Shaun. Onaje is a graduate of George Mason University in Fairfax. Music is in my family's blood, as grandson, Jaylen will enroll in the Kulgan School of Arts in Manassas in the fall of 2020, so the tradition will continue. I am retired and lives in Portsmouth, Virginia. I will always love Charlottesville and cherish the memories and the friends I made.

Cynthia DeSue-Grady, Choir Director and Music Education Teacher, 1965 – 1967

I graduated from Virginia State College in Petersburg, Virginia in 1957 with a Bachelor of Science Degree in Music Education. After college, I served 6 months of active Duty in the U.S. Army.

My first teaching assignment was at Jackson P. Burley High School in the City of Charlottesville. I began in the fall of 1958 and taught through 1963. I was the Choir Director and taught social studies.

The choir had been organized by Mrs. Virginia Word, and I carried on the work she had started. I was a young teacher and was very proud of what I was doing, as I loved music and working with the students. The students were just youngsters, but wanted very much to be a part of the choir and music program and were eager to learn. The choir was very successful and we travelled and performed in local, district and state festivals. The performances were evaluated and judged, always receiving a favorable rating. The choir also performed for the community, churches, and other local events and activities, as well as the school's winter and Christmas concerts, high school graduations and other events at the school. The students were proud of their accomplishments.

While at Burley High, I attended the University of Virginia and received a Masters of Education in Music Education. I left Burley High in 1963 to teach Instrumental Music in the Baltimore Public School System. In 1967, I taught 10th grade Choir, and Band at Cardozo High School in Washington, DC. While at Cardozo High School, I began further study in music education at the Catholic University of America, in Washington, DC. Beginning in 1970, I taught orchestra, music theory, music literature and administered the Music Program at Catonsville Community College, retiring in 2003. In 2008, I began teaching orchestra at the Waldorf School of Baltimore.

I married Fellisco Edwards on June 8, 1957. Fellisco was a native of Charlottesville and a 1953 Burley High School graduate. She taught one semester of Physical Education at the school beginning in January 1959. We have 3 children; Kenneth Douglass (deceased), Willis Eugene III, and Thomas Courtney. I retired in 2020 shortly after COVID-19 closed the schools.

Willis E. Keeling Jr., Choir Director and Social Studies, 1958 – 1963

Mr. George F. Tinsley is a 1948 graduate of the Jefferson School, in Charlottesville, Virginia. Mr. Tinsley grew up in the City of Charlottesville on Preston Avenue. Hard work was a part of his nature, as he grew up with twelve siblings. He is a lifelong member of Zion Union Baptist Church.

He began working at Jackson P. Burley High School in the fall of 1951 with the Cafeteria Staff. In 1956, when Burley's head custodian was transferred to Albemarle High School, Mr. Tinsley became the head custodian.

From 1951 – 1956, Mr. Tinsley worked with the cafeteria staff in the cooking, preparation, serving and lunch clean-up. There were 2 lunch periods each day.

As head custodian, there was lots of work, as the school was a three story building. The industrial arts classes, which included brick masonry and carpentry were held in the basement, along with the home economics classes. The custodial staff consisted of 2 custodians and 2 housekeepers.

Mr. Tinsley had a great relationship with the students, parents and other faculty and staff. The students were well mannered and happy. If a student cut class and he was aware of it, he would speak with them, encouraging them to stay in class, serving as a counselor and advisor. He recalled on many occasion, after school had closed and a student left a book or something in the school they needed, they or a parent would call him. He never failed to return to the school and meet them to open the door, so they could retrieve what was needed.

Mr. Tinsley, worked with many students who were enrolled in the Charlottesville Opportunities Industrialization Center (OIC) Training Program. The program sent students to the school for training in Custodial Services and life skills.

When asking any Burley alumni if they knew Mr. Tinsley, they would eagerly respond, "Yes, I will never forget Mr. Tinsley." For many, he was a father figure for students away from home, a stern disciplinarian and always provided words of wisdom when asked or needed. Mr. Tinsley said, to this day many of the students from Burley High School still keep in touch with him, and on occasion some will stop by for a visit.

George Tinsley married Helen Carter and they had four children: Bertha (D), Bruce (D), Boyd and Betty. He remained at Jackson P. Burley High School after desegregation in 1967. The school became the Jack Jouett Annex and in 1973 became Burley Middle School. Mr. Tinsley retired in 1991 with 40 years of service.

In his honor, George Tinsley Drive was dedicated on November 9, 2013, by the Burley Varsity Club. It is located on the campus of the now Jackson P. Burley Middle School.

George F. Tinsley, Cafeteria Worker and Head Custodian, 1951 – 1991

CHAPTER 6

WE ARE THE BURLEY BEARS

REMEMBERING THE GOOD OLE DAYS

School Colors
Kelly Green and Old Gold

Coach Robert "Bob" Smith used his influence in 1951 to name the Burley Mascot the *"Burley Bears" after* his Alma Mater the Morgan State University Bears.

Burley Bear

Burley Student Handbook

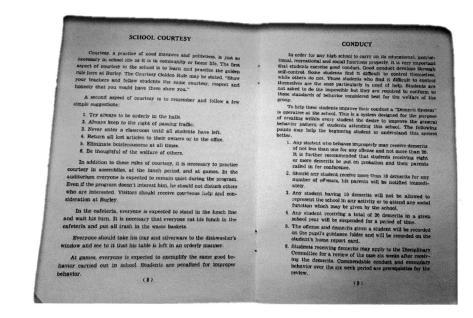

Courtesy of Agnes Ivory Booker
Class of 1963

Daily Schedule

Period	First Bell	Second Bell
Homeroom Attendance	9:05	9:08
First Period	9:17	9:20
Second Period	10:13	10:16
Third Period	11:09	11:12
First Lunch Period	12:05	12:32
Fourth Period	12:32	12:35
Second Lunch Period	1:02	1:30
Fifth Period	1:30	1:33
Sixth Period	2:26	2:29
Dismissal	3:20	3:25

School Day

The school day for students began at 9:05 AM and ended at 3:20 in the afternoon. At the ringing of the first bell, all students went immediately to homeroom for attendance and morning devotion. Students were considered tardy if they were not present in their homeroom when the second bell rang at 9:08 AM. Before going to any class, students reported to their homeroom for attendance, which began at 9:05 AM and concluded at 9:17 AM. The ringing of the bell indicated the beginning of the school day, homeroom periods and the beginning and end of a class period, lunch period and the end of the school day.

School Song
Written by Mildred Jones

Ode to Burley
Majestically among the hills
Neath God's great azure sky,
Stands proudly with its arms outstretched
Our own dear Burley High.

Within thy walls, O sacred one
Is found a guiding light;
The enchantment of thy tender care,
Forever beaming bright.

Chorus:
O Burley High, dear Burley High,
Our pride shall ever be.
Our songs of love and joy we sing,
With kindest thoughts of thee.
With faithful hearts and thoughtful minds,
We pledge our loyalty.
To God and thee we will e'er be true,
Oh hail to dear **Burley High**!

Activities, Clubs and Organizations

Art Club
Burley Band
Burley Bulletin Staff
Burley Chorus
Cheerleaders
Debate Society
Dramatics Club
French Club (Le Cercle Francais)
Guidance Committee
Industrial Cooperative Training Club (ICT)
Industrial Arts and Vocational Club
Latin Club
Library Club
Majorette Corp
Math Club
Music Appreciation Club
National Honor Society
New/Future Business Leaders of America
New/Future Farmers of America
New/Future Homemakers of America
New/Future Teachers of America
Quill & Scroll
Rainbow Art Club
School Safety Patrol
Science Club
Student Participation Association (SPA)
Student Council Association (SCA)
Student Patrol
Thespian Society
Triangle & Siphon Club
Tumbling Team
Vocational Industrial Arts Club (VIAC)
Yearbook Staff

Sports

Baseball Team
Boys' Varsity Basketball
Boys' Junior Varsity Basketball
Golf Team
Girls' Basketball
Girls' Field Hockey
Girls' Softball
Girls' Soccer
Varsity Football
Junior Varsity Football
Track and Field Team

Band Uniform

Uniform without belt and braid
Courtesy of June Hopkins Banks
Class of 1967

Uniform with belt and braid
Courtesy of June Hopkins Banks
Class of 1967

Athletic Attire

Letterman Jacket
Courtesy of Harry Nicholas
Class of 1964

1956 Letterman Sweater
Courtesy of Isaac "Ike" Curry
Class of 1958

Cheerleader Sweater
Courtesy of Dorothea Lewis
Class of 1964

Letterman Sweater
Courtesy of Raymond Curry
Class of 1967

Athletic Attire

Football Cleats
Courtesy of Phillip Jones
Class of 1963

Drill Team Uniform
Courtesy of Wanda Carter Stevens
Class of 1964

Basketball Warm-up Jacket
Courtesy of Aurthodius Haden, III
Class of 1967

Burley High School Trophies

Burley High School Trophies

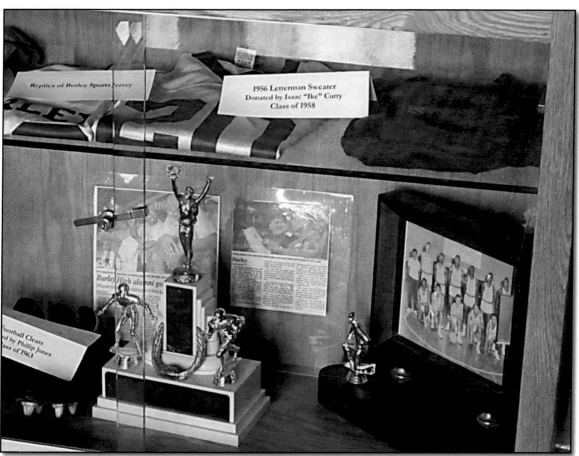

Keepsakes

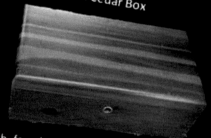

Mini Cedar Box

Each female graduate was presented with a Mini Cedar Box with key. The gift was presented to each student from the furniture companies of Gilmore, Hamm & Snyder, MC Thomas Exchange and MC Thomas Furniture.

Courtesy of Maxine Holland, Class of 1967.

The Cedar boxes were manufactured by Lane Furniture. The company founders were John E. Lane and son, Edward H. Lane who resided in Esmont and Altavista, Virginia.

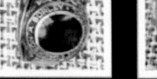

1956 Class Ring
Courtesy of Beatrice Washington Clark

1966 Class Ring
Courtesy of Rauzelle J. Smith

1967 Class Ring
Courtesy of Maxine Holland

Future Teachers of America Pin
Courtesy of Maxine Holland

115

Quill and Scroll Pin
Courtesy of Patricia Bowler Edwards

Quill and Scroll

Miss Louise Pankey was the original sponsor of the Burley Quill and Scroll. The school received its charter in 1954. Mrs. Pauline Garrett became the Sponsor in 1956.

The Quill and Scroll is an International high school Journalism Honor Society which recognizes and encourages outstanding individual and group achievements in scholastic journalism. The members were students from the Burley junior and senior class. Their work was outstanding in journalism and school publications, such as staffers of the Burley Bulletin, or yearbook, as well as excellent writers.

Mr. Stephen Waters became the sponsor of the Burley Quill and Scroll in 1963.

1965 Quill and Scroll

Student Newspaper
Burley Bulletin Last Edition – June 1967

Courtesy of Albemarle Charlottesville Historical Society

Year	Burley Bulletin Editors
1953-54	Edwina Sellers Carter & Carrie Meadows
1954-55	Anita Ray Smith Pankey
1955-56	Althea Mosby Anderson
1956-57	Mary Helen Whiting Payne
1957-58	Pearl Nightengale Thomas
1958-59	Alicia Bowler Lugo
1959-60	Marshall Garrett
1960-61	Alice Henderson Knight
1961-62	Carolyn Mitchell
1962-63	Geraldine Harris
1963-64	Doris Gardner
1964-65	Patricia Bowler
1965-66	Ida Johnson
1966-67	Elizabeth Conway

1967 Burley Bulletin Staff

Jackson P. Burley High School
Yearbooks (1952–1967)
'Jay Pee Bee'

1967 Yearbook Staff

Yearbooks (1952 - 1955)

Yearbooks (1956 - 1959)

Yearbooks (1960 - 1963)

Yearbooks (1964 - 1967)

Jackson P. Burley High School
First Five–Year Graduating Class
Class of 1956

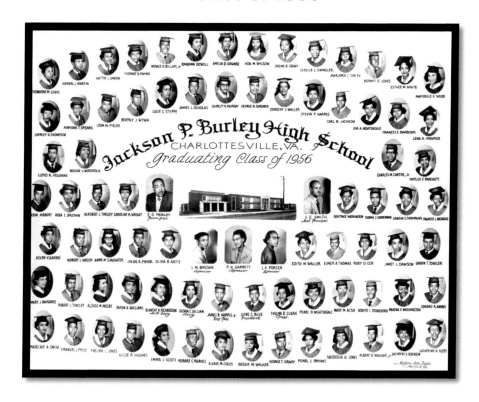

Jackson P. Burley High School, made history when it graduated its first five year class, the "Class of 1956." Graduation was Friday night, June 2, 1956 in the Burley High School auditorium. Dr. Thomas Henderson, Dean of Virginia Union University, delivered the Commencement Address. Seventy-three diplomas were awarded to the graduates.

A capacity crowd attended the graduation ceremony. Burley High School principal, Mr. Eugene Mobley, introduced Dr. Henderson. The theme of Dr. Henderson's timely and inspiring address was, "You're Living in a Critical Age." Dr. Henderson challenged the graduates to ever strive to attain perfection in their chosen fields of endeavor, not to be satisified to just "get by." He told them the rapidly changing world required an ever-increasing number of intelligent young people to do everything in their power to stamp out prejudice based on race.

Immediately following the commencement address, the Burley Choir thrilled the audience with its rendition of, "A Mighty Fortress is Our God" by Mueller and "Hallelujah Chorus" from Handel's "Messiah." The choir was directed by Mrs. Virginia Word.

Mrs. Lillie Mae Brown presented the graduating class. Pearl Nightengale was the Class Valedictorian and Marjorie Smith was the Class Salutatorian. Rev. E.D. McCreary, Pastor of the Ebenezer Baptist Church in Charlottesville gave the Invocation and Benediction.

1956 Graduation Announcement

Graduation Invitation

Courtesy of the Albemarle Charlottesville Historical Society

Diploma

Elsie M. Johnson, Class of 1959

Jackson P. Burley High School educated students from 8th through 12th grade. Students planning to attend college needed 20 academic credits for admission.

 Subjects
Business Education – 1 credit
English – 1 credit
Foreign Language – 1 credit
Home Economics – 1 credit
Mathematics – 1 credit
Nursing – 1 credit
Science – 1 credit
Social Studies – 1 credit
Performing Arts – ½ credit
Physical Education – ½ credit
Visual Art – 1 credit
Vocational/Industrial Education – 1 credit

Courtesy of Elsie M. Johnson

123

Class of 1952

Class of 1953

Class of 1954

Class of 1955

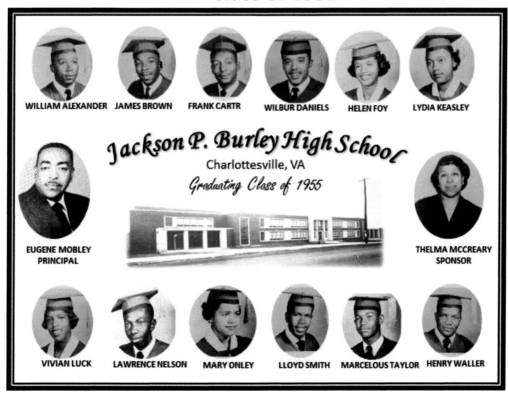

Class of 1956

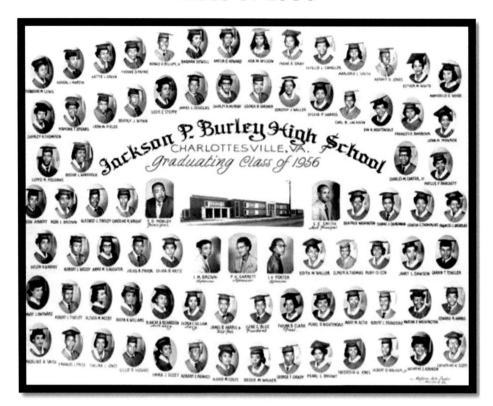

Class of 1957

Class of 1958

Class of 1959

Class of 1960

Class of 1961

Class of 1962

Class of 1963

Class of 1964

Class of 1965

Class of 1966

Class of 1967

The best thing about

Memories

...is making them

Miss Burley 1953 and Attendants

L to R: Constance Green, Yvonne Washington 'Miss Burley' and
Marybelle Wood

1954 Burley Beauties
L to R: Julia Johnson, Marguerita Smith, Carolyn Hurley,
Emma Jane Scott and Thelma Clark

Miss Homecoming 1956-57
Phyllis Carter

Miss Burley 1959
Madelyn Anglin

Miss Homecoming 1963
Betty Perry

Miss Senior Class Beauty 1962
Verden McCoy

Homecoming Queen 1966
Patricia Bowler

Miss Burley 1967
Maxine Holland

Joyce Jackson and
mom Mildred

Alfred Martin and
Janice Witcher

L to R: Barbara Jean Nicholas, Vera Ford, Edward 'Dopey' Sims and Carrie White

George R. Grady and
Pearlie Mae Currington

Russell Scott and
Katherine Robinson

Guidance Department - 1963

Carolyn Burton and Mrs. Pauline Garrett

Executive Board of Student Participation Association (SPA) - 1965

Using the Audio Visual Equipment - 1961

1961 Business Education (Typing Class)

1965 Future Teachers of America (FTA)

1965 Industrial Arts and Vocational Club (ICT)

Art Class with Mr. Waldo Johnson

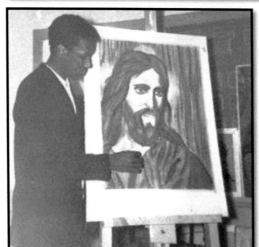

Mr. Waldo Johnson, Art Instructor

1953 Le Cercle Francais

1959 Home Economics

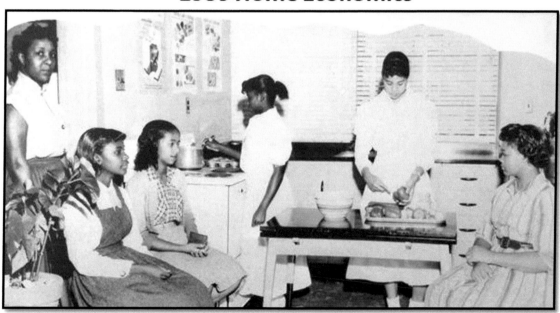

1959 Masonry

1963 Building Trade

1953 General Woodwork

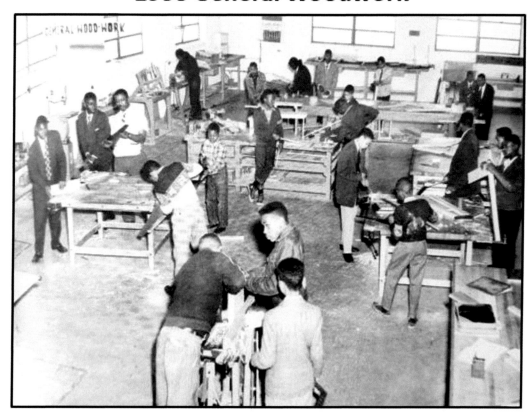

1961 Farm Mechanics

CHAPTER 7

STUDENT REFLECTIONS
CLASSES OF 1952 – 1967

Burley
Bears

Bernard W. Washington
Class of 1952

Upon arriving at Jackson P. Burley High School, via a yellow school bus, as part of the Senior Class of 1952, I was awe struck by its size and brick structure. This reaction was the result of attending the six-room wooden Esmont High School, built in 1916. I thought this new school, Jackson P. Burley High was as good as the schools for white students I had passed for years' enroute to the Esmont School. However, before graduation I learned it was "separate but not equal."

The size of my senior class composed of students from the other two area high schools and the teachers, faculty and support staff, established a great atmosphere for a new learning experience that included vocational education. My home room teacher, Mrs. Alma Pleasants, guided us through the daily routine and ensured that we were aware of and took advantage of the extra curriculum courses, the sports programs and other activities. However, riding the big yellow school bus every day, made that all but impossible.

All the teachers and student counselors were dedicated and had a passionate determination that all of us seniors acquired and completed the requisite studies for graduation this first year.

I regret that my time at Burley was only one year, however, it sparked the desire to pursue a college education. I enrolled in the ROTC Program while attending Hampton Institute, now Hampton University, graduating in 1957. I retired from the U.S. Army as a Lieutenant Colonel (LTC) after 20 years of service, serving two tours of duty in Vietnam.

John J. Gaines, III
Class of 1953

In 1951, I moved from Jefferson School in the City of Charlottesville to Jackson P. Burley High School. Burley High was a very pleasant experience, and I was very happy to be there. The new school was much talked about and was more than we ever expected.

I grew up in the well-known 10th and Page Street neighborhood in the City of Charlottesville. It was great to always be surrounded by family, mentors and neighbors who knew each other well. Their guidance played a great role in my life. I always knew I wanted to be an influencer who helped children.

At Burley High, I played 'center' on the Burley Bears Football Team. We became champions under Coach Robert Smith after such a short time of working together as a team. In 1952 the Burley Bears were the Virginia Inter-Scholastic Athletic League (VIAL) State Champions.

In 1953, after two years at Burley High School, I graduated at the age of 16. I was leaving behind so many memories.

I enrolled at Hampton Institute, now Hampton University in Hampton, Virginia. I received a football scholarship to attend there and graduated with a Bachelor of Arts Degree. I returned to Charlottesville, and in 1958 my first full time job was a teaching assignment at Jefferson Elementary School in the City of Charlottesville.

I later enrolled at the University of Virginia, and in 1965 received a Master's in Public School Administration. I also taught at Buford Middle School, and later became the Assistant Principal of McGuffey Education Center. I spent my 40 year career as an educator, working as a teacher, principal and administrator.

The preparation provided by the teachers at Jackson P. Burley High School brought about an awareness, as they helped to prepare me for much of what I could expect outside the walls of Burley High School.

Clariece Coles Harris
Class of 1954

During my childhood, I always enjoyed school and learning. My experience in elementary education commenced in a 2-room, Rosenwald School with grades first through fifth.

I attended Albemarle Training School for grades six and seven. During that time, families were notified of the expected move to a new school, in the City of Charlottesville, Jackson P. Burley High School.

Over the summer, kids in my community of Eastham, and the surrounding areas, were excited as we realized, we would be attending a new school in the fall.

On our first day, waiting for the bus to arrive, was all we talked about. When the bus came into view at our new school, we were lost for words, seeing this enormous building. The parking area was huge also, it was unbelievable, realizing the conditions from which we had come. Once inside the school, we were ushered to this huge, beautiful, auditorium, one of which we had never seen, as our old school did not have one.

Oddly enough, the teachers from our school transferred to Burley with us. Our teachers were caring, dedicated, concerned and eager to make sure we received the best that was available and offered. There was an immediate bond of students and teachers.

Even now, when I pass my old school, Burley High and see the beautiful structure, I feel a sense of pride, gratitude and elation. I was a part of the many blessings we received in that building, one that produced some of the best doctors, nurses, teachers, engineers, athletes, lawyers, business owners and other professions.

I am presently a nurse of 55 years, and I owe it all to Jackson P. Burley High School. I owe much gratitude to the staff and the people of higher authority who recognized, we deserved to have the best, as well as an equal opportunity.

Marcellous B. Taylor Sr.
Class of 1955

I grew up in Stanardsville, Virginia with 12 siblings. We attended a small two room school. I owe much thanks for my successful, educational journey to my very supportive parents. I arrived at Jackson P. Burley High School in 1953 as a 10th grader. I was completely overwhelmed, as the school was so large and beautiful, unlike my old school. The Greene County students attending Burley were transported to

school in a station wagon, but later travelled by school bus.

There was so much to do at Burley and I was a natural athlete, but sadly, was unable to participate in any sports or extra-curricular activities. Each day after school, I walked to Route 29 to work at the Howard Johnson Hotel. I had little time to study, as I worked from 4:00 – 12:00 each night. Later, a friend and I from Greene County shared a room at a boarding house in Charlottesville, making it easier for us to attend Burley and work after school.

I sang in the chorus, which I enjoyed, but didn't have the time to practice, so I stopped participating. I still have fond memories of several of my Burley teachers. My English teacher, Mrs. Thelma McCreary, was an extraordinary individual. I was failing in an English class taught by another teacher, and under Mrs. McCreary's tutelage and encouragement, I received an "A" in English. Mrs. Gladys McCoy taught my government class and provided so much support. When the thought crossed my mind to quit school and go to work, she told me, "Anybody can get a job and go to work." She provided the motherly advice I needed at the time, so I was determined to follow through and graduate. Mr. Clevester Logan taught Vocational and Industrial Arts and I thrived in his class, as I was interested in Agriculture. He took us on trips to Virginia State College to compete in competitions, where I was successful. He also pushed me into public speaking.

After graduating from Burley High School, I moved to Washington, D.C. with family and later entered the U.S. Marine Corp serving several years. I attended American University and the University of Maryland, where I was interested in Business Enterprise and Police Administration. I retired as a Detective with the Metropolitan Police Department in Washington, DC.

What I learned at Burley has served me well. In my retirement years, writing has been of great interest to me. I have published two books, The Lane and Lane Two, A Boys Journey to Maturity. I am currently in the process of writing my third book. I owe much gratitude to the Burley teachers that nurtured and supported me.

Pastor Lloyd Feggans
Class Reunion Committee, Chairman
Class of 1956

My education through 7th grade occurred at the six-room Esmont High School. There were no inside facilities or running water, but happy students and caring teachers.

To go from Esmont High School to Jackson P. Burley High School was quite a change for the better. I loved Burley High then, and I love it even more today. I began Burley as a proud 8th grader.

My 1956 Burley High graduating class made history as the first five year class. My classmates and I continue to keep in touch and have remained friends.

At Burley, I received a very good education from great teachers, who showed sincere interest in all the students. They were not only instructors, but were guardians of the students when they were away from home. I especially loved my Industrial Arts class taught by Mr. James McDaniel. He would take his students to Virginia State College and Hampton Institute to compete in carpentry projects with students from other black high schools. One year, I won the top prize for building a small revolving bookcase. I was so proud of my work and to this day still have the bookcase and love working with my hands. I will always have fond memories of Mrs. Theresa Walker, who taught business and Mrs. Pauline Garrett who taught English.

I began playing sandlot baseball with the Esmont Giants at the age of 13. I broke my arm as a player, but healed and carried my love of the sport to Burley High School and played under Coach Robert Smith. I was fortunate to be able to attend practice at Burley, as I had a friend with a car. I have never lost my love for the game of baseball.

My teachers were a great influence during my early youth and as a Burley student. They helped to mold me into the man I became. I have nothing but praise for my teachers and the staff at Jackson P. Burley High School.

Many times I reflect on my time at Burley High and what I was taught. I became a minister in 1982 and have pastored several churches over the last 35 years. I married my high school sweetheart, Marie Smith who was a 1957 Burley High School graduate and we forever reminisce of the days gone by and how blessed we were to be graduates of Jackson P. Burley High School.

Ellie Constance Witcher Shackelford
Class of 1957

I'm excited, there is a new school, one street over from home, "Jackson P. Burley High School!"

Every day, I watched the construction of the building of the school. Just think, walking one mile or more to school verses walking one quarter of a block to school. Oh! I thought I could sleep just a little longer in the mornings. Well, it did not happen, my mom, Mrs. Ruby Witcher, made sure I was out of bed at the same time. I would hear, "Get ready for school Connie." When I opened my eyes, my sisters, Barbara, Janice and Claressia would be smiling, because they knew I was not yet ready. Barbara was already attending Burley.

On my first day at Burley High School with all the other students, I was overwhelmed, excited and very happy. I was entering 8th grade and finally in high school with my sister. We entered the school through the door nearest the auditorium. My homeroom was completely at the opposite end of the building, near the gymnasium. On my first day, Barbara walked me to my classroom. I laid back in my bright yellow dress my mom had made me, and strutted down that hallway very proudly with my sister. I was confident and full of smiles. When Barbara left me at my homeroom door, I began to feel nervous. I was facing a room full of unknown people, but my smile remained. We were all introduced, and everyone was very friendly, so I was okay.

My days at Burley moved right along. I was a good student, made good grades and appeared on the 'Honor Roll' from time to time. I participated in many activities; basketball, cheerleader, Tumbling Team, band, and Operetta, I even entered several contests for Operetta.

As a senior, I was chosen, "Miss Versatile", best athlete, most popular and Class Secretary. Jackson P. Burley was the family home that sat high on the hill and will forever shine in our lives from generation to generation. I thank "My God" for the life I've lived, and the people I've met, then and now and for the school I love.

Barbara Churchman Fleming
Class of 1958

In 1953, a very anxious and excited 13 year old entered the halls of Jackson P. Burley High School. This new, three-level building, with its long hallways, spacious library, huge gymnasium and auditorium, were so different from Albemarle Training School. The difference was like night and day, I felt so small, but I knew this was where I belonged.

The teachers at Burley taught more than the basic school lessons. Through their guidance and tough love, they instilled in us values, such as accountability, good citizenship and how to live in our racially charged environment. My two favorite teachers, Miss Henrietta Spotts and Mr. John Clay were devoted to us educationally and personally. Miss Spotts, was my homeroom and home economics teacher. She encouraged her students to become strong minded, responsible individuals. She started each day with a morning devotion, she was well aware and knew being strong in our faith would be a driving force that would help us throughout our lives. Her reprimands were stern, but loving, she only wanted the best for me and the others she had the pleasure of teaching. I remember when she reviewed our report cards, she would look over the grades, to make sure we were working at our maximum potential. She would not accept anything less, and she believed in us.

Mr. John Clay taught history class with so much flair, you hated to miss one. He addressed each of us by "Mr. or Miss" (last name) letting us know at an early age, we deserved respect. Mr. Clay taught us that respect was something you had to earn; we were not entitled to anything in life for which we did not work.

I thank God for having the privilege to attend Jackson P. Burley High School and for the teachers and friends, I made along the way.

My years at Jackson P. Burley High School taught me many things. Even though the times have changed, and some of my teachers and classmates have passed on, the memories are everlasting. I am so proud to have been a Burley Bear, during those precious years. It was those years that profoundly shaped the person I am today.

Charles W. C. Yancey
Class of 1959

I entered Burley High School in September 1954 as a skinny 87 pounder. Coach Smith (Robert) confirmed in our gym class that I was the only boy in the eighth grade that weighed less than 100 pounds. I grew up playing various sports on the sandlots and play grounds, but it was obvious to me that I had better focus on academics.

The "pre-arranged marriage" that was Burley resulted from combining three previously separate school communities. In my class, there was a nice blend of students from each of the three schools and I enjoyed the experience of making new friends. Looking back, it was probably my introduction to what we now call diversity.

I held deep admiration and respect for our caring administrators, teachers, coaches, support staff and classmates. I particularly remember Mrs. Lillie Mae Brown, my math teacher throughout my years at Burley, for fostering the spirit of academic competitiveness. A number of my classmates provided me with friendly academic competition. But, it was Alicia Bowler who set the standard of academic excellence that I attempted to live up to. Also, I am reminded of Richard "Hawk" Monroe who was the all-around athlete that I wanted to be.

To me, 1959 was a year that brought a wide spectrum of emotions and aspirations. On the one hand, we were coming to the end of one of the most turbulent decades in this country's history. On the other hand, most of us were hopeful that our Burley years had prepared us for the next phase of our lives – attending college, trade school, or business school; serving in the military; securing a meaningful occupation; or marrying our high school sweetheart.

Mary Nicholas Nightengale
Class of 1960

What Burley means to me: It was truly an honor to be voted and recognized as Miss Burley for the class of 1960. My best friend Sarah K. Moore, was crowned the same year as Miss Homecoming. I was spotlighted in the Hall of Fame by my peers. I was recognized in four categories to include: best dressed, best dancer, best figure and neatest. All my siblings attended Jackson P. Burley High School and almost all were in the Hall of Fame, athletics, band, or on the cheering squad.

Being an active member in my class, I developed leadership skills, problem-solving skills, and survival skills. Burley had some awesome teachers, they served as role models and taught me, I could do almost anything by applying the skills I was learning.

Burley High was a school like no other! The entire community supported our athletic teams and of course enjoyed our band. The Burley Bears displayed high team spirit, and the baseball, basketball and football teams were all outstanding during my senior year. I was a cheerleader and loved every moment of it, "Hey Burley Bears." I acquired many lifetime friendships while attending Jackson P. Burley High School.

"A friend sticks closer than a brother."

Dora Brown Brooks
Class of 1961

I entered Jackson P. Burley High School in the fall of 1956. I spent the first seven years of my education at the two-room Terry School in Ivy, Virginia. My first time entering my new school, I was intimidated and in awe of this "massive building," called Burley High School. However, once inside, the teachers were an extension of my parents, as they cared about me and wanted me to succeed. While at Burley, I participated in band, member of the Home Economics Club, and Future Business Leaders of America. I credit the teachers for jump starting my career, especially Mrs. Teresa Walker. Mrs. Walker made her students take the Civil Service exam in our senior year and it served me greatly. Because of her and Mrs. Lorraine Williams, I majored in Secretarial Science at Virginia State University. After leaving Virginia State, I went to work for the Department of Health, Education and Welfare, in the City of Charlottesville, as their second Black employee.

Throughout my 35 ½ years with the federal government, I worked my way from Secretary to the first Black and first woman Division Chief at the National Ground Intelligence Center.

Whenever I walk through the doors of Burley High School, I say "thank you."

Zelda DeBerry Mitchell
Class of 1962

My years at Jackson P. Burley High School were, truly, some of the happiest and most carefree years of my life. As these were the beginning and trying years of desegregation in Virginia, we were not oblivious to all of the happenings around us. Some of our schoolmates left Burley to help the cause, but most of us stayed the Course at Burley.

Our high school was our, "home away from home." Most of our daily activities and extra-curricular activities were held at Burley High. Since the school was consolidated at that time, we were able to make lasting friendships with our classmates from surrounding counties. I feel this was a unique and enriching experience for us all.

Our teachers and instructors were both accomplished and caring. I was later able to realize this and appreciate their earnest attempts at preparing us for our life's endeavors. During my matriculation at Burley High School, I was inducted into the National Honor Society, participated in the band, SPA, French Club, Latin Club, Yearbook Staff, and Burley Bulletin Staff.

I found my education at Burley to be, in no way, inferior for I discovered that after graduating valedictorian of the class of 1962, I was, indeed, well prepared to continue my education at the college of my choice.

Reflecting on the words of our Burley alma mater, "Within thy walls o' sacred one, is found a guiding light", I find that this guiding light and the lessons learned therein, have helped guide me thus far through my life's journey, and is still guiding my passage.

Burley was, indeed, unforgettable!

Carolyn Burton Byers
Class of 1963

Entering Burley from the little two room North Garden School was both daunting and exciting. I worried about not finding my classrooms, would I make friends and would I excel academically. I soon felt a sense of belonging. I had many friends and teachers who were invested in me. Because of their devotion to teaching I was motivated to do my best. We were a team working towards a common goal of developing a well-rounded student.

My freshman year, I had a study hall in the band room with one of my favorite teachers, Mr. Sampson. I became interested in being in the band. Mr. Sampson taught me how to play the clarinet during my study hall. The following summer, I enrolled in intermediate band for six weeks. In the fall, I was placed in advanced band. Band was a lot of fun. We were welcomed where ever we went with cheers and applause. I would be bursting at the seams with pride for our achievements. I especially looked forward to marching in the parade in Culpeper, because afterwards we would go to the carnival. I won a big teddy bear at one of the carnivals. My mom would pick me up after band trips and my little brother and sister would be with her. Of course, I gave the teddy bear to them.

Another one of my favorite teachers was, Mrs. Garrett, although I was never in one of her classes. I got to know her when I participated in the Debutante Ball. She was also my Guidance Counselor. My senior year, I spent hours with Mrs. Garrett trying to select a college. I spent so much time with her that I was with her when the photographer came to take pictures for the year book. So, guess who took pictures with Mrs. Garrett to represent the Guidance Department? Oh, by the way I chose Saint Paul's College.

I am the person I am today because of my experiences at Burley. I became a teacher, because of the admiration I had for my teachers. I still live by principles and values instilled in me through my experiences at JACKSON P. BURLEY HIGH SCHOOL.

Berdell McCoy Fleming
Class of 1964

I am a proud graduate of Jackson Price Burley High School, class of 1964. As I stroll through the cauldrons of my mind, I am flooded with so many vivid memories, I will share.

We entered Burley as eager 8th graders, many of us from the Jefferson Elementary School had been together from first grade through seventh grade so we were solid in our ties.

Having been introduced to Burley early in my life, because my beloved mother Madame Gladys W. McCoy upon learning that she had been hired as the French teacher for the new High School had purchased a house on Charlton Avenue, right around the corner from the school. She had taken my sister, who was in the class of 1962 to the school on a few occasions before the school opened. We had become very familiar being there. Knowing some of the teachers from my visits, as well as having community ties, from church, helped with my comfort. We were surrounded by a village safety net.

In 1962, twenty or more of the girls were presented at a Debutante Ball, the gym was decorated so beautifully and after weeks of practice, we waltzed with our escorts across the floor. Beautiful young ladies, peaches and cream, ginger and walnut hued in billowy white gowns.

Becoming a majorette for the famous Burley Band was a milestone in my life. Our band was the first and only one from Central Virginia to be invited to the Cherry Blossom Festival parade in Washington, D. C. The thrill of marching past the reviewing stand and having President John F. Kennedy stand and salute us was an immensely proud moment.

As we moved toward our senior year the defining memory was surreal and somber. On the eve of our senior trip and senior college night we heard the devastating news, President Kennedy had been shot and killed rocked our souls by late afternoon. The decision for us to go to Washington and see the live stage play Macbeth was a difficult one. Our English teacher, Mr. Stephen Waters had planned the trip and insisted we go. We were very sad and against this journey, but I was very glad he was a visionary, he explained this was history and we would tell our grandchildren.

The bus pulled out early that morning bound for Washington. We arrived on a murky, gray day. Washington was in a deep state of mourning. Mr. Waters asked the driver to drive past all the important landmarks, everything was draped in black. We saw very few folks on the streets it was surreal.

I'm thankful for all the teachers who helped to shape and mold us. I'm so glad I went to Burley High, singing Glory, Glory Hallelujah! I went to Burley High.

James "Jimmy" Locker
Class of 1965

Attending Burley High School was a goal we looked forward to as students. While the foundation received from Jefferson Elementary school equipped us well, it was with wide eyed anticipation, we embarked on a new adventure of success. The academic reputation of Burley High School, its athletic accomplishments, excellent scholastic activities and competitive awards earned from regional and state tournaments was an effective drawing card. Students, teachers, administrators and advisors exuded pride in

Supporting and representing the remarkable "Burley Bears." The dedication of the teaching, coaching and mentoring staff at Burley reflected an attitude of caring that was heartfelt and unquestionable.

Burley was a source of community pride as evidenced by the support and attendance at all Burley events. The true testament of "Burley Pride" is the support and attendance at reunion events.

We left Burley, well equipped to face the future, with the confidence to leave an impressionable footprint on life's journey. The life giving experience at Burley produced many lasting friendships that are still maintained today after so many years.

Rauzelle J. Smith
Class of 1966

When I entered Jackson P. Burley High School in the fall of 1961, I was prepared for my five-year journey through high school. My two older sisters, Doris and Vernell had attended, and had told me so much about the school. As I walked into the building my first day as an 8th grader, I stopped, stood still, and began to look around. I was overwhelmed, as the school was more impressive than they had described. Growing up in Covesville, I had previously attended the two-room school in North Garden. Upon its closure in 1959, I attended Rose Hill Elementary School.

My homeroom teacher at Burley High was Mrs. Lyria Hailstork. She was a great source of comfort, support, and guidance.

The musical training I received during my last two years of elementary school, under Mrs. Evelyn Carter enabled me to qualify for the advance band after one year as a beginner. The Burley High marching band was well known by everyone in the city and surrounding counties, and was the magnet that drew many of us toward music. The upper classmen in band, mentored me, to assure I was performing and meeting the high expectations of Mr. Sampson. But, being a member of the band was a real challenge for me, as I lived 17 miles outside the city. The only way I could remain in Charlottesville after school to attend evening band practices was to stay at the home of my cousin, Eileen who lived on Dale Avenue. While there, I had time to complete my homework and get a snack before returning to practice, which lasted until 9:00 PM. After practice, even though tired, I would hurriedly walk to the Trailways Bus Station to catch the last bus headed down Route 29 South to Lynchburg. I could get off the bus in Covesville. It was all worth it, as band class was one I could always rely upon to brighten my day and fulfill my musical needs. I am thankful, I had the good fortune to have trained under Mr. Elmer Sampson, as he demanded perfection from all his students and we gained so very much under his tutelage.

When I reached the 10th grade my interest turned to Business Administration. I studied business law, business formation, litigation and business math. Burley's Business Education teachers were outstanding. I am forever grateful for the guidance and support Miss Gloria Thaxton, Mrs. Teresa Walker and Mrs. Lorraine Williams provided. The training and guidance I received led me to pursue a career in Business Administration at Durham Business College in Durham. North Carolina and later Information Technology, which lasted my 45 year career.

As students, we deserved the best, and the teachers at Burley High School provided it! Most importantly, they challenged us to give our best and be a role model for others.

Raymond L. "Frog" Carey
Class of 1967

As I reflect on my high school days attending Burley High School, I contend that it was the best high school in the state of Virginia. My entire family attended Burley between the years of 1955-1967. We all went on to further our education and obtain degrees. This was made possible by having parents who expected the best out of us and teachers that demanded excellence in the classroom. Our teachers lived in the neighborhood, attended church with our parents, and some were even friends of our parents.

I was totally involved with everything happening at Burley. I enjoyed math, English, industrial arts, music, health and physical education. My favorite teachers were, Mrs. Lillie Mae Brown, Mrs. Bowler, Mr. McDaniel and Coach Jones. Mr. Sampson was also very instrumental in supporting me with my music.

There were two low points, I experienced while attending Burley. I was suspended from school for three days for fighting. My friend tore my shirt, and I struck him. The other was, I was acting out, right before graduation, and one of my teachers told me, "I would be nothing." That statement motivated me to prove to myself that I would be somebody, and I wanted to prove her wrong.

Our football team won the western district championship my senior year by finishing 9-0-1 and was runner up in the state, finishing second to Huntington High. Some highlights of my high school career other than football was our marching band, which excelled in all competitions, especially marching in the Dogwood parades, Apple Blossom and Cherry Blossom parades. People would line the streets and wait for the "Marching 100" to approach and watch us "break down" with our magnificent drumline. The drum major and majorettes were the very best. Our band was the tops!

Following graduation, I attended Virginia State College (now Virginia State University). I wanted to major in math, but my teacher,Mrs. Brown, said I was too reckless to major in math. She said I wasn't patient enough and she would know, because she also majored in math at Virginia State University and she told me to trust her. I did! After briefly considering a major in Elementay Education (my brother did), I settled on Recreation Education with a minor in Health and P.E.

I taught school for five years and after working for State Farm with 30 years of service, I retired. Everything that I learned at Burley and from my favorite teachers, was a blessing to me throughout my career.

The comraderie between our classmates and teachers was second to none. My principal, Mr. Scott, Asst Principal, Mr. Griffin, my football coach, Coach Jones and two of my brothers were very instrumental in my joining, "The Omega Psi Phi Fraternity." These men were truly role models in my life but none more important than my dad, who taught me to be honest and true, because my word was my bond.

I can truly say I was glad to attend Jackson P. Burley High School!

From Jackson P. Burley High School to
Lane High School and Albemarle High School

In the spring of 1967, the lives of the remaining Jackson P. Burley High School students would forever change. For those who had wanted so desperately to wear the green and gold of the Burley Bears when they graduated; it was not to be. Many of the students said they knew their lives would never be the same. Some of the students spent their summer with high anxiety for what would await them when school began their first semester at different schools. The comfort of family and their home away from home, was going to be pulled away like a security blanket. They would need to put their survival skills front and center to past the test.

Through it all, the former Burley students had no choice, but to adjust to new environments at different schools. It was all up to them, some were confident and met the challenge, some wanted the school year to end quickly, and some were angry and disappointed with the law of the land, "Desegregation." The students wished desegregation could have waited just one more year, better yet, many more years.

In the fall of 1967, a short walk from Burley High School heading east, down Preston Avenue, the "Mighty Burley Bears," who were residents of the City of Charlottesville, became the Lane High School "Black Knights," the yearbook became the "Chain," and the Literary Magazine became the "Bumblebee." The mascot, "Black Knights" and the yearbook, the "Chain" didn't sit well with many of the students. But, they had more to worry about than a mascot and yearbook name change. Their beloved green and gold school colors, changed to the black and orange colors of Lane High School. Many of the students experienced high anxiety during the summer months, thinking of their educational future at their new school.

During the 1967–68 school year, the Lane High School Principal was Mr. Williams I. Nickels Jr., and the Assistant Principals were: Mr. Blakeslee B. Anderson and Mr. Willie T. Barnett Jr. The Guidance Counselors were Mr. Pickford, Mrs. Reaves, Mr. Barnes and Mrs. Garrett. The first day of the fall classes the Guidance Staff, assured and reassured more than 1,300 students of their future at Lane High School and the challenges they would face together. Although, many African American students began classes at Lane High School on September 8, 1959, it had not been easy, but the plus

161

for the incoming students was the current African American students would serve as a support system for the arriving students.

At their new school, many of the Burley students who had been well prepared academically and were active participants in the many extra-curricular activities, felt cheated. Many students did not participate in the many activities, clubs and organizations at Lane High School their first year. The question was, how would the year play out? Former Business teachers, Mrs. Teresa Walker and Mrs. Lorraine Williams were of great comfort, and offered shoulders to lean on.

Across town from Burley High, the students who lived in the County of Albemarle, the "Mighty Burley Bears," became the Albemarle High School "Patriots," the yearbook became the 'Peer', and the school newspaper became the "Highlight." The green and gold school colors, changed to the red and blue colors of their new school.

During the 1967–68 school year, the Albemarle High School Principal was Mr. Benjamin Hurt and the Assistant Principal was Mr. Julian King. The Guidance Counselors were: Mrs. Virginia Duffelmyer, Mrs. Mattie Lee Fornes and Mr. Anthony Laquintano. At the first assembly, the students were told they needed 23 units before they could be admitted to the 11th grade. Students in the National Honor Society at Burley were curious about the amount of participation they would be allowed on the Student Council Association (SCA). They wondered whether any of their officers would be placed on the SCA at Albemarle. The students were informed if any of the Burley students wanted to hold office of any kind in the SCA, they would need to make a speech. Their performance would be reviewed and a decision would be made for admittance. They discussed it among themselves and the best representatives agreed to move forward. Some students knew they were as talented and academically prepared as many of the Albemarle students. They vowed not to disgrace the good reputation of their school and would make their classmates proud. Their journey was not easy.

As the years went by, the students who were assigned to Lane High School and Albemarle High school, proved to be strong and resilient, therefore they persevered. It was not easy, but some made friends with their white classmates and some chose not to, they preferred to hang in their own cliques. At Burley some would have been at the top of the pecking order, but now they didn't know where they belonged, as they fought for school equality and having a voice. The students were carefully assigned to the different classes, it was like the old saying, '"They stuck out like a sore thumb," or they were the grain of pepper in the salt shaker, you couldn't help but notice.

The review, "From Jackson P. Burley High School to Lane High School and Albemarle High School" is a collection of thoughts from former students and an assessment by the author. – **Lucille Smith**

Olivia Ferguson McQueen, Junior Class of 1958
Virginia Change Maker

In 1958, Olivia Ferguson a 16 year old rising senior at the all-black Jackson P. Burley High School, led a group of Charlottesville students to challenge school segregation. Olivia's father, George Ferguson Jr., was President of the NAACP in Charlottesville. In the late 1950s, her parents wanted her to be a plaintiff in a lawsuit challenging the city's segregated schools. Olivia was the principal plaintiff in the successful lawsuit to integrate Charlottesville City Schools.

After a federal district court judge ruled in the students' favor, rather than integrate, Governor James Lindsay Almond closed the all-white Lane High School, where Olivia and the other plaintiffs were to attend. In January 1959, state and federal courts simultaneously ruled that closing the schools violated Virginia's constitution. An early 1959 Virginia Supreme Court ruling overturning Massive Resistance would have allowed Olivia to attend the previously all-white Lane High School, but the Charlottesville School Board, continued to resist. Despite Olivia's victory, she was barred from Lane High School, along with the other plaintiffs in the suit. She spent her senior year, as well as the other plaintiffs, being tutored in the Charlottesville School Board office.

With encouragement from teachers and activists, her senior year was still difficult. She was isolated from her peers and did not get to enjoy the many activities in which they participated. While she watched her friends from Burley High School receive their diplomas in June 1959, she wore no cap and gown. She had no ceremony and received only a makeshift certificate with the classes she had completed. The classes were typed onto plain paper, rather than a formal diploma.

Olivia persevered, and in 1963 earned a bachelor's degree in childhood education from Hampton Institute (now Hampton University). She later earned a master's degree in education from Trinity College, in Washington, D.C.

In the auditorium, where she watched her peers graduate in June 1959, the school system and the Burley Varsity Club, celebrated Olivia's contribution to generations of African American school children who came after her. It was fifty-four years later, on May 25, 2013, after spending her career as an educator outside Virginia, Olivia a Civil Rights Pioneer, received her official high school diploma. Charlottesville Public Schools Superintendent, Rosa Atkins and Albemarle County Public Schools Superintendent, Pamela Moran, awarded Olivia her diploma in the ceremony at what is now Burley Middle School. Decades after her challenge of segregation and personal sacrifice, Olivia became a symbol of resilience and hope for the cause of equal access to education for all children.

Lillian M. Jackson, Burley Junior Class of 1967
From Jackson P. Burley (JPB) to Lane High School (LHS)

In 1967, I was in the junior class at Jackson P. Burley High School. This was a bittersweet year for me as a Burley Bear. Burley was the only black high school in the area and this was the last year it would be opened, due to desegregation. If you lived in the City of Charlottesville, you would complete your senior year of high school at Lane High School.

The end of the year saw many tears, because we all wanted so badly to graduate from our beloved Burley High School. Knowing this was the last year at Burley, as one of many juniors, we tried to make the year as memorable as possible.

Entering Lane High School in the fall of 1967, was so very traumatic. There were so many fights between the black and white students. There was hatred on both sides, which was portrayed from the Administration down to the students. Nothing had changed to show us, that all people, no matter what color, were created and treated equally.

Sadly, Burley cheerleaders knew it would be their last year, because the trials were held during the summer before we entered Lane High. At Lane High, those of us sharing the same lunch break tried to sit at the same table for comfort and support. Many of us wore the same colors once a week to show our unity at the dissatisfaction of the decision to close Burley High School.

Many of the Black students thought, there was very little and sometimes no support from the white teachers at Lane High. Very few of our teachers and administrators from Burley, joined us at Lane High School and we missed the support they provided.

During the year, a group of Black students went to a basketball game, as we were now Black Knights, and began chanting the cheers used at Burley. The Lane students knew the cheers, but did not participate. At halftime, one of the Lane High administrators informed the Black students they had to be quiet or they were going to be put out. During the school year, things had gotten so bad, about 200 Black students walked out of Lane High School and marched to Trinity Episcopal Church on Preston Avenue. The next day, we returned to Lane High with some demands, but nothing changed.

The white students did not want the Black students at their high school and we did not want to be there. Looking back in 2020, I can truly say very little has changed. Inequality exists today, just as it existed in the 1960s. Justice for all, still does not apply to Black people. I've never, ever attended a Lane High School Class Reunion. As some of my family had the opportunity, my dream of graduating from Burley High School was not a reality for me!

Barbara Henderson Jacques, Burley Junior Class of 1967
From Jackson P. Burley (JPB) to Albemarle High School (AHS)

It was the summer of 1967 and my 11ᵗʰ grade school year had just ended at Jackson P. Burley High School as the school closed its doors as an all-black school. Desegregation had become a reality. The fun times at JPB became a memory, and no one wanted to talk about the elephant in the room. As the lives of the students were about to change, no one talked to us or explained what we should expect when we got to Albemarle High School. How would we handle the anxiety we were experiencing, as we were not prepared mentally for the change in our lives. We were going from a school where we knew everybody and everybody knew us, to a school knowing almost no one. But Burley High School had laid the foundation for me to become a successful adult.

As summer progressed, and apprehension grew, questions swirl through my head; "what would it be like, would I fit in, would I make new friends, would my teachers be compassionate?" At 17 years of age, this was a heavy burden. I was about to become an Albemarle High School student and it was my senior year! What should have been the most fun year of school was now basically like the first day of school all over again. It was met with a lot of sadness. It was like going into hostile grounds. Even though I never experienced any racial violence, I still knew the potential was there and we knew we really weren't welcome. For me it was a very emotional year. The things I looked forward to in my senior year didn't happen. The excitement of going to school games, proudly wearing the school colors, and attending senior prom, none of these things happened for me. I did not attend senior prom, not that I couldn't, but I had no desire to do so.

My senior year was mostly spent trying to maintain my class work. It was amazing to realize how far behind I really was coming from an all-black school. My grade point average was relatively good at JPB, but a whole different thing at AHS. Although I didn't fail any classes, I had to study extra hard just to maintain. The most astonishing thing was to learn that the books used at AHS were more advanced and up to date. The struggle was real! I felt I had been robbed, and all the hurt and pain still comes back. We were placed in classes when at times you were the only Black student in the room. Even to this day, I have not been back to AHS for anything, because it is a reminder of those dark and uncertain days.

Although, I am an AHS alumnus, I still feel like a "man without a country," not that I have denounced the school, but was caught between two schools, JPB for happy, carefree days and AHS which was forced upon me through desegregation. Fifty two years later, and I still feel the pain of having been forced to leave the comfort of JPB and go into the unknown.

CHAPTER 8

PRACTICAL NURSING

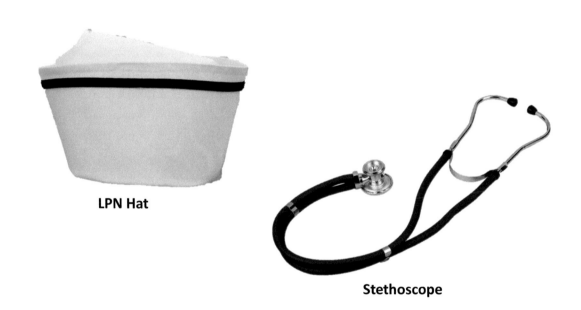

LPN Hat

Stethoscope

Practical Nurse Training
Emma B. Bryson, RN

Driven by a critical nursing shortage after World War II, the University of Virginia Nursing Department Director, Roy Carpenter Beazley, established a yearlong Licensed Practical Nursing (LPN) Program with Jackson P. Burley High School. In 1951, Burley High School partnered with the University of Virginia to create a training course in practical nursing. The Burley classes were taught by Registered Nurse Instructor, Mrs. Emma Bryson. The nursing program was a 13-month diploma program from 1952 – 1966.

The program consisted of two years of training. The first year of training was offered at Burley High School and included courses on: (a) Body structure (b) Group living (c) Community health (d) Feeding the family (e) Meeting emergency needs (f) Care of the newborn, and mother (g) Children and the aged nursing (h) Nursing principles and skills and (i) Personal and vocational relations and conditions of illnesses.[1]

The second year of the program took place at the University of Virginia Hospital, where training consisted of 44 hours of instruction with four hours of classroom and 40 hours of clinical teaching. The program focused on condition of the illness, personal and vocational relationships, and supervised nursing procedures. The subjects were taught by Mrs. Lucy Johnson, a Registered Nurse who served as the Clinical Instructor of Practical Nursing at the University of Virginia from the program's beginning.

Applicants for the program had to be senior high school students, at least 16 years of age and of good moral character. In addition, applicants were required to demonstrate evidence of good physical, mental, and dental health care. Adults with two years of high school were also eligible for enrollment with the same requirements for good health and moral character.

About 150 African American women and a few men were educated in the segregated program. They served alongside white nurses, treated patients of every race, and ran clinics. The graduates ultimately became some of the first Black RNs at the hospital, working first in segregated wards in the basement of the old University of Virginia hospital. But, despite receiving their nursing education in a University of Virginia program, they were not considered University alumni.[2] After the closure of Jackson P. Burley High School, the LPN program continued at the University of Virginia Hospital, at least until 1980 or possibly later.

---

[1] Wikipedia the Free Encyclopedia, "*UVA. Hospital-Burley High School Offers Interesting Course in Practical Nursing*". Charlottesville-Albemarle Tribune (12 April 1957).

[2] Sarah Lindenfeld Hall. *UVA grants full alumni status to Black nurses who earned it decades ago*. University of Virginia Magazine (2019).

LPN Graduating Class of 1954

Front Row – L to R: Anna Jackson, Velonta Murray, Suzane Banks and Estelle Jackson
Back Row – L to R: Martha Tyree, Mary Breckenridge, Carrie Walker, Gloria Barbour and Margaret Grigsby

LPN Graduating Class of 1956

Left to Right: Ruth White, Juanita T. Fleming, Jean Hill, Geneva H. Johnson, Mollie W. Terry, Chester O. Gray, Nellie Walker, Alzella C. Preston, Josephine Smith and Clariece Coles

LPN Graduating Class of 1957

Left to Right: Annie Mae Merritt, Mary Alice Jones, Marcia Chisolm, Anita Rae Smith, Katherine Banks, Louella Jackson, Grace Tinsley, Helen Miller, Lucy B. Morton and Ella Washington

LPN Graduating Class of 1962

Left to Right: Mary P. Tinsley, Dorothy E. Jones, Elsie Banks Johnson, Lucy E. Harris, Thelma M. Tinsley and Mary E. Johnson

Practical Nurse In-Class Training 1955

LPN Graduating Class of 1963

Front Row - L to R: Charlotte V. Brown, Maude J. Boykin, Ida Mae Lewis, Inez Strothers and Estelle Smith
Back Row - L to R: Shirley A. Blakey, Julia R. Martin, Lucy L. Smith, Grace V. Waller and Emily O. Lewis

Practical Nurse In-Class Training 1964

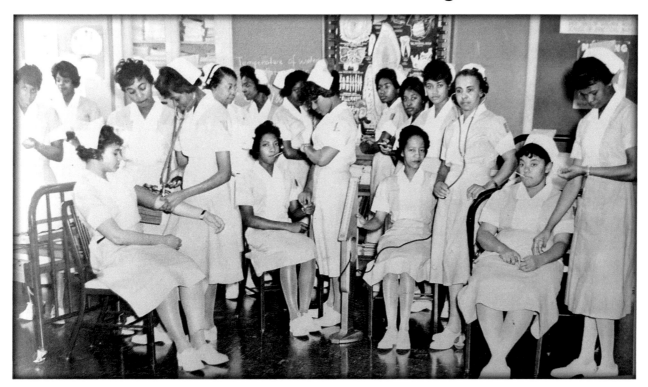

Practical Nurse In-Class Training 1966

Proud Jackson P. Burley High School Trained Nurses

LPN Program Graduates Recognition Program, April 29, 2019 – Photograph by Jennifer Bryne

1st Row – L to R: Barbara Starks, Louella Walker, Anita R. Smith, Mary Washington Jones, Sarah Kelley and Josephine Morrison
2nd Row – L to R: Clariece Coles Harris, Katherine Banks and Ida Rogers
3rd Row – L to R: Phyllis Brackett, Molly Feggans, Barbara Brackett and Evelyn Rogers Gardner

25 UVA LPN graduates of the Burley High School and UVA Hospital program were honored before hundreds on April 6, 2019 "Hidden Nurses" Ceremony
Photo Credit: Jennifer Byrne from the UVA School of Nursing

Becoming a Nurse
Louella Jackson Walker, LPN 1957

I began attending classes at Jackson P. Burley High School in the City of Charlottesville, Virginia in the fall of 1952. I had previously attended Esmont High School in Esmont, Virginia. I was a graduate of the Burley Class of 1957.

My years at Burley were extremely rewarding. I received an excellent education from many outstanding teachers and wonderful guidance from my principals. They taught academics as well as life skills. They were role models for all the students.

After completing my junior year, I knew my family could not afford to send me to college. In the spring of 1956, the Head of the University of Virginia (UVA) Nursing School, Mrs. Roy C. Beazley visited Burley High School and spoke to the students about the Nursing Program. She said the program was offered each year beginning in September and asked us to consider becoming nurses. She gave applications to everyone who were interested. I was very excited because, I knew I had a ticket in my hand for a great career. I went home and told my mother, I would not be spending the rest of my life in someone's kitchen. She was happy for me and readily signed the permission slip so I could enter the nursing program.

Mrs. Emma Bryson was the Nursing Instructor at Burley High School and Mrs. Lucy Johnson was the instructor at the University of Virginia Hospital. Each nursing class had 10–15 students. After completing my first year of Practical Nursing training at Burley High School, I entered the program at the University of Virginia Hospital in July 1957 and completed my training in March 1958. I was a graduate nurse until I passed State Boards in April 1958, receiving my license to practice in the State of Virginia.

The program was incredibly challenging, but thanks to God, I made it! I joined the staff at the UVA Hospital and worked there for 50 rewarding years. I cared for patients in different hospital units, and retired in 2010 from the Emily Couric Cancer Center.

The Jackson P. Burley High School and the University Of Virginia Hospital School Of Practical Nurses were given recognition on April 6, 2019. A total of 139 nurses from Jackson P. Burley High School completed the program from 1952 through 1966. We are no longer, "Hidden Nurses." We have been accepted as Alumni of the University of Virginia.

CHAPTER 9

BURLEY BAND AND CHOIR

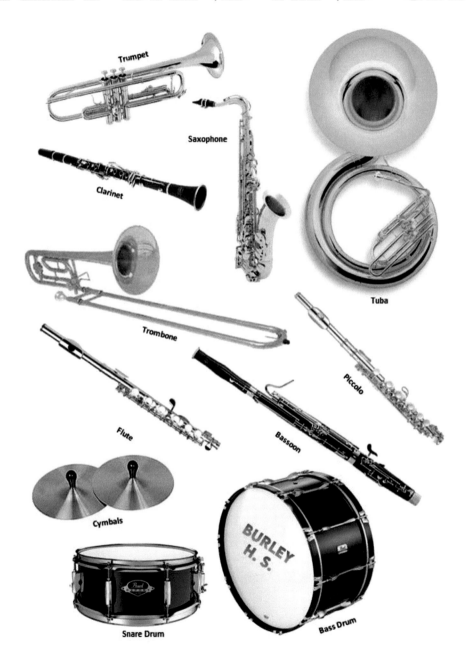

Jackson P. Burley High School
Band Directors 1951 – 1967

George Maxey
1951 – 1953

Henry Shegog
1953 – 1955

Charles Rogers
1955 – 1956

Elmer "Sonny" Sampson
1956 – 1967

Band Director

Elmer "Sonny" Sampson

Band Directors' Uniform

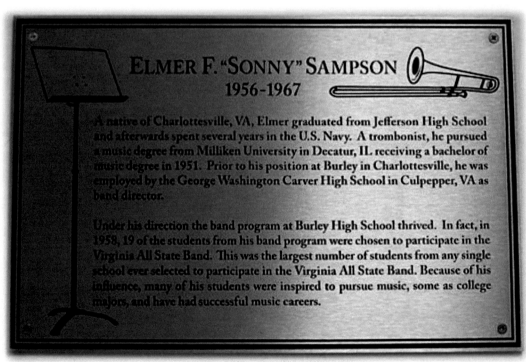

ELMER F. "SONNY" SAMPSON
1956-1967

A native of Charlottesville, VA, Elmer graduated from Jefferson High School and afterwards spent several years in the U.S. Navy. A trombonist, he pursued a music degree from Milliken University in Decatur, IL receiving a bachelor of music degree in 1951. Prior to his position at Burley in Charlottesville, he was employed by the George Washington Carver High School in Culpepper, VA as band director.

Under his direction the band program at Burley High School thrived. In fact, in 1958, 19 of the students from his band program were chosen to participate in the Virginia All State Band. This was the largest number of students from any single school ever selected to participate in the Virginia All State Band. Because of his influence, many of his students were inspired to pursue music, some as college majors, and have had successful music careers.

Band Room Dedication
October 7, 2011

176

Mr. Elmer "Sonny" Sampson, Band Director
Jackson P. Burley High School
1956 – 1967

Mr. Elmer Franklin "Sonny" Sampson, became the Band Director at Jackson P. Burley High School in 1956. He served in the position until desegregation and the closing of the school in 1967.

Elmer graduated from Jefferson High School in the City of Charlottesville in 1944. As a member of the Jefferson Band, he was 1st Chair Trombonist and student conductor.

Elmer served two years in the U.S. Navy during World War II. During the latter stages of the war, he played in the U.S. Navy Band. Following his Naval service, he entered James Millikin University in Decatur, Illinois, remaining for 3 ½ years. He returned to Virginia and received his Bachelor of Music Education Degree from Virginia Commonwealth University in Richmond, Virginia. He also pursued graduate work at the University of Virginia.

Elmer's early musical experience came from playing in his older brother Percy's, Swing Band called, "Sampson's Happy Pals." He was said to be an incredible Trombonist. He also played with the University of Virginia Jazz Ensemble and was a guest soloist with the Virginia Symphony Band. Elmer was a member of the Tommy Miller Quartet for 30 years.

His musical legacy began with his first teaching job at George Washington Carver High School in Culpeper, Virginia. He worked with students to organize and direct the band program.

As the Band Director at Jackson P. Burley High School, the band was supported by a "Band Sponsors Group," consisting of community members interested in supplying many of the needs of the band. He went on to create one of the most successful and exciting Band Programs the City of Charlottesville had ever seen. He chose challenging music at the college level for his students. The Burley band formations were patterned after college and university bands. The band always had the honor of being a, "Virginia All State Band." Each year the band received ratings of "Superior" and "Superior Plus." In 1963, the Burley Band was the first in the local area invited to participate in the Cherry Blossom Parade in Washington, D.C.

Mr. Sampson was known as a talented, easygoing and knowledgeable teacher and musician. His students were eager, dedicated, and precocious musicians. He loved music and shared his passion with his students. He was known to have the ability to teach a student how to play an instrument for the first time while in Study Hall.

When the Burley band performed, people took notice, whether at a parade, recital, football game or other events. The students were advanced beyond their years. They attended All State and Band Camps at Virginia State College to further enhance their skills. Even today, when speaking of him, you only hear praise, and great admiration from all that knew him. Many of his students graduated from Burley High School and attended colleges and universities majoring in music. They became Music Instructors, and Band Directors, as well as performing with professional and other music groups.

Speaking to any member of the Burley High School Band, you will hear many of the same quotes. "Burley had the hottest band in Charlottesville and surrounding counties. We marched with precision. When we played, people stopped and took notice. When the Burley band performed, crowds were drawn to us like magnets. We were proud Burley Bears."

For any local parade the Burley Band would be front and center in the line-up. But, organizers would soon realize, they needed to place the Burley Band at the end of the parade. Because, as they marched the crowd would follow the band along the parade route and would not remain to support many of the other parade participants. The energy and excitement the band generated could not be matched by other participants.

During his career, Mr. Sampson performed in bands for such notable persons as, Bob Hope, Lena Horne, Red Skelton, Mercer Ellington Band, George Hudson Dance Band, as well as the Temptations. He also performed before President Gerald Ford and Queen Elizabeth of England.

Mr. Sampson served the local community as the President of the Music Resource Studio, Board member of the Janie Porter Barrett Day Nursery, Choir Director at First Baptist Church on West Main Street and a member of the Charlottesville Municipal Band.

After the closure of Burley High School, Mr. Sampson taught music at Joseph T. Henley Junior High School, in Crozet, Virginia. He became the Band Director at Albemarle High School in the fall of 1974, retiring in 1985. While at Albemarle High School, he developed an outstanding music program and was an outspoken advocate for music and the arts.

Quote from student, Orlando Carter, "He gave me a purpose, and allowed me to believe in myself."

Elmer "Sonny" Sampson, Trombonist
Photo Courtesy of Orlando P. Carter, Class of 1966

The Tommy Miller Band
Front Center: Tommy Miller **Left to Right**: Elmer Sampson,
Jimmy Lewis, and Calvin Cage - *Photo from Images of America*
Charlottesville: The African-American Community, Tribune Photograph

Buster Scott, PTA Representative shakes hands with Burley Band Director,
Elmer "Sonny" Sampson. The talent of the Burley Band students rivaled any
in the State of Virginia. - *Photo from Images of America Charlottesville: The*
African-American Community, Tribune Photograph

179

1961 Advanced Band

Current Burley Middle School Band Room

1965 Marching Band

THE MARCHING 96

Left to Right: James Locker and Elmer Sampson

Left to Right: Mary Elizabeth Henley, Elmer Sampson and Zelda DeBerry

Members of the 1958 All State Band

In 1958 nineteen members of the Jackson P. Burley High School Band were chosen to play with the black "All State Band" at Virginia State College in Petersburg, Virginia. They represented the largest group of band members ever chosen from one school to participate.

Photo from Images of America Charlottesville: The African-American Community

The highlight of every Charlottesville Dogwood Parade was the Jackson P. Burley High School Marching Band (Leona Porter in the 1963 Dogwood Parade.) Photo from *Images of America: The Charlottesville Dogwood Festival.*

The Jackson P. Burley High School Marching Band in the 1963 Cherry Blossom Parade in Washington, D.C. – Photo from Images of America Charlottesville: The African-American Community, *Courtesy of Elmer Sampson Collections*

1957 Ushers for Uniform Drive

1964 Percussionists

1964 Percussion Section

1964 Wind Section

Jackson P. Burley High School Band Member
Graham Paige, Alto Saxophone, 1961 – 1964

I considered my membership in the Burley High School Band as an honor and privilege. I became a member of the Band as a 9th grader in 1960, and remained through graduation in 1964. I played Alto Saxophone. Band class was 6th period and it was always fun and enjoyable, as we practiced for concerts, parades and half-time shows. Band Director, Mr. Elmer "Sonny" Sampson's choice of music was always appropriate for the occasion, and had the ability to excite the people in our listening audience; parents, students, citizens and other attendees from the Charlottesville and Albemarle communities.

When I think of the many enjoyable highlights of my years in the band, a few examples are always at the forefront. We were proud musicians and one of the most outstanding and memorable band performances for me, was when the Burley Band led the parade for a celebration with the Sons of Esmont Lodge No. 7444, Grand United Order of Odd Fellows in America and Jurisdiction. The pleasure of performing in front of my friends and relatives in the Esmont community was un-describable.

Our annual performance in the Dogwood Parade in Charlottesville and the Firemen's Parade in Warrenton were also exciting and fun, but two parades were especially noteworthy. The Cherry Blossom Parade in Washington, D.C. and the Apple Blossom Parade in Winchester, Virginia were especially enjoyable, because those appearances gave the band a chance to perform in front of a large national audience. In addition, our trip to Washington, D.C. for the Cherry Blossom Festival included an afternoon of skating in an indoor rink in DC. Skating was not my strong point, so I spent the majority of my time stumbling and falling around.

A description of my band experiences would certainly be incomplete without mentioning the half-time performances at the Burley Bear's football games. On many nights, frost partially covered our home field by the end of the game, but we still performed at our best. Our trips with the team were unforgettable, as we were proud Burley Bears! The tale revealed by the scoreboard was usually the deciding factor on when the band would exit to board the buses to head home from Langston High in Danville, Lucy Addison in Roanoke or Dunbar in Lynchburg. If our team was ahead, the band would usually make a quick exit to board the buses. As there was a strong rivalry between the teams, so many times a brawl was quite likely. Beating a team on their home field was not taken lightly.

I will forever treasure all of these memories as a member of the Burley Bears Marching Band.

1960, 1964 and 1966 Majorette Corp

Majorettes

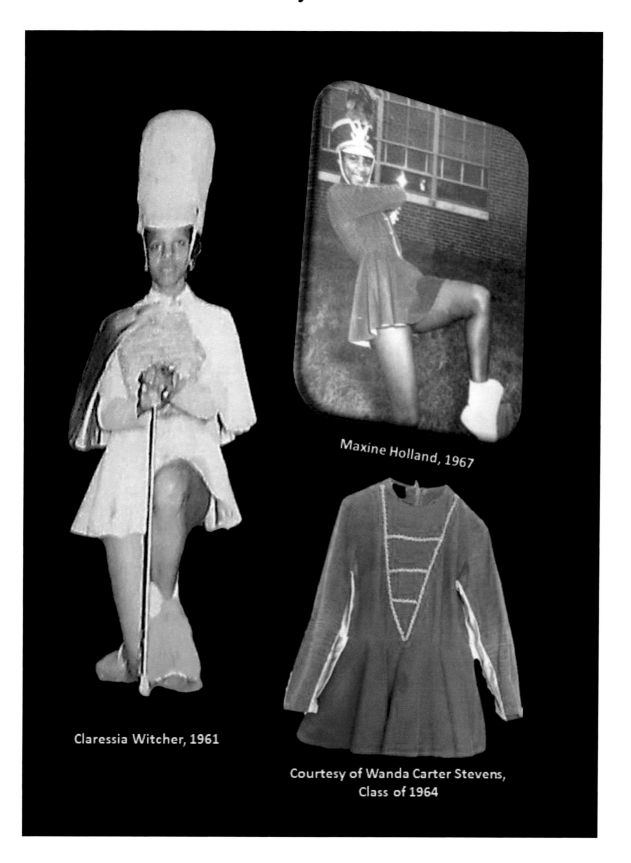

Maxine Holland, 1967

Claressia Witcher, 1961

Courtesy of Wanda Carter Stevens,
Class of 1964

Jackson P. Burley High School Majorette
Claressia Witcher Bell, Lead Majorette, 1961 – 1966

Never in my wildest dreams, did I ever think about being a Majorette, needless to ever think, I would be the Lead Majorette for the legendary, Jackson P. Burley High School Band. However, I loved parades, music and the beat of the drums. When I was very young, I use to stand on our front porch at 906 Charlton Avenue, a block down from Burley, and listen to the band rehearsals outside at the high school. Every, now and then the band would march right by our front door, and I would be so excited I didn't know what to do.

I was just in awe of the instruments and the drums lined across the back of the band. Every person was in step and looking straight ahead. The drums were beating and the feeling I experienced created a movement in my heart and soul that I still feel this very day. What an experience!

When the drums start to beat, my feet start to speak….A Majorette: I AM

During my first year at the great Jackson P. Burley High School, I was asked by the Band Director, Mr. Elmer Sampson, if I would like to be a part of the Burley Majorettes……Wow! What an honor. I couldn't believe it. My answer was yes and from that very moment the drums truly sparked an even more intense spirit in my soul. I thought surely he would march my legs clean off my body. Every day, we practiced and practiced. The older Majorettes had us twirling our batons, kicking up our legs, crossing over 1, 2, 3, 4 and back again. I just didn't know what to make of all of this. I felt as though I was truly working with the pros. I found the older Majorettes to be excellent role models. They embraced me with love and kindness and helped me to become a major part of the team. It wasn't long before I became Lead Majorette and the hard work paid off. What a life fulfilling experience. I marched with the band my entire 5 years of high school. We performed in many parades; the Dogwood Festival, the Cherry Blossom Parade in Washington, DC, the Fireman's Parade in Culpeper, Virginia and Winchester, Virginia. The Burley High School Band and Majorettes were the featured attraction at every home football game and at several away games.

Being a Majorette was a miraculous experience, an honor I shall treasure for life. I had no idea, that it would bring so much fame and so many blessings into my life. I accomplished so much, as a person and as a leader. The Majorettes and the band members were all supportive and we all had the common goal of "being the best". That was instilled in each of us by the great teachers we had at Burley. We all knew that our school work was priority; no work, no play. The teachers were always there for us, providing extra time for help whenever needed. At nearly every performance our parents, as well as our teachers could be found in the crowd. I shall always remember Mr. Elmer Sampson. He was everything, the Band Director, the routine maker, the coach, the friend, and the one who made you proud to be a part of the Burley Band. *He saw in me the Majorette I could truly be.*

I thank God for the opportunity of being a Burley Bear and to have represented the Jackson P. Burley High School band as Lead Majorette, for without God none of this would have been possible.

Cheerleaders

Front and Center: Rosa Brooks **2nd Row L to R:** Lillian Williams, Patricia Farrar and Stella Burkett **3rd Row - L to R:** Margaret Martin and Alice Douglas **Top Row - L to R:** Carolyn Mitchell, Janice Martin and Wilhelmenia Hurley

Front Row - L to R: Alice Douglas, Barbara Nicholas, Stella Burkett and Doretha Burkett **Back Row - L to R:** Rachel Armstead, Doris Henderson, Janice Witcher, Carolyn Vann, Wilhelmenia Hurley and Sheila Jackson

Front Row L to R: Ernestine Hearns, Ruby Stradford Boston, Cheryl Lewis Sheffey, Leona Porter Dawson, Joyce Kelly Mallory, Lillian Jackson, Edwina Curry, Delores Burns Jackson, and Barbara Carey Downs **Standing L to R:** Vivian Tyler and Zelda Johnson

Choir Directors
1951 – 1967

Virginia Word
1953 – 1958

Virginia Wilson
1951 – 1953

Willis E. Keeling, Jr.
1958 – 1963

Horace Cooke
1963 – 1965

Cynthia DeSue-Grady
1965 – 1967

1959 Burley Choir

1964 Burley Choir

Jackson P. Burley High School Choir Member
Marcha Payne Howard, Class of 1964

"EDUCATION IS THE KEY TO SUCCESS!" This was the Class Motto written in our 1964 yearbook, and I am a true believer of this idea!

In June of 1959, I was a member of the last class to attend Albemarle Training School in Albemarle County. This was one of several Elementary Schools in the County for African American Students. Entering Jackson P. Burley High School in September 1959, could best be described as "the end of a short story," and "the beginning of many Chapters", yet to come.

When I began the eighth grade at Burley High, I was twelve years old. The first semester was (without) question, quite intimidating. I had entered a very large, thee story brick building, with many modern conveniences. My previous school was made up of three buildings with stoves in each building, a well for water close to the entrance of the school, and the girl's outhouse in one section of the woods, and the boy's in another section.

It took time to become acquainted with the students just in my class. Burley High School served African Americans throughout Albemarle County and the City of Charlottesville. County Students were bussed in, and City Students walked to School. I was bussed in.

Having the same wonderful Homeroom teacher and French teacher, from grades eight through twelve was most comforting. Madame Gladys McCoy provided an environment that felt safe, and supportive.

There are many great memories from my high school days. A few in particular are: singing with the Choir under the Direction of Mr. Willis Keeling, and during my senior year, with Mr. Horace Cooke. I appreciate the opportunities I had performing with the Choir locally and at State Competitions.

It was also from the Music Department that I was introduced to strings, and learned how to play the cello. I was fortunate to have begun training on the piano, before I began attending Burley.

I always enjoyed participating in the fine arts of music and drama. But, it was Mr. Stephen Waters, my English teacher in my senior year, that broaden my true appreciation for the theatre. Matter of fact, we went on a class trip to Washington, D.C., to see the Shakespearean Play, Macbeth. I will never forget the thrill I experienced from attending that production.

An early observation I noticed between parents and teachers was they seemed to have developed an alliance. The expectations I experienced from the teachers, school administrators, secretaries, and custodial staff were, they wanted you to develop and maintain good work ethics, set your life long goals, and then strive to achieve them. This kind of mindset encouraged us to be lifelong learners. This character building at school was also practiced at home. Parents basically respected the Teachers and were supportive of their methods of discipline, and instructional leadership.

I can also remember my senior year when I had no idea of what college I should even consider attending, and Mrs. Shirley Pope (an Instructor) told me about her alma mater, Johnson C. Smith University in Charlotte, North Carolina. She had nothing but praise for this Music Department. I am very grateful to her, because this was the only school I applied to and was accepted.

I felt privileged when I returned to Burley as a teacher. However, Burley was no longer a High School, but now a Junior High. For my first few years there, the name had been changed to Jack Jouett Annex. By the early 1970s, the School Administration (which was all County at this point), returned the school's name to Jackson P. Burley. Practically all of the High School Administration and Teaching Staff had been relocated in the County. Only one person from the High School Instructional Staff remained, the Librarian, Mrs. Alberta Faulkner. During my first few years of teaching, Mrs. Faulkner was my counselor, confidant, and much needed friend. I will always be deeply indebted to her for her patience and wisdom.

It was around 1974 that a very good friend, and Burley High School graduate, (Evelyn Yancey Jones), encouraged me to join her in a class at the University of Virginia. After one class, I decided to continue and work on a Masters. I received my Master's Degree in August 1976.

After teaching at Burley for twenty-eight years, serving as the Assistant Principal for nine years, and Principal for three years I feel very Blessed and humble to have had the opportunity to begin and end my career in a place that I have always appreciated and respected.

CHAPTER 10

MIGHTY BURLEY BEARS ATHLETICS

ARCHITECTS OF SUCCESS

Jackson P. Burley High School had on staff some of the most successful coaches in Central Virginia. They were legends, still remembered today and spoken of with much love and affection. They were: Coach Robert "Bob" Smith, Coach Clarence "Butch" Jones, Coach Walter "Rock" Greene and Coach Albert "AP" Moore.

The Virginia Interscholastic Athletic Association League (VIAL) was created in the late 1920s to support sports for African American schools in the state of Virginia. In 1954, the Virginia Interscholastic Association (VIA) was formed from the VIAL. The VIA was later reorganized to include sports, academic activities and marching bands. The VIA was in existence from April 1954 through August 1969, the year all the state's public schools were desegregated. Afterwards, all high schools joined the Virginia High School League (VHSL).[1]

The VIA produced some of the best African American athletics in the state of Virginia, they would go on to break records, win championships and enter into professional sports leagues. The VIA governed all non-academic activities of African American high schools in Virginia. During the years of operation, over one hundred high schools with a student population of more than forty thousand had membership in the association. It was one of the most influential athletic organizations in the State of Virginia, serving young African American students who attended segregated high schools.[2]

The role of the association was to provide opportunities for athletes to participate in a number of athletic competitions with other African American high schools. Sports were an integral component of students' lives in high school and an opportunity for them to build teamwork skills and showcase their athletic abilities. The VIA provided athletic, art, academic, and leadership opportunities from 1954 – 1970.

The impact the VIA had on shaping the lives of the student athletes went far beyond governing athletic events. The association brought together students, parents and mentors who worked to develop a strong foundation for young men and women as they supported them in becoming successful athletes and productive adults.

During segregation, there were 115 African American high schools in the State of Virginia. VIAL and the VIA original home was Virginia State College from 1954 – 1969. The records of the VIAL and the VIA are now stored at Virginia State University in Petersburg, Virginia.

---

[1] VIA Heritage Association. *From the VIAL to the VIA.* Virginia State University Special Collections and Archives (1969).
[2] Virginia State University, *Role of the Virginia Interscholastic Association.* Virginia State Special Collections and Archives, (1969).

JACKSON P. BURLEY
INDUCTEES INTO THE

VIRGINIA INTERSCHOLASTIC ASSOCIATION
HERITAGE ASSOCIATION (VIAHA)

2016 - Robert W. "Bob" Smith, Coach
2016 - Clarence "Butch" Jones, Contributor
2016 - Elmer F. "Sonny" Sampson, Contributor (Band)
2017 – Garwin L. DeBerry, Contributor (Coach, teacher and mentor)

Jackson P. Burley Team Champions of the VIAL and VIA

1952 State Football Champions
1954 State Football Champions
1957 State Co-Football Champions
1964 State Runner-up Boys Basketball Champions

Unbelievable "Burley Bears" Football Team set a scoring record still standing more than 65 years later!

In 1956, the Portsmouth's Israel Charles "IC" Norcom High School and Charlottesville's, Jackson P. Burley High School secured very unique positions in the Virginia high schools sports history books. The very unique event happened during the era of racial segregation of the state's public schools.

In 1956, the two schools were elite among Virginia's 115 African American high schools. They both completed the regular football season with a 9–0 record with none of their opponents scoring against them. But, which of the schools would reign supreme was never determined. Leaders of the respective school divisions could not decide where the championship game would be played; so they were named co-champions.

Jackson P. Burley VIAL and VIA Team Champions

1952	VIAL State Football Champions	Coach Robert "Bob" Smith
1954	VIAL State Football Champions	Coach Robert "Bob" Smith
1955	Northern District Football Champions	Coach Robert "Bob" Smith
1956	Northern District Co-Football Champions	Coach Robert "Bob" Smith
1957	VIA State Football Champions	Coach Robert "Bob" Smith
1960	Western District Basketball Champions	Coach Walter "Rock" Greene
1961	Western District Basketball Champions	Coach Walter "Rock" Greene
1963	Western District Football Champions	Coach Clarence "Butch" Jones
1963	Western District Basketball Champions	Coach Walter "Rock" Greene
1964	Western District Football Champions	Coach Clarence "Butch" Jones
1964	State Runner-up Football Champions	Coach Clarence "Butch" Jones
1964	Western District Basketball Champions	Coach Albert "AP" Moore
1964	State Runner-up Boys' Basketball Champions	Coach Albert "AP" Moore
1965	Western District Basketball Champions	Coach Albert "AP" Moore
1965	Western District Baseball Champions	Coach Albert "AP" Moore
1966	Western District Football Champions	Coach Clarence "Butch" Jones
1966	State Runner-up Football Champions	Coach Clarence "Butch" Jones

Robert S. "Bob" Smith Jr.
Burley High Athletics 1951 – 1960

Robert "Bob" Smith (1917 – 1997) was born in Paterson, New Jersey to the parents of Ola Holmes Smith and Robert S. Smith Sr. He has one sister, Anne Louise Knox. Robert was a graduate of the famed Eastside High School in the Paterson section of Passaic County, New Jersey.

Robert received honors from the Central Intercollegiate Athletic Association (CIAA) as an offensive end for the Morgan State University Golden Bears. He graduated in 1941.

Robert married Marian Elizabeth Haskins and they had five daughters; Beverly Ann Woolfolk, Carolyn Hussain, Roberta Dunn, Shirley DeLaine and Robina Puryear Castro. Daughter Beverly, was a 1960 graduate of Jackson P. Burley High School. Each of his daughters became teachers and Robina became a principal. Coach Smith has nine grandchildren, twelve great-grandchildren and one niece, Linda Anne Knox.

Beginning in 1945, Coach Smith, coached football, basketball and baseball at Jefferson High School in the City of Charlottesville. While at Jefferson High School, Coach Smith persuaded a 6-foot-3, 225 pound Jefferson band member named, Roosevelt Brown to join the football team. Roosevelt Brown went on to have a stellar NFL Hall of fame career with the New York Giants.

When Burley High School opened in 1951, Coach Smith became the Athletic Director, head football, basketball and baseball coach. From 1952–1958, the Smith led Burley Bears teams won four Virginia Interscholastic Association State Football Championships. The 1952 Burley Bears became the Virginia Inter-Scholastic Athletic League (VIAL) State Champions.

In 1956, Coach Smith led the Burley Bears to a remarkable perfect season, Undefeated, Untied and Unscored upon! To date, the record still stands! The 1956 team had the most impressive football season for a team in the state of Virginia. An unimaginative run where the opponents were held scoreless for an entire season. Under Coach Smith's leadership, the Burley Bears compiled an impressive 41 wins, 12 losses, and 5 ties, and won 5 District Championships. His team won 28 consecutive games from 1955–1958.

Coach Smith left Burley High School and became the coach at St. Paul College in Lawrenceville, Virginia from 1960–1966. He returned to Patterson, New Jersey and coached at John F. Kennedy High School until retirement.

The Smith Aquatic and Fitness Center in Charlottesville was named in honor of Coach Robert Smith in 1975. The center is located on the Buford Middle School Campus on Cherry Avenue.

The beyond legendary, Coach Robert "Bob" Smith was inducted into the Virginia High School League Hall of Fame in 2012, 15 years after his death. He became the first former Burley coach or player to be given such an honor.

Naming of the Smith Aquatic and Fitness Center

On December 1, 1975, Mayor Charles Barbour dedicated the Robert S. Smith Recreation Center in honor of Jefferson High School and Jackson P. Burley High School, Coach Robert "Bob" Smith. The center is located on the campus of Buford Middle School, 1000 Cherry Avenue in Charlottesville, Virginia. Coach Smith distinguished himself among his peers, teams and the community, as a leader in the athletic world.

In the fall of 2010, the Smith Recreation Center became the Smith Aquatic & Fitness Center. The Aquatic & Fitness Center is an $8.25 million facility. It is a 27,290 sq. ft. indoor aquatics and fitness facility. The facility features: Two Indoor Pools (one competitive pool and one leisure pool), two water slides, in-water play structure, lazy river, fitness area with cardio and strength training equipment, group fitness classes, and more.

Photos by Daily Progress

Clarence "Butch" Jones
Burley High Athletics 1960 – 1967

Clarence Jones (1924 – 2006) born in Charlottesville, Virginia to the parents of Anderson and Lula K. Jones. Clarence was a graduate of Jefferson High School in Charlottesville. He received a B.A. degree in Physical Education from St. Augustine College in Raleigh, North Carolina and continued his education at the University of Virginia earning a Master's Degree. He was a lifetime member of Omega Psi Phi Fraternity, Inc.

Clarence served in the U.S. Army during WWII. He was a faithful member of Trinity Episcopal Church.

Clarence married Betty Dowdy in 1950 and they had three children: (Patricia, Clarice and Clarence Jones Jr., "Tony". The grandchildren are Constance Torian, Stacey Jones and Derrick Jones.

Before coming to Burley High School, Coach Jones had a six-year coaching career in Rustburg, VA at Campbell County High School. He became the Assistant Football Coach under Coach Smith. After the departure of Coach Smith in 1960, he assumed the role as Head Football Coach. Under his leadership, he immediately molded the team into a cohesive unit, compiling an impressive football record. He had an overall 14 year football coaching career with a record of 102–7–8 and a 48–13–9 record at Burley High School.

Coach Jones team won three Western District Football Championships and two Virginia Interscholastic Association State runner-up finishes in football. During the 1966–67 school year the Burley Bears went undefeated 9–0–1 and Coach Jones was the Western District Coach of the Year.

Coach Jones was selected as a Paul Harris Fellow by the Rotary Foundation of Rotary International in appreciation of tangible and significant assistance given for the furtherance of better understanding of the world.

Coach Clarence Jones earned a Distinguished Service Award from the National Federation of Interscholastic Coaches. He was inducted into the Virginia High School League Hall of Fame in 1992 and the St. Augustine's Athletic Hall of Fame in 1994. He served as the Officials Program Supervisor of the Virginia High School League until his retirement in 1985.

The Clarence A. Jones Scholarship Foundation was established by the XI IOTA Chapter of Omega Psi Phi of Charlottesville, Virginia. It was granted a tax exempt status on May 23, 2008. The scholarship foundation awards academic scholarships to support students of promising ability and a record of community service, who has a financial need in order to continue their education. The students must be a resident of Albemarle County, City of Charlottesville, Fluvanna County, Louisa County, and City of Waynesboro.

Pictured: Coach Smith, Dorance Banks, Albert Walker, & Gillie Hughes – 1954

Pictured: Coach Smith, Garvin Tonsler, Leon Fields and Carl B. Jackson

Pictured: Coach Greene and Co-Captain William Vest - 1959

1952 State Football Champions

With a loss of many of the athletes who held key positions on the 1951 football squad, the outlook for a successful 1952 season looked rather dim for the Burley Bears. But, under the skillful guidance of Coach Robert Smith and Assistant Coach, Bishop Patterson, a championship team evolved. The season ended with a record of 8 wins, 0 losses and no ties. The 1952 Burley Bears became the Virginia Interscholastic Athletic League (VIAL) State Champions.

1952 State Football Championship Team

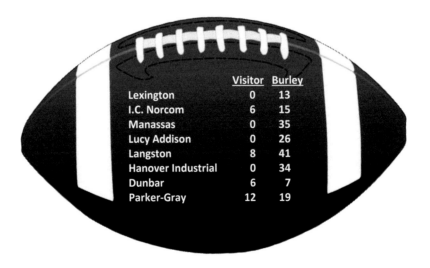

	Visitor	Burley
Lexington	0	13
I.C. Norcom	6	15
Manassas	0	35
Lucy Addison	0	26
Langston	8	41
Hanover Industrial	0	34
Dunbar	6	7
Parker-Gray	12	19

1954 State Football Champions

Under the successful coaching of Coach Robert Smith, Assistant Coach, George Quarles and Volunteer Coach, David Burns, another championship team took top honors. The season ended with a record of 11 wins, 0 losses and 1 tie. The 1954 Burley Bears became the Virginia Interscholastic Athletic League (VIAL) State Champions.

1954 State Football Championship Team

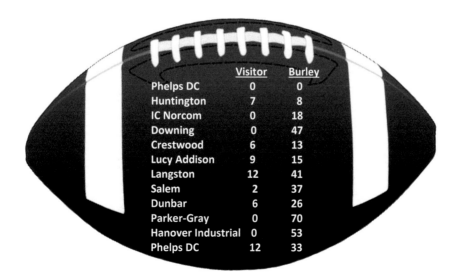

	Visitor	Burley
Phelps DC	0	0
Huntington	7	8
IC Norcom	0	18
Downing	0	47
Crestwood	6	13
Lucy Addison	9	15
Langston	12	41
Salem	2	37
Dunbar	6	26
Parker-Gray	0	70
Hanover Industrial	0	53
Phelps DC	12	33

1956 Perfect Season

The 1956 Mighty Burley Bears were **Undefeated**, **Untied** and **Unscored** upon with a school football record of 9–0–0. Coach Robert "Bob" Smith and Assistant Coach, George Quarles were the leaders of the most successful football team in the State of Virginia. The record stands today, more than 64 years later! The Burley Bears were the 1956 Northern District Co-Champions with IC Norcom High School in Portsmouth, Virginia.

1956 Mighty Burley Bears Football Team

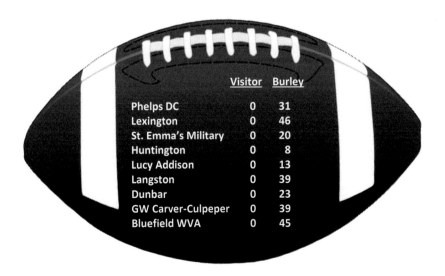

	Visitor	Burley
Phelps DC	0	31
Lexington	0	46
St. Emma's Military	0	20
Huntington	0	8
Lucy Addison	0	13
Langston	0	39
Dunbar	0	23
GW Carver-Culpeper	0	39
Bluefield WVA	0	45

Friday, November 9, 1956
Burley Football Program

BURLEY
VS.
CULPEPER

Friday, Nov. 9th
8:00 P. M.
Burley Stadium
25c

BURLEY ROSTER

NAME	WHITE JERSEY	OLD GOLD	WEIGHT	POSITION
Raymond Bell	59	27	210	L. End
William Read	70	39	175	R. End
Harry Walker	64	17	160	L. End
Charles L. Barbour	65	19	155	R. End
John Estes	47	46	175	L. Tackle
Robert Ferguson	61	23	235	R. Tackle
Walter Payne	63	32	260	L. Tackle
Louis Wood	69	16	190	R. Tackle
Charles Barbour	48	13	195	L. Tackle
Junius Jordan	57	40	188	L. Tackle
Linwood Carr	55	29	150	R. Guard
Waddell Brown	45	45	195	R. Guard
Pete Jones	44	41	160	L. Guard
James Read	66	35	150	R. Guard
Bernard Nelson	62	15	145	L. Guard
Merle Estes	71	26	150	R. Guard
Isaac Curry	42	25	175	Center
Harold Jackson	53	31	165	Center
Richard Monroe	61	24	170	Quarterback
James Shackelford	30	36	170	Quarterback
William Douglas	46	21	150	Quarterback
Pete Johnson	50	18	150	L. Halfback
Phillip Gardner	60	20	165	L. Halfback
Robert Williams	44	11	145	L. Halfback
Russell Scott	21	10	160	R. Halfback
Herbert Churchman	49	28	150	R. Halfback
Lester Washington	49	14	155	R. Halfback
Kanuso Breckinbridge	43	22	185	Fullback
William Vest	51	38	170	Fullback

Program Courtesy of the Albemarle Charlottesville Historical Society

Football smashed barriers

Blacks, whites all backed Burley

Second in a three-part series.

By Jerry Miller
Daily Progress staff writer

Norman Terrell knows Charlottesville more than most.

Born and raised during segregation, Terrell spent his impressionable years on Anderson Street just behind the Pepsi-Cola building and a few blocks from Jackson P. Burley High School.

Today the 72-year-old Terrell still has that zest for life and mischievous chuckle that surely got him into a little trouble here and there as a student at Burley High.

With a belly full of laughter, Terrell can have a group roaring in seconds, but when his tone gets serious, the chatter stops and the ears perk up.

THE PERFECT SEASON

"If not for football in this area, segregation wouldn't have changed as quickly," Terrell explained. "You might think I'm exaggerating, but Burley football was about the only team that was any good during the 1950s and '60s.

"We were the talk of the town. The Burley Bears, that's all we had at the time."

A stocky teen with good explosion off the line of scrimmage, Terrell played two-ways at tackle before graduating from Burley in 1953.

"When we played, it was standing room only," Terrell said. "Everyone came — whites and blacks. It was a packed house and you had to find a place to sit or stand wherever you could.

"It didn't make no difference who you were or whether you were white or black. People were quiet and they watched us play football."

Ray Carey, a towering man who played on the last Burley team in 1967 before integration phased out black

In 1956, no team could score against the Jackson P. Burley High School football team. Burley alumni have gathered for a reunion. First row, from left: Norman Terrel, Bob Ferguson, Philip Bell and Wilson Dooms. Second row: John Gaines, Ray Carey and Richard Nitengale. Standing: Robert Mickie, Robert Monroe and Garwin DeBerry.

The Daily Progress/Matthew Rosenberg

schools, remembers more of the same.

"We were football players," Carey said. "At that time we were primarily in a segregated school system, but football was a way to bring everyone together — black, white and the university students. Everyone came out and everyone knew who could play."

Four-time Pro Bowler and 1959 Virginia graduate Sonny Randle said he

See RACE on A7

Daily Progress Article October 6, 2006
Courtesy of Garwin DeBerry

The Series

Thursday: The two captains of the celebrated 1956 Jackson P. Burley High football team reflect on the team's undefeated season and how it has affected their lives.

Today: Football's effect on race relations in Charlottesville in the days of segregation.

Saturday: A retrospective on Burley football, and its meaning to the community in the 1950s and '60s.

On the Web: Share your thoughts and memories at DailyProgress.com.

Race

Continued from A1

attended as many Burley games as he could while pursuing an education at UVa.

"Those guys were all great players at a time when we didn't realize just how great they actually were," Randle explained. "They used to play with a little rhythm. They'd dance a bit at the line of scrimmage and have a good time, but when the ball was snapped, they were all business."

Football is a simple game and a tremendous unifier. Take the pigskin, cross the goal line, score a touchdown and watch as fans shower you with praise regardless of your skin color.

"Sure this is the South and sure you'll have incidents, but Burley was carrying this town and people loved us," said Richard Monroe, a co-captain of the 1956 Burley football team. "See, people like a winner, and at that time, Lane [High School], Albemarle [High School] and the university weren't very good. So people — black, white and even the uni-

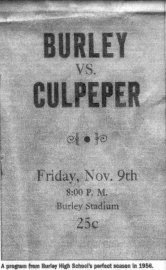

BURLEY VS. CULPEPER

⚜ ● ⚜

Friday, Nov. 9th
8:00 P. M.
Burley Stadium
25c

A program from Burley High School's perfect season in 1956.

versity students — came and saw us win. They would all come."

Garwin DeBerry, the head coach at Charlottesville High for the past 26 years, can offer tremendous perspective on football and race relations.

DeBerry started his high school years at Lane when integration was first phasing in but transferred to Burley because he wasn't permitted to play football at Lane.

"Burley football was the pride of this town," DeBerry said. "We had such great teams so everyone followed us closely. We brought people together. Any kind of interaction between races plays a part in mending fences.

"I've been fortunate to coach white kids and black kids. That would have never happened if not for football and integration."

Terrell put it simply: Burley football transcended racism and hatred because the Bears were good football players and even better people.

"It didn't make any difference if we were black or white," he explained. "People cared because we represented Charlottesville and we did it well."

Contact Jerry Miller at (434) 978-7258 or jmiller@dailyprogress.com.

Bob Ferguson (left) and Richard Monroe led Jackson P. Burley High to an undefeated 1956 season in which the team gave up no points.

The Daily Progress/Matthew Rosenberg

Burley team captains look back

First in a three-part series.

By Jerry Miller
Daily Progress staff writer

Overcoming adversity on the playing field is discussed ad nauseam.

If a team is hit with injuries or handcuffed with suspensions but still manages a victory, the headline in the paper or the subject of talk radio will undoubtedly reference adversity or courage in the face of defeat and despair.

THE PERFECT SEASON

In the grand scheme of things, it couldn't be further from the truth. For true adversity and valor, con-

sider what Bob Ferguson, Richard Monroe and their 27 teammates that comprised the Jackson P. Burley football team endured in the fall of 1956.

Ferguson, a chiseled tackle who tipped the scales at 235 pounds, and Monroe co-captained the Burley Bears to an undefeated, untied, unscored upon season in the height of segregation in Charlottesville.

Ferguson can vividly remember trucking down the sidelines, itching to make a tackle when a referee's whistle sliced through the air to stop play.

See BURLEY on A7

The Series

Today: The two captains of the celebrated 1956 Jackson P. Burley High football team reflect on the team's undefeated season and how it has affected their lives.

Friday: Football's effect on race relations in Charlottesville in the days of segregation.

Saturday: A retrospective on Burley football, and its meaning to the community in the 1950s and '60s.

On the Web: Share your thoughts and memories at DailyProgress.com.

Daily Progress Article October 6,
Charlottesville Albemarle Historical Society

208

1964 State Runner-up Football Team

Under Coach Clarence "Butch" Jones, and Assistant Coach, Walter "Rock" Greene, the 1964 Mighty Burley Bears were the State Runner-up Champions. They had 7 wins, 2 losses and 0 ties.

Quarterbacks

Halfbacks

Ends

Coach Jones & Captains

Linebackers

Guards

Offensive Line

	Visitor	Burley
Woodson	0	34
Covington	15	7
Dunbar	12	6
St. Emma	0	6
Albert Harris	7	40
GW Carver-Culpeper	21	52
Langston	12	29
Addison	6	21
Northside	0	2

Fullback

Tackles

Tackles

1966 Western District Champions

The 1966 Mighty Burley Bears were **Undefeated** (10–0–1) during the season. They were the best in the Western District and second only to Huntington High School of Newport News, Virginia. Head Coach, Clarence Jones, Western District Coach of the Year, and Assistant Coach, Albert "AP" Moore developed a small and typical team into a powerhouse, which utterly destroyed every team they faced. The Bears scored 257 points during the season and gave up only 48 points to their opponents.

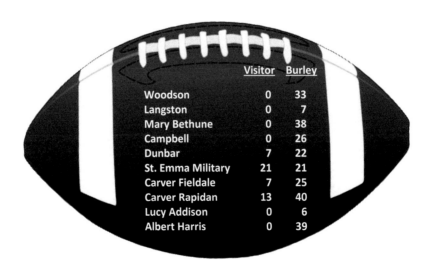

	Visitor	Burley
Woodson	0	33
Langston	0	7
Mary Bethune	0	38
Campbell	0	26
Dunbar	7	22
St. Emma Military	21	21
Carver Fieldale	7	25
Carver Rapidan	13	40
Lucy Addison	0	6
Albert Harris	0	39

Junior Varsity Football Coach
Lorenzo Collins

1963 Junior Varsity Football Team

Jackson P. Burley Football
Carl B. Jackson, Class of 1956

I left Jefferson High School for Jackson P. Burley High School in the fall of 1951 to become an 8th grader. I entered Burley with pure excitement.

As a Burley student Mrs. Lillie Mae Brown, who taught math was my favorite teacher.

I joined the Burley Football team in 1952 and played each season through 1955. During the four years I played, the coach was Robert Smith, known as "Coach Smith." He was a person who believed in discipline. He did not allow any smoking or staying out late. He believed in good, clean living. As players, we practiced hard and played hard. I vividly remember, there was a hill we had to run at least twice after each practice. The athletes were in great physical condition. Coach Smith was a hands on "Coach", he would show you how to block, tackle or run. I played "Center" for the Offense and 'Linebacker' for Defense. We only had 30 players on the team, so we rotated between playing offense and defense.

During the years I played football, our record was steadfast. In 1952 our record was 9–0, in 1953 (7–3), in 1954 (10–0–1) and in 1955, 10–1. During the 1954 season we had two players to make the Virginia High School All-State Team; Arthur Morrison and I made the team. The 1955 team had two players to make the Virginia High School All-State Team. I made the team that year, along with Robert Ferguson.

I was always happy to represent my team, "The Mighty Burley Bears." I was Captain of the football team during the 1954 and 1955 season. We, as a team enjoyed each other's company. We were one big happy family, full of love, trust and support for each other.

I will always remember and love Jackson P. Burley High School!

Albert "AP" Moore
Burley High Athletics 1963 – 1967

Albert P. Moore (1930 – 1987) was born in Kansas City, Missouri, to Wiley Moore and Mary Gordon Moore. He graduated with a Bachelor of Science and Master of Science Degree in Physical Education from North Carolina Central University, Durham, North Carolina. He was a member of the Charlottesville Alumni Chapter of Kappa Alpha Psi Fraternity.

Albert served in the U.S. Army during the Korean Conflict. He married his college sweetheart, Roxie Holloway in 1960 and they had three sons: LeRoi (deceased), Rodney and Jeffrey Moore.

Albert was a faithful member of Trinity Episcopal Church in Charlottesville, Virginia.

Coach "AP" Moore came to Burley High School in 1963 at the request of his long time coaching mate, Coach Clarence Jones, from their days at Campbell County High School. Coach Moore became the Head Basketball Coach after the departure of Coach Walter Greene. He also served as the Assistant Football Coach beginning in 1963.

During his first season, he led the 1964 Basketball Team to the Western District Championship. The 1964 basketball team went on to become the Virginia Interscholastic Association (VIA) State Runner-up.

In 1965, Coach Moore led the Burley Baseball Team to the regular season Western District Championship. The 1965 baseball team became the District Tournament Runner-up for the VIA State Championship. Coach Moore was named the Western District Coach of the year in 1967.

After the closure of Jackson P. Burley High School in 1967, Coach Moore taught at Albemarle High School.

Coach Albert P. Moore was honored by the Burley Varsity Club on September 23, 2010 with the unveiling of a Historical Marker for the Walter "Rock" Greene and Albert "AP" Moore Gymnasium, honoring them as outstanding Burley High School basketball coaches.

Albert P. Moore died on February 1, 1987. He is buried at Holly Memorial Gardens, Albemarle County, Virginia.

1956 Baseball Team

Front Row – L to R: Samuel Williams, Huneal Martin, Curtis Minor, Lester Washington, Leroy Stevens, Charles Douglas, and Lloyd Feggans

Second Row- L to R: Coach Robert Smith, Leroy Jones, Mack Burton, Harold "Ski" Jackson, Silas Jordan, John Estes, Ray Bell and Earl Williams

1960 Baseball Team

Front Row – L to R: James "Boo" Waller, Arthur Brown, Charles Jones, Odell Gardner, John Vest, Johnny Carr, Charles Nelson, Edward "Dopie" Sims and Curtis Byers

Second Row - L to R: Lloyd Burton, Charles Gilmore, John Burton, Leonard Wayne, Clarence Ivory, Andrew "AJ" Shelton, Leonard Medley and Coach Walter Greene

1965 Baseball Champions

Under the leadership of Coach Albert "AP" Moore the Burley Baseball team was the 1965 Western District Champions.

Front and Center: Jack Ridley (Water boy)
Pictured Left to Right: Robert, Carey, Douglas Henderson, Moses Agee, Jr., Floyd Monroe, Mitchell Carter, Albert Singleton, Alvin Howard, William Alexander, James Fitch and Keith Jackson
Coach Albert "AP" Moore is not pictured

	Visitor	Burley
Addison	2	3
Addison	2	6
Carver Culpeper	8	6
Campbell	0	1
Langston	7	15
Langston	5	6
Carver Fieldale	6	8
Carver Fieldale	6	5
Albert Harris	8	5
Albert Harris	3	10
Rosenwald Waynesboro	1	21
GW Carver Culpeper	8	9
Langston	1	7

Jackson P. Burley Baseball
D. Mitchell Carter, Class of 1966

From an early age, baseball excited me. I ran the bases after watching my father and his friends' community baseball games. The team traveled throughout the counties surrounding the Charlottesville area. I started playing little league baseball at nine years old on a field overlooked by Jackson P. Burley High School. When I was 12 years old, I joined our adult community team, "The South Garden Tigers", playing alongside my cousins, their friends, and men well into their twenties and thirties. My father had given up the game a few years before. I played outfield and learned how to pitch under the tutelage of Wayne Stevens, a catcher and pitcher on the team.

Baseball challenged me to be good at something and competition forced me to be better. When I entered Jackson P. Burley High School in 1961, I was playing with or competing against players who were naturally good at the game and who had established strong reputations on Burley's baseball field; people like my cousins, Donald and Curtis Byers, Johnny Carr, Odell Gardner, the Sims brothers, Esters and Edward, and the legend himself, Alfred Martin. They had graduated, but I spent my time at Burley chasing these guys. I wanted to be mentioned in the same breath with them. They set the standard by which my era was measured. My first game as a Burley Bear was in the spring of 1963. I was in the ninth grade. Our team played a double-header in Roanoke against Addison High School. I pitched a complete game in the opener and won 2–1. Albert Singleton threw a 1–0 shutout in the second game and our careers were off and running. I was psyched about being a Burley Bear.

The Addison games were a precursor to many games during my baseball career at Burley; tight defensive battles that were won or lost by one or two runs. We played under Coach Albert P. Moore. He was a tough, no nonsense coach. Conditioning was important to him. He believed, rightfully so, that games were not won with your arms and bats. They were won with your legs and mind. We ran a lot. Because we were not heavy hitters, our teams had to be fundamentally sound executing our offense and defense. We were built on speed and accuracy. Our practices were considerably harder than our games. Base running drills were emphasized heavily during batting drills. Hitting the cutoff man was as important as catching fly balls and fielding grounders. Coach Moore also expected us to work as a team. Wind sprints were a favorite end of practice drill. Everyone lined up across one goal post on the football field and sprinted the one hundred yards to the other goal post. We sprinted down, back, down, back (400 yards total) and the last three players ran it again. After a few practices of sprinting as hard as we could, we realized that he was killing all of us. Consequently, we agreed that the first three 100-yard sprints would be done at three-quarter speed and on the last 100-yards it would be all out, everyone for himself. When Coach Moore realized what we were doing, he made us all run again. We stuck with our plan and he relented. After all, he was getting what he wanted; a cohesive team that stuck together.

Representing Jackson P. Burley High School and playing with the group of guys that I did was special. I was a centerfielder/pitcher and leadoff batter. Whether I was the starting pitcher or the leadoff batter, I saw it as my responsibility to set the tone and tempo for the game. Most of the time, if I did my job, we won. I do not recall our record for each season, but we won a whole lot more than we lost. In 1965 we won the Western District Championship. As I look back on my time at Burley, its culture, faculty, and students set the tone and tempo of my life. And, I would have to say I have won significantly more than I have lost.

1966 Senior Diamondmen
D. Mitchell Carter, James Fitch and Albert Singleton

1964 – 1965 Track Team

1966 – 1967 Track Team

Walter "Rock" Greene
Athletics 1957 – 1963

Walter "Rock" Greene was a native of Washington, D.C. He graduated from Phelps Vocational High School in Washington, D.C. in 1953. He was a graduate of Delaware State University and a member of the Kappa Alpha Psi Fraternity. While at Delaware State, he lettered in four sports.

He began his coaching career at Burley High School in 1957 as an Assistant Basketball Coach under Coach Robert Smith. He became the Head Basketball Coach in 1960 and they became the Western District Runner-up. The following year in 1961, the Burley Bears basketball team became the Western District Champions.

Coach Greene taught physical education, was an Assistant Football Coach and served as the Burley Bears Head Baseball Coach. He served as the Athletic Director from 1960-1963.

At the request of the Assistant Superintendent of Adult Vocational Education for the District of Columbia Public Schools, Mr. Lemuel A. Penn, Coach Greene left Jackson P. Burley High School in 1963. Mr. Penn wanted him to return home to teach and coach, as he had earned so much success at Jackson P. Burley High School. Coach Greene was the first student to return to the school as a teacher and Coach.

Walter married Estelle Lockert in 1969. They have two children: Walter Jr., and Lisa.

Coach Greene was inducted into the Athletic Hall of Fame at Delaware State University in 1986. He was inducted into the Washington, D.C. Sports Hall of Fame in 2000 and the Phelps Vocational High School Hall of Fame in 2007.

Coach Greene returned to Charlottesville in 2010 for the unveiling of a Historical Marker for the Walter "Rock" Greene and Albert "AP" Moore Gymnasium. The marker was dedicated by the Burley Varsity Club on September 23, 2010 to honor outstanding Burley basketball coaches.

1959 Varsity Basketball Starters

Charles Yancey
Guard – 1959

Gerald Smith
Center – 1959

Sam Brown
Guard – 1959

1963 –1964 State Runner–up Boys' Basketball Champions
Coach Albert "AP" Moore

Opponent	Score	Burley Bears	Score
Campbell County High School	49	Jackson P. Burley High School	74
Bethune High School	46	Jackson P. Burley High School	99
Addison High School	51	Jackson P. Burley High School	63
Albert Harris High School	44	Jackson P. Burley High School	58
Southside (Blairs) High School	48	Jackson P. Burley High School	65
Carver (Rapidan) High School	32	Jackson P. Burley High School	92
Campbell County High School	53	Jackson P. Burley High School	71
Addison High School	62	Jackson P. Burley High School	66
Bethune High School	62	Jackson P. Burley High School	64
Albert Harris high School	63	Jackson P. Burley High School	78
Carver (Fieldale) High School	34	Jackson P. Burley High School	61
Dunbar High School	77	Jackson P. Burley High School	69
Langston High School	47	Jackson P. Burley High School	61
Carver (Rapidan) High School	45	Jackson P. Burley High School	85
Northside (Gretna) High School	43	Jackson P. Burley High School	49
Southside (Blairs) High School	49	Jackson P. Burley High School	52

State Runner-up Boys' Basketball Champions

Left to Right: Thomas Carey, Clarence Nickolas, Ronald Sheffey, Halliard Brown, Keith Jackson, Leonard Stewart, Herbert Carter, Garwin DeBerry, Grandville Carthorne, and Harry Williams

Jackson P. Burley Basketball
Garwin L. DeBerry, Class of 1965

As an alumnus of Jackson P. Burley High School, I have so many memories of times and events at the school. I was fortunate to be able to play on the football team, basketball team, baseball team, and a member of the band and Quill and Scrolls.

Burley was well known all over the state of Virginia for its excellence in academics and athletics. We always had great teachers and coaches to encourage and push us to do well.

I was a member of the Burley Basketball Team from 1962 – 1965. My 10th grade year, I went out for the team and made it, but as a substitute, there was so much competition. My 11th grade year, I became a starter at the point guard position. Being a member of the team and this experience will always be a big part of my life, as we made it to the State finals. Starters on that team were: Rudolph Carey, Woody Dooms, Richard Stewart, Leonard Stewart and myself, Garwin DeBerry. We had a great year, as we won the Western District title over Langston High School of Danville, Virginia. We always had a tough time, because District Teams were so strong.

Our main competition came from Dunbar (Lynchburg, VA), Langston (Danville, VA), Addison (Roanoke, VA) and Mary Bethune (Halifax, VA). Making it to the State tournament was a goal set at the beginning of the year, making it something I will always remember. The State tournament was played at Hampton University. It was such a big deal for all of us to be able to play on a college campus, in a college gymnasium, in front of so many people. Coach "AP" Moore had prepared us well for the challenge, and I think we represented Burley and Charlottesville very well.

To my amazement, after graduation and attending Virginia State University, I ran into a lot of people who remembered our team and boasted about how well we played. As a teacher and coach, I would always tell my students and players, "You never know who is watching you, so always represent yourself well in a positive light."

Hail Burley High School!

Jackson P. Burley Girls' Basketball

	Visitor	Burley
Downing	21	26
Downing	35	41
Simms	40	36
Simms	32	15
Rosenwald	16	24
Rosenwald	16	18
Carver	37	21
Carver	16	15

Emma Jackson
Head Basketball Coach

Alma Pleasants
Assistant Basketball Coach

1952 – Girls' Basketball Team

Girls' Basketball was a sport only through the 1959 school year.

223

CHAPTER 11

MONUMENT WALL

GROUND BREAKING CEREMONY
AND MONUMENT WALL UNVEILING

Jackson P. Burley High School
Monument Wall Committee

Front Row - L to R: Katherine Banks, James "Jimmy" Hollins, Joyce Jackson Colemon, Elsie M. Johnson, Dirie Payne Harris and Berdell McCoy Fleming

Middle Row - L to R: Patricia Bowler Edwards, Dr. Pamela Moran, Phillip Jones, Donald A. Byers, Carolyn Brooks and Lucille Stout Smith

Back Row - L to R: Ernest Allen, Carolyn Key Allen, Nelson Jones, William Redd Sr., James "Jim" Asher and Rauzelle J. Smith

Mission of the Monument Wall Committee

The Jackson P. Burley Monument Wall Committee was established in February 2017.

The mission of the Monument Wall Committee was to perform research on constructing a Monument Wall on the former campus of Jackson P. Burley High School, now Jackson P. Burley Middle School, located in the City of Charlottesville.

The wall will honor all students, (including those who did not graduate from the school, but attended), as well as administrators, faculty, and staff of Jackson P. Burley High School. The history of Jackson P. Burley High School represents a very significant era in the life of the Charlottesville community and in the lives of the African American students who passed through its halls.

Monument Wall Committee

Donald A. Byers	– Chairperson
Rauzelle J. Smith	– Project Manager
James "Jimmy" Hollins	– Event Chairperson
Lucille Stout Smith	– Communications Manager and Graphics Designer
William Redd	– Construction
Phillip Jones	– Construction
Nelson Jones	– Construction
Carolyn Brooks	– Secretary
Carolyn Key Allen	– Assistant Secretary
Dirie Payne Harris	– Treasurer
Katherine Banks	– Assistant Treasurer
James "Jim" Asher	– Member
Dr. Pamela Moran	– Member
Joyce Jackson Colemon	– Member
Patricia Bowler Edwards	– Member
Elsie M. Johnson	– Member
Berdell McCoy Fleming	– Member
Earnest Allen	– Member

Advisors

Mr. James Asher, Principal
Jackson P. Burley Middle School

Dr. Pamela Moran, Superintendent
Albemarle County Public Schools

Dr. Rosa S. Atkins, Superintendent
Charlottesville City Public Schools

Jackson P. Burley High School
Monument Wall Committee
Established 2016

Jackson P. Burley High School – 1951-1967

Donald A. Byers, Chairman	Carolyn Brooks, Recording Secretary	Dirie Harris, Treasurer
PO Box 4746	PO Box 4746	PO Box 4746
Charlottesville, VA 22905	Charlottesville, VA 22905	Charlottesville, VA 22905
(434) 996-9271	(434) 296-8055	(434) 293-2896

May 1, 2016

Greetings Alumni, Former Students and Staff of JPB High School,

The Jackson P. Burley High School Varsity Club is in the early planning stages of one of the most ambitious projects it has undertaken since its inception in 2007. The project is to construct a Monument Wall to honor all students, faculty, staff and others who contributed to the success of Jackson P. Burley High. With your support we can bestow a lasting honor on our beloved Jackson P. Burley High School.

Our goal is to offer all individuals who had any contact with JPB High School the opportunity to have their name engraved on this Monument. We strongly encourage, families of deceased students, faculty, staff and administrators to participate and make this a final memorial to their loved ones.

This Monument Wall will be constructed on the campus of the current Jackson P. Burley Middle School. The cost to construct the Monument Wall is approximately $85,000.00. Our sister high schools, Lucy Addison in Roanoke and Paul Dunbar in Lynchburg have completed their Monument Walls. Please show your love and respect to your former alma mater by supporting the financing of this project with a $125.00 donation to have your name included on the wall.

We are sincerely hopeful you will join us in this tribute to the memories of Jackson P. Burley High School.

Sincerely,

Donald A. Byers
Monument Wall Chairman

Burley Club Members Seek Support from the Community as Wall Groundbreaking Nears
October 5, 2017

Burley Varsity Club Monument Wall Committee Members
L to R: James "Jimmy" Hollins, Class of 1965, Rauzelle J. Smith, Class of 1966 and Donald A. Byers, Class of 1959.

The Groundbreaking Ceremony for the Monument Wall was scheduled for October 14, 2018 on the campus of the now Jackson P. Burley Middle School.

The Monument Wall Committee invited all who attended Burley High School or were administrators, faculty, staff, custodians, cafeteria workers and others — to have their names engraved on the wall.

The wall will contain three sections. The middle section will honor Mr. Jackson P. Burley, the school was named in his honor. The left section will contain the names of all administrators, faculty, staff, custodians, and cafeteria workers. The right section will contain the names of all alumni and special participants.

Signing of Contract for the Monument Wall
February 10, 2018

Monument Wall Committee witness signing of Construction Contract with
Michael Baer of Baer & Sons • Lynchburg, VA

Ground Breaking Ceremony
Saturday, October 14, 2017 @ 1:00 PM

Campus of now Jackson P. Burley Middle School
901 Rose Hill Drive • Charlottesville, Virginia 22903

Monument Wall
Groundbreaking Ceremony
October 14, 2017

The Jackson P. Burley Monument Wall Committee and the Burley Varsity Club held its Ground Breaking Ceremony on Saturday, October 14th at 1:00 PM on the campus of what is now Burley Middle School. It was a beautiful, crisp, fall day, where the attendees were surrounded by the brilliance of the season, with bold, cheerful colors, that matched everyone's mood for the wonderful occasion. The attendees were former students, administrators, friends, family, supporters and officials from the City of Charlottesville and Albemarle County.

Event Chairman, James "Jimmy" Hollins, class of 1965 was the Master of Ceremony for the event. The Invocation was provided by Reverend Lloyd Cosby Jr. of Zion Union Baptist Church in Charlottesville. Reverend Cosby provided inspirational words of wisdom to all the workers and supporters of the Monument Wall. The attendees received a warmhearted welcome from Committee member, Joyce Jackson Colemon, class of 1966 and a Statement of Occasion from Committee Chairman, Donald A. Byer, class of 1959.

After the ceremony, Dr. Pamela Moran, Superintendent of the Albemarle County Public Schools provided remarks. She stated, "Over the years, I've worked with the Burley Varsity Club and their President, Jimmy Hollins, as they have made many accomplishments toward their goal of keeping their school memory alive. The Club members are builders, and they are creating a lasting legacy for Jackson P. Burley High School." Dr. Moran applauded them for their ability to organize and work together to create a permanent history of their school for the community and future generations.

Monument Wall Committee Members

Front Row - L to R: Carolyn Allen, Joyce Jackson Colemon, Berdell McCoy Fleming, Lucille S. Smith, Dirie Payne Harris, Katherine Banks, Donald A. Byers, Elsie Johnson, Nelson Jones, Phillip Jones and Patricia Bowler Edwards
Back Row - L to R: William Redd and Rauzelle J. Smith

Monument Wall
Ground Breaking Ceremony
October 14, 2017

Monument Wall Unveiling
September 29, 2018

Finally, the long awaited day had arrived, beautiful blue and white clouds filling the sky. The Monument Wall Unveiling Ceremony was held on Saturday, September 29, 2018. Many stood outside and socialized as they waited for family and friends. The radiant, bold, and cheerful fall colors matched everyone's mood for the wonderful occasion. On this clear fall day, the atmosphere was electric, as the smiles from the attendees, sparkled with the sun.

The crowd inside buzzed with anticipation and waited patiently, as they registered and picked up their Burley Souvenir Booklet, t-shirt, and hat. The attendees quickly headed to the auditorium to get the best seats available and wait for the ceremony to begin.

The Monument Wall Committee members were very proud of their accomplishments. They were charged with contacting all faculty, staff, students and others who were a part of the history of Jackson P. Burley High School. For more than a year, the committee forwarded letters, Invitations, and newsletters. They conducted fundraisers and compiled an address database of all responses from interested individuals. They wanted to ensure all were aware of the project and had an opportunity to participate in having their name engraved on the wall. Their hard work paid off, as the participation was great from alumni, as well as members of the Charlottesville Community and surrounding counties.

The Monument Wall was a 19 month long project and is now a permanent history. The wall honors all students who attended Burley High School (including those who did not graduate before the school closed). Administrators, faculty, and staff at the school are a part of the history. The wall also pays special recognition to several volunteers who contributed to the success of the project.

The Committee worked with Baer & Sons Memorials, Inc. from Lynchburg, Virginia to create a design and coordinate construction of the JPB Monument Wall.

Mr. Jackson P. Burley

Jackson P. Burley High School • 1951 - 1967

Burley Bear

Jackson P. Burley High School

Monument Wall

'Dedicated to Preserving the Educational Legacy' of Jackson P. Burley High School

Saturday, September 29, 2018
1:00 PM

901 Rose Hill Drive • Charlottesville, VA 22903

Monument Wall Unveiling Program

'THE GLORY YEARS'
1951– 1967

MASTER OF CEREMONY: RAUZELLE J. SMITH, CLASS OF 1966
MONUMENT WALL PROJECT MANAGER

Invocation.. Reverend Lloyd Feggans, Class of 1956

Welcome...Joyce Jackson Colemon, Class of 1966

Pledge of Allegiance..

Burley School Anthem....................'Ode to Burley'....................... Isaac (Pete) Carey, Class of 1960
Accompanied by Marsha Howard, Class of 1964

Greetings from the City of Charlottesville...............................Honorable Mayor Nikuyah Walker

Greetings from the Albemarle County Public Schools..............Dr. Matthew Haas, Superintendent

Greetings from the Albemarle County Board of Supervisor ....Ann H. Mallek, Chair

Statement of Occasion........................ Donald Byers, Class of 1959 – Monument Wall Chairman

Presentation to Burley Family.. Delegate David J. Toscano

Musical Selections...Jackson P. Burley Middle School Chorus

Introduction of Guest Speaker..Patricia Bowler Edwards, Class of 1966

Guest Speaker...Charles W.C. Yancey, Class of 1959

Remarks...................................... Dr. Bernard Hairston, Former Principal of Burley Middle School

Remarks... James Asher, Principal Burley Middle School

Remarks............... Dr. Pamela Moran, Former Superintendent, Albemarle County Public Schools

Reflections................ James (Jimmy) Hollins, Class of 1965 – Monument Wall Event Coordinator

Jackson P. Burley Monument Wall

UNVEILING CEREMONY
SEPTEMBER 29, 2018

'DEDICATED TO PRESERVING THE EDUCATIONAL LEGACY' OF
 ### JACKSON P. BURLEY HIGH SCHOOL

MASTER OF CEREMONY: RAUZELLE J. SMITH, CLASS OF 1966
MONUMENT WALL PROJECT MANAGER

Prayer of Dedication...Bishop-Elect Frank Reeves Sr., Class of 1967

Formal Removal of the Covering.....................Jackson P. Burley Monument Wall Committee

Benediction and Blessing of Food.......................Bishop-Elect Frank Reeves Sr., Class of 1967

REFRESHMENTS WILL BE SERVED IN THE BURLEY SCHOOL CAFETERIA
CATERED BY ADA'S KITCHEN

Alumni, visitors and friends, please feel free
to take pictures at the Monument Wall.

WALL ARCHITECT DESIGNER
BAER & SONS MEMORIAL INC. • LYNCHBURG, VA 24502

Unveiling of Monument Wall
September 29, 2018

Unveiled Monument Wall

CHAPTER 12

JACKSON P. BURLEY VARSITY CLUB

Established 2007

Jackson P. Burley Varsity Club

Row 1 - L to R: Katherine Banks, James "Jimmy" Hollins, Clariece Coles Harris, Curtis Byers, Elsie Johnson and Dirie Payne Harris

Row 2 - L to R: Frank Reeves Sr., Donald A. Byers, Mary Brown, Agnes Ivory Booker and Beatrice Washington Clark

Row 3 - L to R: Nelson Jones, Joyce Jackson Colemon, Phillip Jones, and Bernard Nelson

Row 4 - L to R: William Redd, Richard Jones, William Byers, Roland Luck and Herbert Carter

Not pictured: George Lindsay Jr.

Mission Statement

The mission of the Jackson P. Burley Varsity Club (BVC) is to conduct research on all sports records from 1951 – 1967, and to pay tribute to the achievements of Burley High School athletes by determining the number of sports championships accompanying trophies, photographs, and any other pertinent sports paraphernalia. The BVC will continue to accomplish its mission by creating and sponsoring events to educate and bring about an awareness to inspire and preserve the school's history, as we all look back on the days of yesteryear, and what a difference change can make. We will keep the name of Jackson P. Burley High School alive (The Mighty Burley Bears!)

James "Jimmy" Hollins
Burley Varsity Club, Chairman (2007 – Present)

When the Jackson P. Burley Varsity Club was established in January 2007, Club members agreed the right choice for Chairman was, James "Jimmy" Hollins. Since establishment of the Club, he has been actively engaged and a man on a mission accomplishing many great things in the name of Jackson P. Burley High School.

Jimmy attended the Jefferson School in Charlottesville and later Jackson P. Burley High School, where he became very active in academics, and extra curricula activities to include football and band.

After graduating from Burley High School in 1965, he attended trade school and later enlisted in the U.S. Army, serving a tour of duty during the Vietnam War. After discharge from the military, he began working for Amtrak, remaining in their employment until he retired on disability in 2005. Throughout his work career, he maintained a home in the City of Charlottesville.

Jimmy has always been very interested in his school and community, and began to think about what could be done to improve the community, as well as things to keep the spirit of Jackson P. Burley High School alive. On January 27, 2007, four former Burley High School athletes, Donald Byers, James "Jimmy" Hollins, George Lindsay Jr., and Beverly McCullough, came together to form the Burley Varsity Club. Jimmy was elected Chairman, Donald elected as the Secretary, Beverly was elected Sergeant-at-Arms and George Lindsay Jr., elected as Treasurer. The first goal for the Club was to recruit former athletes. The club wanted to make a difference in the community and give back to their school.

Jimmy has been forever grateful for the support provided to the Burley Varsity Club by the Albemarle County School System and the City of Charlottesville, as well as community leaders, alumni, volunteers and the greater Charlottesville community.

The Varsity Club is pleased to have the opportunity to keep Burley High School from ever being forgotten. They are doing so through the various events they have sponsored, and the creation and awarding of scholarships through the Stephen D. Waters Scholarship Fund is very heartwarming.

In addition to his work with the Varsity Club, Jimmy is an active member of Zion Union Baptist Church, where he is an Usher and serves on the Capital Improvement Project Team. He is the current vice president and past president of the Rose Hill Neighborhood Association, and chairman of the newly formed VIA Heritage Association, which was founded in 2014. In addition, he serves on the Piedmont Housing Board and eagerly participates in other community activities and projects.

Jimmy says, he has enjoyed a good life and feels a responsibility to give back to his community.

Burley Varsity Club Accomplishments

The Jackson P. Burley Varsity Club (BVC) was established in January 2007 with four members: James "Jimmy" Hollins, Donald Byers, George Lindsay Jr., and Beverly McCullough. The Club meets monthly on the 2nd Saturday. The Club is a nonprofit 501(c) (3) organization, which exists to improve the awareness, history and maintain the legacy of Jackson P. Burley High School. While the organization does not have direct staff, there are dedicated and hardworking members and volunteers.

BVC Membership	Position	BVC Membership	Position
James "Jimmy" Hollins	Chairperson	Dirie Payne Harris	Member
William Redd	Vice-Chair	Elsie M. Johnson	Member
Nelson Jones	Secretary	Rose Johnson	Member
George Lindsay Jr.	Treasurer	Phillip Jones	Member
George Lindsay III	Assistant Treasurer	Richard Jones	Member
Donald A. Byers	Chaplain	Roland Luck	Member
Joseph Agee	Member	Tiffany McCullough	Member
Katherine Banks	Member	Bernard Nelson	Member
Agnes Ivory Booker	Member	John Nelson	Member
Mary Brown	Member	Ralph Poindexter	Member
Curtis Byers	Member	Ada Saylor	Member
D. Mitchell Carter	Member		
Herbert Carter	Member	William Byers	Deceased Member
Beatrice Washington Clark	Member	Robert Ferguson	Deceased Member
Joyce Jackson Colemon	Member	Beverly McCullough	Deceased Member
Clariece Coles	Member	Frank Reeves Sr.	Deceased Member
Burley Varsity Club Program Committee and Volunteers Patricia Bowler Edwards Graham Paige Edwina St. Rose Dede Smith Lucille S. Smith Rauzelle J. Smith			

In the mid 2000's, some alumni found a storage area at Charlottesville High School where the lost Burley High School trophies had been stored for decades. In the spring of 2008, the Youth Leadership Initiative of Burley Middle School held an event and invited Burley High School alumni. At the time of the event, the Burley Varsity Club decided something needed to be done to preserve and protect the hard won trophies. So, in May 2009, the Varsity Club became very busy with various fund raisers to acquire new trophy cases. In September 2009, the Club presented Burley Middle School with new trophy cases. Once the trophy cases were in place the Club went on a mission to restore the trophies.

Shortly thereafter, the work of the Club began to gain support and new projects were undertaken. To this day, the Club has been full steam ahead. Over the years, the Club received much support toward their endeavors from Albemarle County Superintendent of Schools, Dr. Pamela Moran.

The Burley Middle School, Youth Leadership Initiative showed their support and hosted the dedication program with the Burley Varsity Club for the naming of the football field and the gymnasium.

Accomplishments and Dedications over the Years

- In September 2009, the BVC celebrated the unveiling of new trophy cases at the school, which now house all refurbished trophies, from the opening of the school in 1951 to desegregation in 1967.

- On October 8, 2010, a dedication service was held to unveil Historical Markers for the naming of the gymnasium and the athletic field, honoring former basketball and football coaches.

- On October 8, 2010 a plaque was placed on the school by the Historical Resource Committee, stating the school's significance during integration.

- In June 2011, the Varsity Club Chairman, Jimmy Hollins led the charge to have Coach Robert "Bob" Smith inducted into the Virginia High School League Hall of Fame. Albemarle County High School Athletic Director, Ms. Deb Tyson submitted the application for the induction. Many former football players wrote letters of support to accompany the application. After more than a year, finally on July 13, 2012 an announcement was made, that Coach Robert Smith would be inducted posthumously into the Virginia High School League Hall of Fame. This was a glorious day, the induction ceremony was held in October 2012 at the Doubletree by Hilton Hotel, Charlottesville, Virginia.

- On October 7, 2011, under the leadership of Mayor Dave Norris a Proclamation was passed for Rose Hill Drive to receive the honorary name of Jackson P. Burley Drive.

- On October 7, 2011 the Elmer F. "Sonny" Sampson Band room was dedicated and a bronze plaque placed outside the entry to the band room. Mr. Sampson was the Band Director from 1956 until the school closed in 1967.

- In October 2012, Coach Robert "Bob" Smith was inducted into the Virginia High School League (VHSL) Hall of Fame.

- In 2012, the Stephen D. Waters Scholarship Fund was created to serve public school students in Charlottesville and Albemarle County.

− In 2012, the Varsity Club unveiled a sign for Burley Middle School.

− On May 25, 2013, fifty-four (54) years later, the BVC assisted former Burley High School student, Olivia Ferguson McQueen, Civil Rights Pioneer in receiving her official high school diploma from Lane High School in Charlottesville. Olivia's diploma was awarded jointly by Superintendents, Dr. Rosa Atkins, Charlottesville Public Schools and Dr. Pamela Moran, Albemarle County Public Schools. Olivia was a plaintiff in a lawsuit challenging the City of Charlottesville's segregated schools. She should have graduated from Lane High School in the spring of 1959. Instead, at graduation she did not receive a diploma, but a Certificate of Completion. The 2013 event awarding Olivia a high school diploma garnered much local and national publicity.

− On November 9, 2013, George Tinsley Drive was named in honor of Mr. Tinsley. He worked with the Cafeteria and Custodial staff at the school from opening day in 1951 until it closed in 1967.

− On November 9, 2013, the Media Center was dedicated in honor of the Jackson P. Burley High School Librarian, Mrs. Alberta H. Faulkner, who served from the school opening in 1951 until closing in 1967. A plaque was placed outside the entry to the Media Center.

− On November 9, 2013, the Alicia Bowler-Lugo Alumni Hall was dedicated in honor of Ms. Lugo. She had a dynamic presence in the halls of Burley High School, as a student and teacher. She was the valedictorian in the graduating class of 1959.

− On September 29, 2018, the unveiling of the Monument Wall on the now Burley Middle School campus, listing the names of faculty, staff, administrators and former students became a reality.

− In December 2019, a historic Jackson P. Burley Audio tour was written by volunteer Lucille Smith to include voices from former Burley High alumni. The tour can be accessed via the following link: https://izi.travel/en/3c5a-historic-jackson-p-burley-tour/en

− On September 15, 2020, the Virginia Department of Historic Resources approved Jackson P. Burley High School as a historic landmark.

− On November 24, 2020, the National Park Service approved Jackson P. Burley High School to be listed on the National Register of Historic Places.

Howard Hall

Marcha Payne Howard attended Jackson P. Burley High School and graduated in the class of 1964. Through the Burley Music Department, she was introduced to strings, and learned how to play the cello. She began piano training at an early age showing her love for music. After graduation, she continued her musical training at Johnson C. Smith University in Charlotte, North Carolina. Her travels abroad to Europe and Germany further enhanced her love of music.

Mrs. Howard went full circle from Burley student, to teacher, assistant principal and principal at her beloved school. From student to principal, she spent 45 years walking the halls of the Burley School. She taught at Burley for twenty-eight years, served as the assistant principal for nine years, and as principal for three years. Mrs. Howard was loved by her students and peers. She said, "Work was never a chore. Each position built on the other." Mrs. Howard began and ended her career at a place she loved and respected.

In 2006, outgoing Principal, Dr. Bernard Hairston named the hallway on the lower level the "Howard Hallway" in honor of Marcha Payne Howard. The hallway leads to the band room and choral room. Displayed on the wall along the hallway are pictures of the Burley Middle School band and choir members. This dedication was not a Burley Varsity Club project.

Howard Hall Dedicated June 2006

Trophy Cases

The trophy cases purchased by the Burley Varsity Club were unveiled in September 2009. All athletic trophies were refurbished and many other memorabilia donated by alumni and friends are now on display.

Burley High School Trophy Cases

Burley High School Trophy Cases

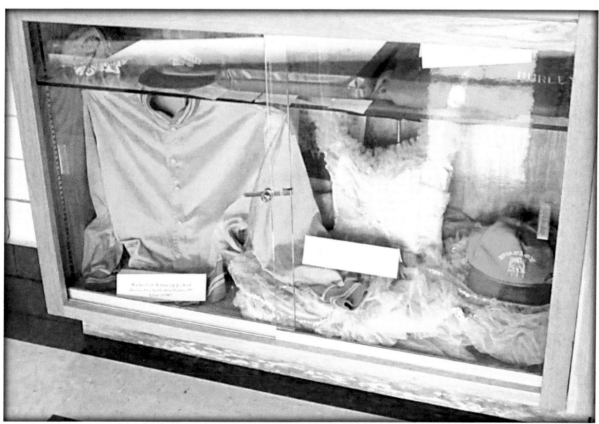

Dedications and Recognitions by the
Burley Varsity Club

Honorary Naming of Rose Hill Drive
To Jackson P. Burley Drive

Rose Hill Drive has the honorary name of Jackson P. Burley Drive, adopted on October 7, 2011.

At the request of the Burley Varsity Club, Mayor David Norris of the City of Charlottesville was asked to proclaim Rose Hill Drive, as Burley Bear Drive on October 8th and 9th of each year.

Rose Hill Drive serves as the main thruway for the Rose Hill neighborhood. Residents of this neighborhood are within walking distance of commercial areas located on Preston Avenue and the Downtown Mall.

In 1820 this neighborhood was part of the Rose Hill Plantation, which was purchased by John Craven.

Adopted October 7, 2011

Historical Markers for Athletic Field

The Burley Varsity Club dedicated a Historical Marker for the Robert "Bob" Smith and Clarence "Butch" Jones Athletic Field. The marker was dedicated on Friday, October 8, 2010 to honor Burley High School outstanding football coaches.

On July 13, 2012 an announcement was made that Coach Smith would be inducted posthumously into the Virginia High School League Hall of Fame. The Induction Ceremony was held at the Doubletree by Hilton Hotel, Charlottesville, Virginia in October of 2012. He was also inducted into the St. Augustine's Athletic Hall of Fame. He served as the Official Program Supervisor of the Virginia High School League until his retirement in 1985.

Historical Marker for Gymnasium

The Historical Marker for the Walter "Rock" Greene and Albert "AP" Moore Gymnasium was dedicated by the Burley Varsity Club on Friday, October 8, 2010 to honor outstanding Burley basketball coaches.

Stephen D. Waters Scholarship Fund

The Burley Varsity Club created the Stephen D. Waters Scholarship Fund in 2011 in honor of beloved English teacher, Stephen D. Waters.

Stephen Decator Waters was a graduate of Wilberforce University and a member of Alpha Phi Alpha Fraternity, Inc.

Mr. Waters began his career in 1963 as an English teacher at Jackson P. Burley High School in Charlottesville. While at Burley High School, he encouraged students who excelled in writing to join the Quill & Scroll Club to further enhance their writing skills.

He also taught at Buford Middle School. He directed the Head Start Program for a summer before accepting a job as Associate Director of the program.

In 1967, Mr. Waters became the first Director of the Upward Bound Program at the University of Virginia. The goal of the federally funded educational program is to help students overcome class, academic, social, and cultural barriers to higher education.

Mr. Waters directed youth programs at the Monticello Area Community Action Agency (MACAA) and then returned to the Charlottesville Public Schools where he served as Attendance Coordinator, Teacher and "Buy Back" Coordinator. He ended his career in public education upon retirement in 2004 after 40 years of service.

The consummate educator, Mr. Waters believed in the genius of simplicity and organization. He believed in exposing rural southern children to the arts and culture in the larger society, which enabled them to examine their own gifts and talents. To each child, he was devoted to establishing clear training and career goals.

Stephen's Vision: Educate young minds and inspire youth to explore, imagine, achieve and conquer unimaginable heights.

In 2012, the first Stephen D. Waters Scholarship was awarded. A minimum of three Scholarships are awarded each year to students in the public schools of the City of Charlottesville and Albemarle County.

Donation of Jackson P. Burley Middle School Sign

Sign donated by the Burley Varsity Club in 2012

Olivia Ferguson-McQueen

On May 25, 2013, fifty-four (54) years later, the Burley Varsity Club assisted former Burley High School student, Olivia Ferguson McQueen, Civil Rights Pioneer in receiving her official high school diploma from Lane High School in the City of Charlottesville.

Dedication of George Tinsley Drive

George Tinsley Drive was dedicated on November 9, 2013. Mr. George Tinsley worked with the Cafeteria and Custodial staff at Jackson P. Burley High School from opening day in September 1951 and remained after desegregation in 1967. While at Burley High School, he was a father figure for the students away from home, always providing words of wisdom when asked or needed.

The school became the Jack Jouett Junior Annex in 1967, housing an overflow of seventh grade students from Jack Jouett Middle School in Albemarle County. In the fall of 1973, Albemarle County reopened Jackson P. Burley High School as a middle school, housing 841 students in grades six through eight.

Mr. Tinsley continued his career with Burley Middle School, retiring in 1991, with 40 years of service.

Dedicated November 9, 2013

Alicia Inez Bowler-Lugo

Alicia Inez Bowler-Lugo attended Jackson P. Burley High School graduating as valedictorian in the Class of 1959. After graduating from Hampton University, Alicia went on to establish a distinguished career as an entrepreneur, activist, educator and community leader. She was a member of Delta Sigma Theta Sorority, Inc. and a member of the Charlottesville-Albemarle Inter-Fraternal Council.

Ms. Lugo began her professional career as a teacher in the Charlottesville City School System and served as the primary administrator for two major federally funded "skills" training programs in the City of Charlottesville; Central Virginia O.I.C. Inc. and the Drewary J. Brown Training Center.

She owned and operated the Rose Hill Market and Radio Station WUMX, MIX 107.5 FM in Charlottesville. This was the first minority owned station in the Central Virginia area.

Ms. Lugo was a fierce warrior for social justice and equality. Long active in the community and with civic affairs, Ms. Lugo was the first African American Chair of the Charlottesville School Board and served eleven years, including five years as Chair. She served on the Board of Directors of Piedmont Virginia Community College, the Advisory Board of Habitat for Humanity, Charlottesville – Albemarle Technical Education Center, Region 10 Mental Health Board, Planned Parenthood of the Piedmont, the AIDS Support Group, the Charlottesville Electoral Board and the Quality Community Council. She also served on the Board of Commissioners of the Charlottesville Redevelopment and Housing Authority.

In 1988, Ms. Lugo created and served as the Director of the *TEENSIGHT* Project, a program for the Focus Women's Resource Center. In 2006 she was promoted to the position of Associate Director of Focus and retired as Executive Director.

On November 9, 2013, the Burley Varsity Club honored Ms. Lugo with the naming of Alicia Inez Bowler-Lugo Alumni Hall. Ms. Lugo had a dynamic presence in those halls as a student and teacher.

In 2014, the Lugo-McGinness Academy was named for Alicia Bowler Lugo and Rebecca Fuller McGinness, two Charlottesville natives and educators. The Academy is located in the Hope Community Center building in the 10th and Page neighborhood. The Academy is an educational facility operated by the City of Charlottesville Public Schools that serves at-risk adolescents. The Center also provides counseling to students and affords them the opportunity for a high school diploma or GED preparation.

Dedication of Alicia Bowler – Lugo Alumni Hall

 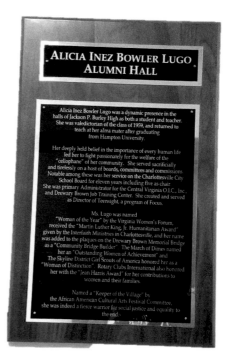

Dedicated November 9, 2013

Alberta Hall Faulkner

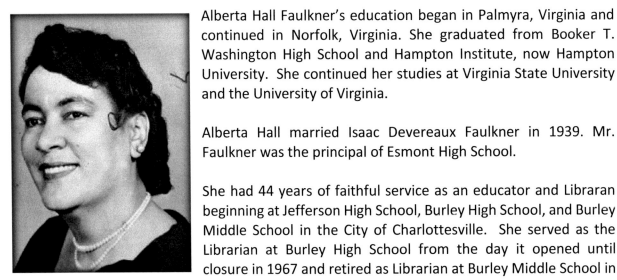

Alberta Hall Faulkner's education began in Palmyra, Virginia and continued in Norfolk, Virginia. She graduated from Booker T. Washington High School and Hampton Institute, now Hampton University. She continued her studies at Virginia State University and the University of Virginia.

Alberta Hall married Isaac Devereaux Faulkner in 1939. Mr. Faulkner was the principal of Esmont High School.

She had 44 years of faithful service as an educator and Libraran beginning at Jefferson High School, Burley High School, and Burley Middle School in the City of Charlottesville. She served as the Librarian at Burley High School from the day it opened until closure in 1967 and retired as Librarian at Burley Middle School in 1972.

Mrs. Faulkner dedicated her life to education and participated in many organizations over the years. She was the Secretary of the Charlottesville Teachers Association and City Librarians. She was the first African American to be elected secretary of the Albemarle Education Association, a charter member and Secretary of the Charlottesville Branch of the NAACP, member of the District "J" Albemarle Education Association, the Virginia Education Association, the Virginia Library Association and the National Education Association.

Mrs. Faulkner took pride in being an educator and wanted all students to live up to their potential by reading books. She was known for always being about business and did not believe in wasting precious time. She would readily assist the students as they came to the Library to find material for class assignments and research.

Mrs. Faulkner had a love of books and for young people. She believed in education and in 2001 contributed $370,604 to Hampton University to meet their unprecedented $200 million "Dreaming No Small Dreams" capital campaign goal. She also contributed more than $300,000 to the Lincoln University Endowed Alumni Scholarship Fund.

Dedication of Alberta H. Faulkner Media Center

Dedicated November 9, 2013

Mrs. Faulkner assisting students in the Media Center

Dedication of Plaques for Cafeteria and Custodial Staff

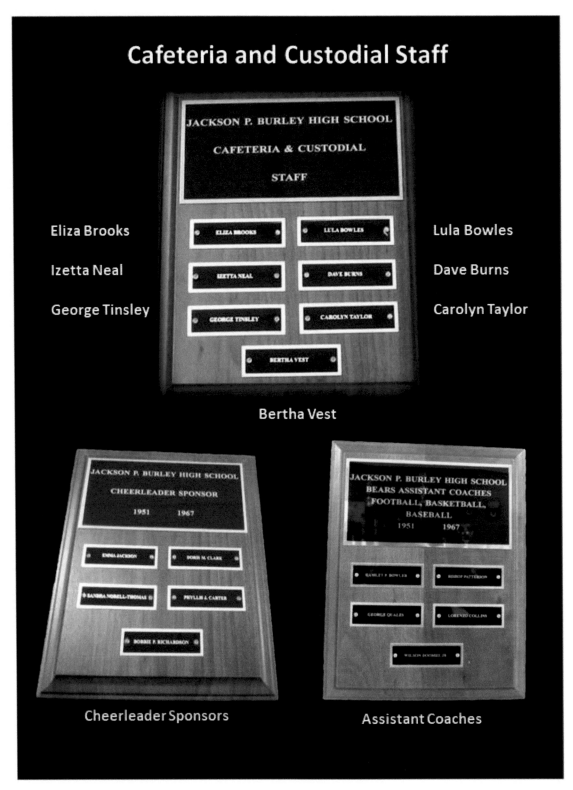

Cafeteria and Custodial Staff

JACKSON P. BURLEY HIGH SCHOOL

CAFETERIA & CUSTODIAL

STAFF

Eliza Brooks   Lula Bowles

Izetta Neal   Dave Burns

George Tinsley   Carolyn Taylor

Bertha Vest

Cheerleader Sponsors   Assistant Coaches

Dedicated November 9, 2013

Monument Wall Unveiled
September 29, 2018

Jackson P. Burley High School Approved for Virginia Landmark Register

Photo Credit: Maral Kalbian, 2019

On September 17, 2020, the Virginia State Department of Historic Resources named Jackson P. Burley High School in Charlottesville as a Virginia historic landmark.

The school was named in honor of local African American Jackson Price Burley. He was an educator, community leader, land owner, and businessman. The united effort by school leaders in the City of Charlottesville and Albemarle County provided a "separate but equal" educational facility for African American students during segregation.

The Charlottesville area is steep in regional African American history and the schools are a very important part of this history. Burley High School opened in 1951 as a result of "the overcrowded and seriously insufficient facilities for African Americans in both jurisdictions," was stated by the board in making its announcement.[1]

The board acknowledged that, "Jackson P. Burley High School proved to be the last substantial effort in Virginia to construct a new and well-equipped separate but equal high school for African American students." [2] The separate but equal approach ended when the U.S. Supreme Court ruled in 1954 in Brown v. Board of Education that segregated public schooling was unconstitutional.

Schools in the City of Charlottesville and Albemarle County were officially desegregated in 1967 and the County took control of Jackson P. Burley High School, which now serves as a middle school. The building is now solely owned by the County of Albemarle.

---

[1] VLR: Virginia Landmarks Register, *Agreement to construct new high school, Statement of Significance Summary Paragraph* (Sep 17, 2020), Section 8, Page 13.

[2] Ibid. *Lack of equal facilities for Black students, Statement of Significance Summary Paragraph* (Sep 17, 2020), Section 8, Page 13.

Jackson P. Burley High School
Listed on the National Register of Historic Places

On November 24, 2020, the Jackson P. Burley High School was approved by the National Park Service to be listed on the National Register for Historic Places.

Bibliography

Books and Booklets

1. Brennan, Eryn S., and Maliszewski, Margaret. _Images of America Charlottesville_, page 75.

2. Cross-White, Agnes. _Images of America Charlottesville: The African-American Community_, Tommy Miller Band, pages 52, Buster Scott and Elmer Sampson, page 91 and Jackson P. Burley Band, Cherry Blossom Parade, page 92.

3. Douglas, Andrea N., Editor. _Pride Overcomes Prejudice: A History of Charlottesville's African American School_, pages 86-87, (Jefferson Band), page 74 (Petition to establish a Colored High School"), page 99 (Massive Resistance).

4. Friends of Esmont with Andi Cumbo-Floyd, _Esmont Virginia: A community Carved from the Earth and Sustained by Story_, Page 41, 44 and 46.

5. Howard, Marcha P., _Souvenir Booklet Commemorating the 1990 Reunion of Albemarle Training School (1885 – 1959)._

6. Vest, Sharon C., _Esmont High School Reunion Booklet, 1991_.

7. Smith, Elizabeth D. Wood., _Images of America: The Charlottesville Dogwood Festival_, Page 50

8. Special Staff Writers for Virginia Biography, _History of Virginia, Volume 6_, Page 101

9. _Papers of the Jefferson School_, (Land purchase and quotes from City School superintendent James G. Johnson) Albemarle Charlottesville Historical Society

10. Virginia Foundation for the Humanities. "Jackson P. Burley High School."

Articles

11. "Charlottesville Dedicates New $1,400,000 High School", Sellers, T., _New Journal and Guide_ (1916 – 2003), Jun 17, 1950 and March 29, 1952.

12. "City of Charlottesville Blue Ribbon Commission on Race, Memorials and Public Spaces" December 19, 2016, Page 33

13. "Phelps-Stokes Fellowship Papers", Issues 5-8, Page 66

Newspapers

14. _CvillePedia_, "Charlottesville Awards Diploma 54 Years after Massive Resistance".

15. _Charlottesville Daily Progress_, Aaron Richardson, 25 May 2013, retrieved 28 February 2014.

16. _The Washington Post_ – "Desegregation Plaintiffs Gets Diploma", By Susan Svrluga, May 25, 2013.

17. _Richmond Free Press_, "Local Civil Rights Pioneer among Statewide Honorees," February 2, 2014.

18. _ProQuest Historical Newspapers_: Black Newspaper Collection Page 26

19. _Charlottesville-Albemarle Tribune_, Charlottesville, Virginia June 8, 1956, Vol 2-No 39, Page 1, Column 2

20. *ProQuest Historical Newspapers*: Black Newspaper Collection Page 12A
21. *The Daily Progress,* "New Schools in the County," Wednesday August 4, 1915, page 1 & 6
22. *Charlottesville Daily Progress,* March 9, 2019, "Finding Segregated UVA Hospital's hidden nurses." Ruth Serven Smith.

Yearbooks (Primary Source)
23. Byers, Donald A., "Jackson P. Burley High School Yearbook - 1952 and 1959."
24. Johnson, Elsie M., "Jackson P. Burley High School Yearbook - 1952."
25. Johnson, James, "Jackson P. Burley High School Yearbook - 1953."
26. Jefferson School African American Heritage Center. "Jackson P. Burley High School Yearbooks – 1953, 1961 and 1963."
27. Jefferson School African American Heritage Center. "Jefferson High School Yearbooks – 1941, 1943, 1944, 1945, 1946, 1947, 1950, and 1955."
28. Grady, George, "Jackson P. Burley High School Yearbook - 1954."
29. Feggans, Rev. Lloyd, "Jackson P. Burley High School Yearbook - 1955."
30. Clark, Beatrice Washington, "Jackson P. Burley High School Yearbook - 1956."
31. Banks, Katherine 'Jackson P. Burley High School Yearbook - 1957.'
32. Berkley, Vivian Woodfolk, "Jackson P. Burley High School Yearbook - 1956."
33. Lindsay, George Jr., "Jackson P. Burley High School Yearbooks - 1958, 1959, 1961, & 1963.'"
34. Allen, Ernest and Carolyn, "Jackson P. Burley High School Yearbook - 1960."
35. Howard, Marcha Payne, "Jackson P. Burley High School Yearbook - 1964."
36. Smith, Rauzelle J., "Jackson P. Burley High School Yearbooks -1965 and 1966."
37. Holland, Maxine, "Jackson P. Burley High School Yearbook - 1967."
38. Ayres, Rosa W., "Lane High School Yearbook - 1968."
39. Price, Teresa Jackson Walker, "Jefferson High School Yearbook - 1942."

References
40. Albemarle Charlottesville Historical Society collection (ACHS), 'Burley High School Folder' (Football article, last edition of the Burley Bulletin and 1956 Graduation Announcement.
41. Yearbooks, 1952-1967, Staff and faculty photos, sports coverage, and social activities.
42. Commonwealth of Virginia Department of Historic Resources, Burley Nomination State Review Board
43. National Register of Historic Place Nomination Form-Jackson P. Burley High School, (NRHP Reference Number SG100005836), VLR Listing Date 09/17/2020, NRHP Listing Date 11/24/2020, Maral S. Kalbian and Margaret T. Peters. Pages 4-10, 14, 15, 17, 19-20 and 22.
44. National Register of Historic Place Nomination Form-Jefferson School and Carver Recreation Center, (NRHP Reference Number 06000050), VLR Listing Date 12/07/2005, NRHP Listing Date 02/15/2006, Maral S. Kalbian and Margaret T. Peters

45. City of Charlottesville. "Application for a Building Permit," (April 19, 1950). "Joint Negro School, Charlottesville and Albemarle County." First floor building layout plan.

46. Charlottesville Circuit Court Real Property Data, Final Decree recorded in (Deed Book, 141:33 (1948).

47. Virtual Books: Real Property Data Type: DEED Volume: 00041 00488, 00141 00034, and 00039 00478.

48. City of Charlottesville Planning Commission Meeting, December 15, 1944 and August 18, 1948.

49. Charlottesville City School Board Minutes, July, 1958 – December, 1958

50. Charlottesville City School Board Minutes, January, 1946 – December, 1947

51. Albemarle County School Board Minutes, January, 1946 – December, 1949

52. Minute Book H, Charlottesville Council, September 1, 1938 – April 1, 1947

53. Minute Book I, Charlottesville Council, April 1, 1947 – August 31, 1953

54. Albert and Shirley Small Special Collections Library, UVA; Records of the Charlottesville City School Board, Petition to the Charlottesville School Board requesting the establishment of a "High School for Colored Youth," ca. 1921

55. Virginia Foundation for the Humanities. "Jackson P. Burley School." African American Historic Sites Database. www.aahistoricalsitesva.org/items/show/220

56. Albemarle County Public Schools Building Services, 1949 Building and Site Plans for the Joint Negro High School, blueprints dated August 1949, revisions December 1949.

57. Plaque on Burley School, entitled, "Jackson P. Burley High School" was provided by the City of Charlottesville in 2010.

58. The Burley-Boggs-Woodson - Payne Family, Genealogy.com

59. Library of Virginia 'Change Maker' - Olivia Ferguson McQueen

60. *Papers of the Benjamin Franklin Yancey Family, Race and Place Personal Papers*, Virginia Center for Digital History and to the Albert B. Small Special Collections Library at the University of Virginia. Box 6 – Papers of Benjamin Franklin Yancey, photograph of Harriet Yancey.

61. *Ancestry.com* - Network of genealogical, and historical records.

62. Find a Grave. (https://findagrave.com) Jackson Price Burley (1865 – 1945).

63. Graduation Composites (1952, 1954 and 1956 – 1967 from the Halls of Jackson P. Burley Middle School, photographed by Ralph Dixon.

64. 1953 and 1955 Graduation Composites, created by Lucille Smith.

65. Jefferson High School, Wikipedia, the free encyclopedia

66. Photographs of Jackson P. Burley High School faculty and staff are from the 1952 – 1967 "Jay Pee Bee", Yearbooks.

67. Photographs if the Burley Middle School principals are from the Burley Middle School yearbooks and other sources.

68. Student Interviews and reflections from the Class of 1952 – 1967 in Chapter 7 are their personal recollections and feelings. Other accounts, may not be quoted verbatim, but provide strong background information of historical value.

Research Log

Contact Date	Person/Place/Group Contacted	Notes
05 Jun 2020	Marsha Payne Howard	Picked up a document to assist in the write-up for Burley Band Director, Elmer Sampson.
18 Jun 2020	Albemarle Charlottesville Historical Society	Reviewed the Burley High School collections folder and retrieved information on the 1956 Undefeated Football Team.
23 Jun 2020	Burley Middle School Principal, Jim Asher	Visited Burley Middle School to speak with Jim and get a walk-through to assess the layout of the school.
17 Jul 2020	Jefferson Madison Library Greene County	Checked out the book, <u>Images of America Charlottesville, and Images of America Charlottesville: The African-American Community</u>.
21 Jul 2020	Albemarle Charlottesville Historical Society Miranda Burnett	Sent an email request for the name of the Principal for Charlottesville City Schools in 1949. Received information from Kay Slaughter, ACHS volunteer.
22 Jul 2020	Jefferson Madison Library Greene County	Checked out the book, <u>Pride Overcomes Prejudice: A History of Charlottesville's African American School</u>.
24 Jul 2020	Dr. Olivia Boggs	Spoke with Dr. Boggs about reviewing my written comments on the Burley family.
5 Aug 2020	Jefferson Madison Library Greene County	Checked out the book, <u>Charlottesville, VA, Images of America and Images of America: The Charlottesville Dogwood Festival</u>.
28 Sep 2020	Charlottesville Circuit Court	Reviewed Deed Books for Burley Land purchase.
29 Sep 2020	City Planning Office	Spoke with Mr. Jeff Werner who provided resources to obtain information to review minutes of the Charlottesville Council. He also emailed documents for review.
5 Nov 2020	Charlottesville City Hall Kyna Thomas, Chief of Staff/Clerk of Council	Reviewed Charlottesville Council Meeting Minutes from 1946-1952.
17 Aug 2020	Albemarle County Schools Building Services	Mr. Joe Letteri mailed an old blueprint of the 1949 Joint Negro High School (Jackson P. Burley)
11 Sep 2020	Albemarle County Schools Public Works Department	Visited Albemarle Public works Department to review additional blueprints and approval dates for the 1949 architectural design for Joint Negro High School (Burley).
09 Nov 2020	Dr. Olivia Boggs	Spoke to Dr. Boggs who provided feedback on Burley Family write-up.
13 Nov 2020	Albemarle County Board of Supervisors-Senior Deputy Clerk, Travis Morris	Emailed Travis about receiving access to meeting minutes for the Board from 1946 – 1952. Access granted on December 10th.

5 Jan 2021	Jefferson Madison Library Greene County	Checked out the book, <u>Holsinger's Charlottesville</u>.
16 Feb 2021	Edward (Beau) Lane	Received a follow-up email from Mr. Lane providing me a few tidbit pieces of information about John H. Lane one of the founders of the first Esmont Colored Schools. He also referred me to his cousin Rick Lane for more information.
18 Feb 2021	Rick Lane	Mr. Rick Lane called this morning and we had a 1 ½ hour conversation about the Lane family, providing a wealth of information. Some info will be used in follow-up book. He also provided me a picture of his grandfather, John. I had follow-up emails from Rick on Feb 22, 25 and Mar 9th.
09 Mar 2021	Laura Stoner	Ms. Laura Stoner of the Virginia Museum of History and Culture reached out at the request of Mr. Rick Lane to offer assistance in my research for the Lane family and the segregated high schools in Charlottesville and Albemarle County.
12 Mar 2021	Carol Coffey	At my request, Ms. Coffey, Director of TJACE PVCC reached out to answer several questions I had and to provide information on a Publishing Event at the Festival of the Book.
12 Mar 2021	Gigi Davis	Ms. Davis, Job and Internship Coordinator at PVCC reached out at the request of Ms. Coffey to assist in getting support on book editing and graphic design.
09 Apr 2021	Albemarle Charlottesville Historical Society	Reviewed the folders on Esmont, Jefferson and Albemarle Training School. Names of African American teachers were included in each folder.
15 Apr 2021	Margaret T. Peters	I spoke with Mrs. Peters, who agreed to edit Chapter 5 of the book, "About Jackson P. Burley High School." The edited chapter was received on May 1st.
30 Apr 2021	Dr. Olivia Boggs	Received a copy of Mr. Burley's marriage license from Dr. Boggs with correct date. Received write-up for Dr. Boggs and Frederick Jr.
07 May 2021	Hampton University Archives	I spoke with Andreese A. Scott, Museum Secretary and Archivists for information on alumni Thomas Cayton and to see if there was anything in their files on the old Delevan Hotel for the Jefferson School site in Charlottesville. We spoke again on May13th, but there was no additional information available.
25 May 2021	Jefferson African American Heritage Center-Dr. Andrea Douglas.	Reviewed Jefferson School yearbooks, 1941-1947 and 1950 and 1955.